Sailing Orders

by

David O'Neil

W & B Publishers
USA

W & B Publishers

For information:
W & B Publishers
Post Office Box 193
Colfax, NC 27235
www.a-argusbooks.com

ISBN: 978-0-6159408-2-3
ISBN: 0-6159408-2-X

Book Cover designed by Dubya

Printed in the United States of America

Chapter one

Ambush

1792... Late autumn. Eastney, Hampshire, England

Martin Forest sat gloomily just inside the door of the barn. He could hear the sound of the animals chomping at their feed: three horses, a pony and a donkey. All were warm and snug in their stalls. *It's all right for them,* Martin thought, struggling to pull the coat round him tighter. His growing frame was suffering from a sparse diet and the damp cold. As he sat watching the odd person hurrying past in the rapidly darkening evening, he noticed the two men across the roadway. Both were wearing cloaks, and he could see the outline of swords under the hang of their cloaks. There was something furtive about their manner. For want of something better to do, he watched them with some interest, drawing back a little more into the dark shelter of the barn entrance where he could not be easily seen. He became aware of another presence on his side of the road. Someone had come and stationed himself by the wall of the barn. Martin realized he was there when he heard him loosening his sword in its scabbard.

He suspected that they were waiting for something or somebody, preparing to act. The men across the road stirred and drew their swords. Martin realized whatever it was must be close at hand.

The jingle of harness came from down the road which was now almost clear of pedestrians. The semi-darkness hid the men across the road. The man on the near side moved out to the middle of the road where he stood and waited his drawn sword in one hand, and a pistol in the other.

Martin ran through to the rear of the barn and out of the trap door at the back. He turned and ran down the lane behind the buildings and then through another alley further down the road toward the sound of the approaching horses.

The lights of the coach appeared round the bend in the road, the horses slowed climbing the short rise. Martin ran down to the coach and jumped up on the step. He leaned in through the open window. "There are men waiting to stop you up the road."

A hand reached out and took hold of his collar. "What did you say, boy?"

"There are three men up the road near the barn waiting for someone. As soon as they heard the coach they stepped out into the road. They are armed."

"Stop the coach." The man called to the driver. The driver whipped up the horses, and tried to get them moving faster despite the call of the man inside. The boy wrenched his coat from the man's grip and hauled himself up to the box where the driver was whipping the horses, leaning forward peering through the rain. Martin held the rail beside the seat and rammed both feet into the driver's side. Unbalanced, the driver pitched over the side of the coach to land asprawl in the road. The reins caught under him and his weight pulled the horses heads round. The already unwilling beasts dragged the coach, rocking dangerously, to a halt.

The two men in the coach got out. The big one pulled the boy from the box. A pistol was fired in their direction. The sound of running feet came from up the hill as the three ambushers came to see what had gone wrong. Both of the men from the coach drew their swords and turned to face their attackers. The big man said to the boy, "Stay by the coach and watch the lady."

Startled, Martin climbed into the coach where he found a lady and a girl, both sitting back in the corner of the seat. Martin saw they were scared. "Don't worry. I'll look after you." He showed them his knife. A hand appeared at the opposite window reaching for the inside handle. Whoever it was missed the handle and a face appeared at the window. The girl screamed, as the man grimaced, reaching for the latch. Martin reached out with the knife and stabbed the man in the hand. There was a spurt of blood, the man yelled as he tried to pull his hand away from the door. The knife had gone right through the palm and stuck in the wood of the door, trapping him there. He saw the other hand appear holding a pistol. Without thinking, Martin grabbed the barrel and wrenched it back toward the man's face. The man's finger caught in the trigger and the pistol misfired. The powder from the pan exploded into his face. He screamed again and fell out of the window, wrenching the knife out with the weight of his body. The other door opened and the big man appeared. He was bleeding from a wound in the shoulder, but otherwise seemed alright. He looked at the woman who was holding the girl in her arms. She said calmly, "We are all right. Your friend looked after us. he drove off the man who attacked us. She pointed to the blood on the door.

The big man said, "Giles is taking the reins. We will soon be home."

Martin was still in the coach and he made to get up. The big man said, "Sit down, lad. You have saved the lady and her daughter. You will join us for some food and I must reward you."

"There is no need, sir. I was just there at the right time. You have no need to reward me."

The big man's cloak moved and Martin saw he was wearing a uniform.

"Your shoulder, sir. You have been wounded."

"Tis nothing, lad. We will be home in a few minutes. It will be attended there."

The coach drew up in the drive of the large house, half a mile beyond the town. The man driving jumped down and looked at Martin as he stepped down from the coach. "What? Who?..." The big man stepped down, lifted the girl down and helped the lady out. They led the way into the house. Martin hesitated at the door, uncertain what to do. The big man said,

"Come in, boy. You must be hungry. Boys of your age are always hungry."

Martin walked into the hallway which was as big as the drawing room of his father's house.

The younger man, Giles, received quietly whispered instructions from the lady. With a grin he took Martin's arm and said, "This way. What is your name, lad?"

"Martin Forest, sir."

"I am not 'sir'. My name is Giles Masters. I am the brother of the Captain's lady. We have some time to wait for dinner, as we were not expected today. So in the meantime, we will find you something to replace your coat which I see has been torn. Now tell me what happened in the coach?"

They walked up the grand staircase and Martin heard running feet preparing for the guest and their returning master.

Giles took him to a room on the landing. It was a bedroom and there were clothes laid out on the bed. There was also a bath standing beside the window and, as they stood watching, three maids came in carrying buckets of steaming water. They poured them, in turn, into the bath and then left. A manservant entered with a bucket of obviously cold water. He stood to one side while the maids returned with more hot water. When they left he closed the door.

"Would you test the water, sir?" He held the cold water ready to add to the bath to cool the water down. Giles leaned over and said, "Half the bucket should do, Parker."

Parker poured half the contents of the bucket into the bath. Giles tested it again." That's fine. I'll see to things now, Parker. Thank you."

"Thank you, sir," said Parker, looking at Martin curiously. He left the room closing the door.

"There are clothes for you to try on the bed but I thought you would probably wish to have a wash before you put on clean clothes. I'm right, am I not?"

Martin looked at the bath. He had not bathed since he had left home three months ago. He smiled and, ignoring Giles, stripped off his clothes and climbed into the bath.

When Giles and Martin entered the drawing room, the others were all gathered. Martin was introduced by Giles.

The big man—now resplendent in uniform, no sign of the tear gained earlier in the shoulder—shook his hand and introduced himself as Captain Bowers, RN. The lady was the Lady Jane Bowers, the Captain's wife. The girl, perhaps twelve years old, was Jennifer Bowers, the daughter of the Captain and Lady Bowers. Giles had already introduced himself as the Hon. Giles Masters, the younger brother of Lady Bowers. At eighteen, newly promoted to Lieutenant RN, he was awaiting delivery of his new uniforms.

The girl, Jennifer, was only one year younger than the thirteen-year-old Martin. She looked at the newly-scrubbed, well-dressed, young man in front of her, and, with the candour enjoyed by the young, said, "My goodness, Martin, that is an improvement."

Seeing the blush appear on Martin's face, Jane Bowers said, "Really, Jennifer. Please remember that, but for this gentleman, we might be very poorly off."

Jennifer looked dismayed, then smiled and said, "But he looks much more comfortable now."

Martin smiled back. "Indeed I am more comfortable I can assure you, and I take no offence at what is patently the truth."

The party was called to dine with Martin seated between his hostess and Jennifer.

As the meal was served Jennifer prepared to instruct Martin in the order of use for the cutlery. When she realized that he was using the correct spoon for the soup, she stopped herself and set to, while still keeping an eye on Martin.

The Captain was forthright. "Tell me, lad. What brings you to Eastney?"

"I'm afraid it is a poor tale for the company, sir."

"Oh, please? Tell us how came you here?" Jennifer asked.

"Well…I am from Eynsham in Oxford. My father was a Major in the 18th Dragoons. He retired just four years ago, having bought Walton Manor. It is not as big as this house but it has land. My mother had died when I was just three. Father met his second wife in Oxford. She did not seem unhappy with me, though I now believe she must have always resented my presence. At first she made herself most agreeable. As time went by she arranged for me to be sent to board in Oxford at a private school. While I was studying there she had my father to herself." Martin paused at this point and accepted the next course, choosing the correct knife and fork to attack it. He smiled as he glanced out of the corner of his eye at Jennifer, noticing her interest in his manners.

He continued at the urging of Lady Bowers. "Oh, do go on, Martin."

At the urging he continued. "My father was killed in a hunting accident. We had several acres of mixed woodland and grazing and he used to ramble with his gun through the area taking the odd rabbit and sometimes a deer. On the day he died there was frost and ice on the puddles. They say he tripped or slipped and fell on a sharp stone striking his head and breaking his neck. He was found later that day when he did not return home.

"I was not told until I returned from school two weeks later. Meredith, my stepmother, was not happy to see me. From that time I was expected to keep out of sight, though I was clothed and fed." He paused once more as the courses changed.

"Then," he hesitated, "Jethro Woods appeared and took up residence with us, apparently as factor for the estate. I was now spending more time with our handyman, Bill Smith. He used to be father's servant in the army. My stepmother disliked him, too, but he knew all about the estate and perhaps a little more as well. I do believe my stepmother was afraid of him. Bill taught me how to fight. He had been a prize fighter in his youth. He had been travelling with a fairground when he was taken by the law, and chose the army rather than prison.

"Four months ago Bill passed away. During the early winter he took the ague, and never recovered. After the funeral, when I was still in my best clothes following the service, Jethro came to me and told me I must leave. My stepmother could no longer afford to keep me."

Jennifer gasped. "How could she?" She said, unbelievingly.

"Quiet, Jennifer", her aunt said firmly. "Let Martin continue.

"I packed my things and set out with a little money I had saved. My stepmother gave me a small purse with five guineas in it. I set off down the road to the south. Just over a mile from the house I was waylaid by Jethro. He warned me never to return. "Come near again and I will kill you", were his exact words'. I said, 'I will come back when I have grown up a little more'."

The steel behind the words made it clear that this young man would do exactly that. The Captain commented to Giles afterward, "I don't envy Jethro somehow. I cannot see Martin being stopped by threats. Can you?"

Giles, five years older than the lad said. "Damn it, sir. I would not like to be Jethro now if I had to face him. That man at the coach will never forget him, if he still lives."

On his way south Martin had decided he would try to get a situation on a ship, perhaps as cabin boy. It did not at occur to him that being able to read and write might be more valuable than a strong back and a willing heart.

His clothes had suffered during his journeying over the past four months, and his money had long gone. He had suffered a few knocks but was eternally grateful for the training received from Bill Smith. He had survived many a scrap with his fists and knife. He had learned a few things, too. At thirteen years he stood five-foot six and was growing fast. His educated tongue had got him trouble, but it had got him out of trouble too. A quick learner he had discovered that survival was never just brute force, and that guile was often easier to use than a knife.

That night he slept in a bed for the first time in weeks. The soft feather mattress cosseted his body and he slept, until wakened by the sunlight through the window. His waking was a struggle as, unused to the enveloping sheets and blankets, he took a few moments to remember his situation. He lay back luxuriating in the comfort of the bed. He dozed a little, too. Finally, hearing voices below the window, he reluctantly left the bed and peered out at the scene below. The grassland rose in a slope to the woods on the hilltop. Immediately below his window was the yard, with a stable block on the other side. The noises he had heard were those of the stable lad grooming the horses.

He pulled on his new clothes and ventured downstairs. Following his nose, and the sounds, he found the kitchen. Jennifer was there already chatting to the cook, a slim lady of middle age, her stern face smiling at the chatter from Jennifer. She looked up and with a wicked smile said, "Why, here is the young man himself. Good morning to you, sir. We were just discussing your bravery last evening."

Martin felt himself blush, and noticed that Jennifer was also blushing as she turned away to look furiously at the cook. She ignored the look and introduced herself. "I'm Mrs.. Hogget, the cook for the household. Normally the young folk come here for breakfast, to the kitchen I mean. It allows the grown-ups a chance to eat their breakfast while the Captain reads the papers.

Martin said, "Good morning, Mrs.. Hogget. Jennifer, I am obliged to you and happy to eat breakfast here with you both."

Jennifer turned and smiled at him. "Hello, Martin. Father suggested you might like to go riding this morning if the weather allows. Would you like that?"

"I would be delighted, provided you will show me where to go. I am a stranger to this area."

"Of course I will. I'll just tell Will to prepare the horses." She dashed out of the door into the yard calling to Will.

As Martin seated himself Mrs.. Hogget said, "She is delighted to have someone here near her own age. Mr.. Giles is very good but he is older, and at her age Giles seems like a grown up. She is still a child in many ways."

"I am only perhaps one year older than she," Martin said.

"Ah, but you have lived in the real world, from what I hear. If you'll forgive me saying so, it shows."

He looked at her, lifting his eyes from the big plate of bacon and eggs placed in front of him.

She looked him straight in the eye and said, "I means' it, Mr. Martin. I look at you and you have a look of a man, even more so than Mr. Giles who is five years your senior. You'll keep an eye on our Jennifer out riding, won't you?"

"Of course, Mrs.. Hogget. And I don't take your words amiss. There are times I have felt very old during the past few months. I presume it shows."

He ate his breakfast, interrupted by Jennifer returning, chattering happily about the horses and the countryside around the house.

Wearing an old pair of riding boots that almost fitted, Martin walked the horse out of the stable yard. Will, the groom, followed Jennifer, who was riding side-saddle on a Welsh cob.

All three cantered up the rise to the tree line where a path followed the tree-line along to a small lake. They rode for an hour before returning to the house, rosy cheeked and laughing as they shared a quip made by Will, the stable lad.

Captain Bowers watched them, noting the easy manner between them. He had an idea that Martin might well become a permanent fixture here, for a time at least. As he looked he thought of the son he had never had. Jane could not have any children. He loved Jennifer, and was happy and proud of Giles, his young brother-in-law, there was still that feeling that something was missing. He shook his head and straightened up, annoyed that he was becoming maudlin. He would talk to Martin as soon as possible.

The two young people came in to see the grown-ups after they had tidied up from their ride. Martin particularly wished to thank them for their hospitality and make arrangements to move on.

It was Jane who was swift to stop him talking about leaving, though when Martin asked why would they wish him to stay, it was the Captain who provided the answer.

"Martin, you spoke of making your way to the sea to search for a job as cabin boy on a merchantman. If you were serious I would like to suggest you stay, as my wife bids you. As you know, I am Captain in the Royal Navy. I am waiting to join my new ship which is re-fitting in the dockyard in Portsmouth. I am taking over the crew of the vessel. Giles, as you know, is passed for lieutenant and must move to another ship. I am short of a midshipman, and with your education, I have no doubt you will in time pass for lieutenant like Giles.

"We still have the midshipman's uniform that Giles had discarded. It will still pass. I would be happy to help with the other things you need. I would deem it a favor as I have no other person in mind for the place, and I would rather appoint someone I judge would benefit from the post."

Martin was stunned. "But you do not know me, sir."

"I know you well enough to trust the lives of my wife and ward to you. I think that will do for a start. That is, if you would consider my offer."

"Consider? I accept gladly, sir. Though I will need to study the things I must know, so that I do not let you down."

"Giles will be back this afternoon. I will ask him to speak to you and he may be able to help you with books." He turned to Jane. "Will that suit, my dear?"

Jane just looked at him. She didn't speak. She didn't need to. She had seen in Martin what her husband had, but had taken the extra step. She saw in Martin the son she had desperately wanted but could never have. She could not be certain. He could turn out to be other than the boy she judged him to be, but she believed in him. Until or unless he proved otherwise, he would call this house home. "Absolutely, my dear. He will be most welcome."

Jennifer laughed delightedly. "You will be like my brother, Martin. Come, I will show you my garden." Quite unaffectedly, she took his hand and towed him off to see her garden.

"Are you sure about this, Jane?" Charles asked his wife. "I confess I had not looked past his appointment to my ship."

Jane took his hand and said fondly, "Charles, you may be able to fool others, but I am not as they. I fear I know you too well. You had every intention of just allowing things to happen, until the lad would have been a fixture here."

"I am so pleased I married you." Charles kissed her and held her close. You know me well, my love."

Chapter two

Sea-time

1793

It was difficult for Martin to believe that only six months had passed since he had been threatened by Jethro Woods. Now fourteen years old, for the past two months he had been accommodated at the Bower's home just outside Eastney, looked after by the Bowers and Mrs.. Hogget, and being chased about by Jennifer and instructed by Giles, who was delighted to have the chance to instruct someone who really wanted to learn. Giles guessed he might well be pushed into training the Midshipmen in his new ship. As junior Lieutenant in a frigate, he was aware that he would in effect command the gunroom, the Middy's quarters, for the next voyage at least.

Martin was grateful for the training. It had involved sailing the small boat owned by the Captain. Since Martin had never been in a boat in his life it was an important lesson, and it revealed an excitement and a talent for the feel of a boat that he was grateful to discover.

The basic teaching of navigation had introduced him to a subject that his school lessons had prepared him for, and the fact of his literacy made the schoolwork on board, while still a task, less so than were he without.

"Mr.. Forest! A word if you will." The voice of the First Lieutenant carried easily across the poop deck of *HMS Arun*. Lt. Sir Archibald Carrington, Bart, was a little distant, almost aloof on occasion, but he was a good First Lieutenant for the ship. Even now, as Martin prepared to receive the rebuke he deserved for day-dreaming, when he should have been studying the horizon for strange ships. There was no rebuke however. Carrington passed Martin his telescope. "Off to the foretop. See if anything is about."

"Aye, aye, sir." Martin took the telescope, slung the strap around his shoulder and made off to the fore shrouds and began to climb.

Happily settled in the foretop, Martin raised the telescope. He then immediately lowered it. He looked at the seaman whose task was lookout. The seaman looked back defiantly.

"Why?" Martin said. "Why did you not report it?"

The man, maybe three years older than Martin's fourteen years, looked as if he was going to cry. "'Coz I don't belong here. I should be at home looking after my mother. They bloody Press-men came and snatched me when I was working in the field. I'm no sailor. I'm a field hand." He sobbed quietly.

Martin raised the telescope, discomforted by the distress of the young man. He called below. "Ship on our port bow, closing under full sail. Looks like..... She's under French colors, a frigate." He waited for the lift of a wave, "Looks like 36 guns."

Carrington called, "Stay there and keep me informed for the moment."

From beneath them the two people in the foretop heard the whistles calling the men to their quarters.

Martin turned to his companion. "What's your name?"

"Peters, sir. Patrick Peters."

"Well, Patrick Peters. I should report you for this, but I won't. You can do nothing about your mother now, absolutely nothing. If you like, I will write to your local vicar when we speak to a homeward bound ship. It's the best I can do. If you do this again it will be the cat, with no option. You put the whole ship in danger. Understand?"

Peters looked shamefaced. "I didn't think of that." He said, "I'll do my best, sir. If you will write a letter I should be obliged."

From below came the call to clear for action. Then, "Mr.. Forest, take your station. Lookout?"

"Peters, sir."

"Peters, call any change in position."

"Aye, aye, sir!"

Martin slid down the forestay and landed on deck with a thump. He hurried to the quarter-deck and passed the glass to Mr. Carrington. "She looks fast, sir. And her sails are clean."

"Well observed, Mr.. Forest." The captain turned to Carrington. "Load the guns, but do not run out until the situation becomes clearer." Turning back to Martin he said, "Your first action, Mr.. Forest!"

"Yes, sir."

Captain Bowers looked thoughtful for a moment before saying, "Keep close to Mr.. Carrington and mark what he does. He is a fine officer and is experienced. You'll do well to learn from him." He turned and walked the length of the quarter-deck before turning and walking back. As Martin had become aware, the walk was the Captain's way of letting the crew know, he was sharing the danger with them. It also allowed him to see what was happening, and issue orders controlling the ship during the forthcoming action.

HMS Arun was nominally a 36gun frigate, captured from the French who had named her *L'Hirondelle (Swallow),* her 9 pounder broadside guns had been replaced in Portsmouth with 12 pounders. Also 2x9 pound bow and 2x9pound stern chasers had been added. In addition 4x24pounder carronades mounted on slides were placed on the quarter-deck to complete her main armament. The carronades were short range because of the short barrels, and only used at close quarters where they were devastating.

Martin watched the approaching French ship. Neither craft was attempting anything spectacular. The course of each ship would bring them to a collision point by late afternoon. According to Mr. Carrington the action would be over before nightfall, which would not be until about 9pm that evening.

The war with France had only officially started in 1792, but clashes with French ships had been intermittent since the Revolution. There had obviously been problems within the French fleet with many of the officers being replaced or eliminated in the name of the people. This resulted in some cases of ships being handled by inexperienced officers. The *Arun* herself had been captured with very little damage because of the inept handling of her captain.

The approaching ship was not however, being handled by an amateur. Identified now as the *Charon* she would not be up with them for at least another hour.

Both ships closed gradually. Neither Captain was disclosing his tactics before it was necessary. The

Frenchman was sailing on a converging course, heeling to starboard under full sail.

The *Arun* was on the port tack, sailing close to the wind. Captain Bowers turned to the Master. "Mr.. Hardy, can we get any extra out of her?" He looked up at the cloud of sail on the three masts.

Carter Hardy scratched his bristly chin. "If we can get her a little more upright, we should ride easier through the water."

"How can we do that, d'ye think?"

Hardy's eyes ranged over the masts and straining sails. Martin, standing next to him, said quietly, without thinking. "What about the guns?"

Hardy looked at him quizzically.

"Suppose we run out the starboard guns. That would shift, what? 25 tons weight to starboard. It should ease the ship a little."

Hardy turned to the Captain. "Sir. Young Mr. Forest here suggests that we run out the starboard battery. By doubling up on the gun crews for the task they should be able to manage it. It could shift just enough weight to make a difference. At least it's worth a try."

The Captain looked at the pair of them, considering what had been suggested. Then he turned to Mr. Carrington. "Run out the starboard guns, and chock them in place. We will have to remember when we use them to remove the chocks."

Carrington raised his speaking trumpet. "Starboard guns run out. Port watch double up for the run out. Lively there!"

The men crouched on deck sprang into activity. The gun ports on the starboard side were opened and the guns standing on the sloping deck, with huge effort, were hauled up by the double crews to the fully run-out position. The barrels of the 12 pounders projected from the gun ports for the full length of the gun deck, like the thorns on a rose stalk.

Hardy was watching the sails and he called for slight adjustments to the trim. The Captain ordered the log to be checked and the speed marked.

As the ship settled down to the alterations to her trim, Hardy commented, "It's made a difference, I vow. I can feel it. She is lighter, by God."

Martin was looking at the French ship when Mr. Carrington, who was using his telescope, called, "We are headreaching on her, sir. We are outsailing her." He snapped his telescope shut and turned to Martin with a quiet "Well done, lad!" Then he strode to the quarter rail and called down to the main deck, "Mr. Green, Mr. Harper. Be sharp when the orders come. The Frenchy looks well-handled and new. She'll be full of men so our gunnery is important."

Both Lieutenant Green and the senior Midshipman Robert Harper responded, eagerly awaiting the chance to use the guns they commanded.

Captain Bowers turned to Martin. I think we'll hoist the battle ensign, just to make sure our friend there knows who he is fighting. As Martin saw the huge Union Flag raised, snapping and rippling in the fresh breeze, he thought his heart would burst with the pride it inspired.

The two ships closed the gap between them with the British frigate drawing gradually ahead. The effect of this was that for the Frenchman to bring his broadside to bear he would need to give way to port. The other danger he faced was that the *Arun* would gain sufficient lead to allow her to cross the bow of her opponent, firing her broadside guns in turn, with the effect of sending her shot the full length of the French ship, creating mayhem in their passing.

On the other hand, if the French ship could keep close to her opponent, a skilled Captain may be able to come starboard and cross the stern of the British ship and use her broadside against the stern of the *Arun.* This action would now be a battle of wits between the two Captains.

There was no way that Martin could describe the action with any accuracy. It started at 5.00pm, and it was all over by 6.15 pm. Between times, for Martin, the action was a confusion of smoke and noise from the guns, and the shriek of passing bullets. Men cheered. The gun carriages rumbled out and were thrown back by the recoil from firing. Enemy shot hit the fife rail, sending a swathe of splinters across the deck. The only man standing upright on the quarter-deck was one of the helmsmen who had managed to hang on to the wheel when everyone else was thrown down. He managed to remain upright. Sadly, he was caught in the shower of splinters. Riddled and bleeding he collapsed on deck, coughing his life away in seconds.

Martin was back on his feet in time to see the foremast of the French ship lean back and collapse in a tangle of rigging and torn sails. The *Charon* fell off to port and the smoke ripped apart in the freshening wind. There were a series of holes smashed into the French ship along her exposed sides. Only seven of her cannon were still were still firing. There were red streaks down the side of her hull, that Martin realized were tracks of blood from the dead and wounded strewn across the decks. Men were hacking away at the rigging from the foremast trying to clear room to move it out of the way. The mainmast was rocking dangerously and another group of men were trying to carry a hawser from the truck of the mainmast to the bow of the ship to brace it and stop it from collapsing and bringing the mizzen down with it.

All the time the relentless crash of the guns from the British ship, as they were sending their heavy shot to add to the carnage on the enemy ship. As he watched he heard the swishing noise of the canister shot and saw men on the enemy deck struck down. All the men with the hawser were gone, cut down with the one shot. The collection of half inch lead shot spread in a wide swath and took them all.

Martin heard his name called and turned to see Mr. Carrington struggling to rise from the deck where he had fallen. There was blood on his sleeve. He ran across and sat him up, looking in horror at the splinter of wood that projected from the sleeve.

"Get me back on my feet, Martin. Come, help me up." Carrington gasped. Martin hauled the wounded man up to his feet and held him while he caught his balance. The Captain came across and saw the wound. "Get Mr. Carrington down to the surgeon! Quickly now."

"But, sir, my place is on deck here with you." Carrington was still finding difficulty in standing upright.

Martin called one of the spare hands over to help him. Between them they carried the First Lieutenant down to the orlop deck where the surgeon was performing his duties, in what looked like hell to Martin Forest. They set Carrington down and told the surgeon he was there.

The Surgeon came and looked at the wound. He tied a bandage tightly round the arm above the splinter, the blood flow slowed though it did not cease entirely. "I'll get back to you shortly," he said and returned to the man he had been working on, still held down by his assistants.

Martin returned to the quarter-deck where he realized that the guns were silent. The Frenchman had struck her colors.

Mr.. Green spoke to the Captain, who ordered him to take a party across to the captured ship and accept the surrender of the French Captain. As he turned to leave he called to Martin, "Collect your sword and accompany me to the prize. Tell the Bosun to bring the longboat alongside, and get it manned. I'll arrange some marines."

Martin called the Bosun and gave him his orders, then ran down to the gunroom and collected the sword given him by Mrs.. Bowers. He was back on deck in time to follow the crew down the side into the longboat. He was followed by ten red-coated marines, who crouched down the middle of the boat trying to keep clear of the men settling to row.

At the French ship's side there was nobody to stop the boarding party from hauling themselves aboard. On the deck the men were still clearing the raffle of torn sails and tangled rigging. On the quarter deck the Captain was leaning on the binnacle, his shoulder bandaged and the arm hanging loosely down. Beside him another officer stood arrogantly facing the British party.

"Have you come to surrender?" He said in accented English.

The Captain wearily lifted his head and drew the sword awkwardly from its scabbard. He reversed it and presented it to Lieutenant Green. He turned to the man beside him "Armand, your sword!"

The arrogant one drew his sword and Martin, not trusting the man's temper, lifted the pistol he carried. In the event the man ungraciously passed his sword over with a nod of his head. Lt. Green turned to Martin. "Return to the ship and inform the Captain we need help to keep the prize afloat, and, if they can be spared, more of the marines."

Martin took the longboat back to the *Arun* and informed the Captain.

He watched as Bill Swan, Master's Mate, and Robert Harper, the senior midshipman took the loaded longboat across the darkening gap between the ships. They all climbed aboard including the longboat crew who went to help with the securing of the prize.

They kept company for two days whilst repairs were carried out on both ships. After 48 hours of backbreaking work the prize parted company with *HMS Arun*, and they resumed their voyage to Gibraltar. The *Charon* made for Falmouth, perhaps two day's sailing north-east back the way they had come.

Both the officers and the crew were for several days involved in the restoration of the rigging and the remounting of one of the forward broadside guns which was dismounted during the action with the *Charon*. The absence of Lt. Green and Midshipman Harper was also felt as the remaining deck officers were pressed to cover the gaps. John Reed was elevated to acting Lieutenant, having had three years' experience as a Midshipman. The captain thought the responsibility would be good for him. His chances of retaining the post were slim, as it was known that there were several officers in Gibraltar from the Mediterranean, men wounded in action and taken to Gibraltar for treatment, now recovered and looking for places. The unsuccessful would be returned to England where they must compete with many others for berths.

Captain Bowers was indeed depending on the pool of men available in Gibraltar to make up the numbers short in the crew due to being shorthanded when they sailed, a situation made worse by the need to produce a prize crew for the captured French frigate.

He at least was only one of the people who sighed with relief when the Rock hove into view.

For Martin the arrival at Gibraltar was an occasion in his young life, it being his first visit to anywhere out of England. The warm climate and the exotic fruits in the market were a delight and a source of wonder. Though he had seen a monkey before, the sight of the Rock apes running free was odd and he very quickly learned that they were not tame.

The ship had acquired a new third Lieutenant, as Alan Powers was elevated to second with the arrival of newly promoted Lieutenant Michael Walker, who now commanded the gunroom with his own particular set of rules. The addition of two more Midshipmen reduced Martin once again to junior in the gunroom. Though both seemed reasonable, only time would tell. Sufficient that on this day the young men were able to enjoy the freedom of the Rock for twelve hours. The ship was under orders to sail in company with a convoy to Naples the following day in the afternoon. In view of the labors of the voyage to Gibraltar the Captain had given them the chance to stretch their legs ashore.

They sailed in company with the frigate *HMS Jupiter*, 38 guns, to join the convoy passing through the straits under the protection of the fleet of Lord Hood. The Flagship, *HMS Victory* 100 guns, paused in the roads outside the harbor. The Captains of the frigates, *Arun* and *Jupiter,* were ordered to repair on board.

Jupiter had been waiting in Gibraltar when the *Arun* arrived. Both had been sent to Gibraltar for assignment. Now in the great cabin of the *Victory* the two Captains were told that they would be part of the fleet bound for Toulon. The so-called Naples convoy was actually a provision convoy for the force involved in the blockade of the French port. The addition of the two frigates to the fleet was welcomed by Lord Hood who like most British admirals of the time complained that he was always short of frigates, essentially the eyes of the fleet.

They arrived off Toulon in July and waited to be joined by the Spanish fleet of seventeen ships, when they arrived. Martin was most impressed until the now recovered Mr. Carrington informed him that the crews were poorly led. He pointed out the uneven brails on the furled sails and, through the telescope, the rattails in the rigging.

"The problem is, young Forest, leadership is not gained through the whip. Captain Bowers has shown that the best results are obtained by fair treatment. This ship has not seen the cat used for the entire voyage up to now. I hope you have observed the way the men respond? Being of the nobility does not automatically mean that you are fitted to lead men into battle. Happily, in that regard, though the field is still slanted in that direction, skill and training have an important place in the selection of naval officers. In fact, Prince William, the Duke of Clarence, has just passed for Lieutenant, having, like you, served as a midshipman, on *HMS Barfleur.* He learned his trade just as you do now."

Martin was impressed by the information and even more so by the fact that the already famous Captain Nelson was serving with the fleet in the blockade, in command of the *Agamemnon* 64 guns. A ship he could see with his naked eye across the bay from the *Arun*.

For the first two weeks, the bustle and activity of the ships, and the back and forth boat traffic, kept Martin entertained and very busy. But as the time passed and nothing seemed likely to happen, matters began to become routine.

From the masthead he was able to study the ships of the French fleet anchored in Toulon. All twenty of the ships of the line, that is ships that stood in the line of battle, including only ships of sixty guns or more, were manned, though none showed any sign of coming out to give battle to the combined British/Spanish fleet.

Chapter three

Toulon and points East

1793 December

The town of Toulon favored the Royal cause, but, though the French Admiral was also Royalist, a large proportion of his men including his second in command were Republicans.

Lord Hood had landed two regiments of troops he had brought from England in August, after the authorities in Toulon surrendered the town and the ships to the blockading fleet. Though the troops were not sufficient to defend the town from the Republican army, they were able to hold matters up for sufficient time to enable 14.000 loyalists to be brought aboard the fleet.

During this time parties went ashore for various reasons and Martin was included on several of these excursions because he had a basic knowledge of French. His usage of the language improved with practice. The only other French speakers in the ship were Lieutenant Carrington and Midshipman Troop, one of the new arrivals from Gibraltar. The shore duties were varied and when Martin was chosen he found himself expected to command a battery of naval guns, now in regular action against the growing army of the Republic. They would be used to assist in strengthening the defences, then perhaps to help move some of the more important families from their houses to the harbor, where often private ships were available to take them off elsewhere to safety out of the reach of the clutches of the mob.

The bulk of General Carteau's Republican forces were still massing and getting organized when Lord Hood decided to abandon Toulon. Whilst the refugees were being loaded onto the fleet ships, arrangements were made to blow up the arsenal and destroy the French ships in the harbor. Parties from several of the smaller ships of the fleet were told to burn the French ships. Martin found himself with a party of six seamen including a gunner boarding a French 28 gun Corvette. This was in effect a frigate and, though not new, was a fine ship. The crew had abandoned her with most of her food and useable stores removed. They had however left the magazine untouched. Under the eyes of several grim looking men on the quayside, Martin and his men boarded the Corvette and set to work. The gunner was disgusted, "I could have left our powder in the ship. The bastards have left her with enough powder and fuse in the magazine to blow up half of Toulon."

"Let's put a few of the kegs in the boat, just in case." Martin said, "We might need it on the other ships."

The gunner nodded and called for the men to lower some of the barrels already brought on deck down into the longboat that they had used for the trip from the ship.

The corvette was anchored off in the harbor and Martin noticed that the drift of the tide was pulling her towards the moorings where four of the other frigates or corvettes were moored. When the gunner had been round all the guns except the one he was going to use to blow a hole in the bottom to sink the ship. Martin pointed out his observations.

"If we cut the cables we will drift down on the next two ships to be destroyed. From what I can see, if we cut them loose they will collide with the next in line. Is it worth a try, d'ye think?"

The gunner looked. "You devious…." He corrected himself hastily, but couldn't help grinning as he said, "That would do nicely, sir." He bellowed out to the big seaman who was chopping open barrels of powder. "Carter, take that axe and cut us loose."

"Aye, aye, Mr. Gunner, sir." He grinned as the gunner swore at him and made his way to the eyes of the ship to hack through the strops holding the anchor cable. He then tripped the ratchet. The anchor cable ran out with a roar, the bitter end flying through the hawse hole releasing the ship to drift with the tide.

The gunner turned to Martin. "Perhaps you would like to do the honors with the next two, sir."

"I'll take the boat." Martin called the men to the boat and they left the gunner with one man while they rowed down to the next in line.

Carter climbed on board and did his trick with the anchor cable. Then clambered down into the boat once more to visit next in line.

As he went to climb on board Martin stopped him. "Collect some line and grappling hooks. We may have to persuade these ships to stay together."

Carter nodded. "I'll take Andrews with me, sir. He can find the ropes while I cut the cable."

"Good! Off you go, Andrews."

Andrews returned with ropes while Carter was still trying to release the anchor cable.

When he eventually returned he said, "There is someone aboard the last ship, sir."

"Well, let's go and see. Shall we?" Martin checked the pistol he had brought, replaced the sword he had put aside, in the frogs on his belt and called the men to row to the last ship in line.

He boarded first, Carter and his axe behind him. The other men followed. He called out in French for the person to come out and a girl appeared carrying a baby. She came out followed by two more children and a wounded man who could hardly walk. The man wore the uniform of a Royalist soldier.

Martin asked him who he was and why was he here.

It seemed he had been wounded in the fighting and returned home to recover, only to find his home taken by Republicans and his children on the street. His wife was dead, raped and murdered by looters.

"We will take you back to our ship, then. I don't know what my Captain will say, but you cannot stay here."

The man shrugged his shoulders helplessly.

Martin turned to the man nearest to him. Recognizing him he said "Peters, take the family down into the boat and keep them company until we finish here. Andrews, let's hook onto our neighbor." He indicated the ship drifting down towards them, followed by the others in turn.

He sent the others down to the boat leaving himself Carter and Andrews to arrange the incendiaries. The gentle nudge of the next in line was followed by small collisions of the other ships. Andrews was off leaping from ship to ship with the lines, tying off the ships just to keep them together long enough to get a good fire going. The corvette with the gunner on board was now attached to the next in line and the roar of the last gun signalled that the hole had been punched in the hull to make the corvette sink in place.

Carter had brought several barrels of gunpowder on deck and was trailing fuse to the entry port where the boat was attached. Andrews was on the next ship hauling powder from below, the gunner was on the second last ship now with a flame lit and burning well, in the pile of sails left on the deck by the departed crew. Martin waited for the others to join him. Then when they were all safely in the boat, he lit the fuse and descended hastily into the now crowded boat. They pulled away. As they stood off to watch, the flame from the piled sails suddenly leaped up into the rigging and the brailed sails of the next ship and the next. Then the powder on the last ship blew, showering the other ships with burning debris, and suddenly the entire group was ablaze. The sole anchor hawser on the last ship burned through, and three of the burning ships broke away from the sinking corvette and drifted inexorably down to the three-deck ship of the line anchored at the end of the row of line-of-battle ships.

Horrified Martin saw the collision and the subsequent burst of flame from the mast and sails of the French ship.

A boat appeared round the stern of the now burning ship with a lieutenant in charge.

"What ho? What ship?" He called.

"The frigate, *Arun*," he called back. "Midshipman Forest, sir."

"Much obliged, Mr.. Forest. Lieutenant Graham *HMS Victory*. I will be happy to buy you supper, if we meet ashore. You have saved me a deal of trouble by setting fire to the Frog."

Martin remembered the soldier and children. "Sir, perhaps you can assist me here. The boats drew alongside. Heexplained about the children and their father. Graham looked at him, "I see there would be little room on a frigate. We have people already on the *Victory*. Pass them over into my boat. We should find room for them."

With a sigh of relief Martin passed the family across to the other boat and called his crew to give way back to their own ship, with a parting wave to the other boat.

The month of December 1793 was busy, with the retrieval of the troops from the town of Toulon, and the collection of the remaining loyalists. For *Arun* there was movement out into the Mediterranean, escorting cargo ships to Italy. It was on a voyage in January 1794, that Martin discovered just how much he had learned during the past year he had spent at sea.

They had delivered three ships to Naples and were escorting one ship loaded with provisions for the fleet.

The masthead lookout reported two sails to windward. Both changed course towards the frigate. The lookout was unable to identify the ships for some time, but eventually he reported the pair to be privateers under the new Tricolor flag of France. The ships were armed, each carrying a 15gun broadside. Though the guns were 9 pounders they were still a formidable challenge. The provision ship was armed with ten guns, and under orders from Captain Bowers, her guns, 12 pounders, were loaded and run out. The *Arun* took the initiative and placed herself between her charge and the enemy. Opening fire, she disabled one of the ships with a lucky shot. The foremast of the brigantine fell, stopping her in the water. She was helpless to fire her guns because of all the flammable canvas strewn about her decks.

The other ship committed to the action, came on and fired her broadside guns as the *Arun* turned to meet her. Her guns managed to bring down the foretopmast of the *Arun* which was snapped off just above the platform where the lookout had been stationed. The loss of the top section of the mast caused the ship's head to fall off line and enabled the *Arun* to fire her entire broadside into the unfortunate ship. She had literally brought about her own defeat. The weight of shot smashed in her side, the mainmast fell and she took an immediate list that worsened, while the men of the frigate watched.

The crash of the guns from the merchantman shocked them all, unexpected as it was.

It seemed that the privateer had launched boats on its sheltered side and the merchantman suspected that she would be boarded. Her canister shot had wreaked havoc among the boats, but it was the two round-shot from the merchantman that killed the privateer. They had struck the ship as she recovered from the *Arun's* broadside, striking the exposed bottom as the ship heeled. As the vessel stabilized, the holes under water allowed the water to flood in and she immediately started to settle in the water. There was little to be done with her, except take off her survivors.

The other ship struck her colors and it was possible to see her crew taking to the boats, even while there were still men working on the deck trying to clear the litter from her decks. The bulk of the crew including the privateer Captain took to the boats, raising masts and sails and making off towards the distant loom of the island of Sardinia.

As far as Captain Bowers was concerned it was good riddance, He sent a prize crew over to the stricken ship under the command of the 3rd Lieutenant Wales with Martin Forest, now 14years old, as second in command. Detailed to collect a prize crew, Martin called on Carter, as senior hand, with Peters.

Martin had written to the Parson in Peter's home village. The letter had gone with the prize taken before they reached Gibraltar. A reply had come whilst they were stationed in Toulon. It seemed that Peters' mother was well and was now keeping house for the Parson. Peters had settled down to his work and had earned his place as a top-man in the ship. Now with the other members of the crew of the boat, there were fifteen men in total going across to the damaged privateer, which they now knew was named *La Corbeau (The Crow)*

Carter was named acting Bosun. He had the remaining crew members, abandoned by their fellows, brought together, where with the help of Martin, he pointed to the worsening weather and the shattered mast. The leading hand still on board shrugged, said something in a local dialect to the others. They all moved forward to return to the work they were doing when the ship first struck her colors. They grappled the mast from the sinking privateer. Peters, from the prize crew, jumped down onto the floating wreckage, slashing the stays at the metal cringle where they attached to the mast. The spar was hauled up using the windlass, with all hands at the bars. Meanwhile Peters hacked off the ropes around the rescued mast as they appeared. Carter guessed they would be able to fish the spar to the stump of the fore/mizzen mast. It was darkening before they cleared the mess on deck. The stern lights of the merchantman and the *Arun* were fading into the distance as they offered up the new spar, and lashed it to the trimmed-off stump. The sea was rising, so Lieutenant Wales ordered the rigging to be set before work could be stopped for the night.

With the shattered piece of the ship's own foremast, floating and still attached, acting as a sea anchor, the prize rode out the night. Martin fell into his berth well after midnight, exhausted.

The following day dawned with angry skies and the waves piling higher and higher.

The work, swaying up the yards for the sails, took most of the morning watch, the fourteen privateers working alongside the British seamen. For the rest of the day the sails were hoisted to the yards and attached. With the rigging back in place the jib sails were re-rigged and the sea anchor released, they now had the chance to make way to re-join the fleet.

It seemed that the privateers from the crew were a mix of Sardinians, fishermen pressed from the fishing fleet from Corsica and the northern parts of Sardinia, and three Irish. Their accent had made Martin's job of translation much more difficult. Their native language was a patois of Italian, though they spoke and understood French as a matter of survival. The two Corsicans among them were treated with suspicion until it was discovered that both were fugitives from the law and quite happy to serve the ship whatever flag she carried.

What was not good was the weather. The sirocco was blowing from the south. The hot dry wind had brought rough seas, and the short-handed ship was still unbalanced, pitching and rolling in the uneven waters. Wales had life-lines strung along the deck and the entire crew were called out for all sail changes. The sharp twitches in the movement of the ship caused several accidents, that first night. When Martin reported to take the morning watch he found that disaster had struck. Lieutenant Wales had disappeared. He had been last seen at the change of watch at 8 bells (4am.). The movement of the ship had been violent and all the men awake were holding on for their lives.

"Carter, let's search the ship."

"Aye, aye sir." Calling for men to accompany him he set off, still hanging on for his life.

Within a few minutes he returned. "Sir, we have found him. It's bad news I'm afraid. We found Mr. Wales at the bottom of the forward stairs. He has a broken leg and damaged his head. The men have taken him to his cabin. The carpenter is setting his leg and he has bandaged his head but he is still unconscious. You are in command, sir."

For Martin the quiet last words from Carter sent a chill up his spine. He looked about him. The grim weather was still a problem. As he watched, the wind stripping the peaks of the waves, and sending the spray in sheets across the deck, hammering at the men hanging on to the rigging for their lives, he realized that this would be no easy task.

"We'll ease her head northwards to take the pressure off the jury rig. Running with the wind should let her ride better."

"What about the French, sir?" Carter sounded just a little anxious.

"They'll just have to cope with the weather on their own." Martin said with a hint of a smile.

Carter grinned, satisfied that his own opinion of this young man was confirmed. He may not be very old, or experienced, but he had the sort of strength that was already coming through. This situation would not send him into a panic. He would benefit from a little advice, of course.

The weather did not improve, and the ship labored through the angry waters of the Mediterranean. It was late in the afternoon when a new sound was heard through the racket created by the storm.

In the distance a brief flash of light appeared. It was followed by the crack of gunfire. A ship was fighting for its life. Still sailing downwind *Le Corbeau* approached the battle unseen or at least disregarded by the combatants.

Without thinking, Martin took the telescope captured with the ship up with him to the main top. From there despite the wild swings of the mast he was able to see over the intervening rain and surface spume. Two ships locked in combat. The bigger of the two was a French ship, by her rig. The other had a lateen sail. He guessed she would be a pirate from the Barbary Coast to the south.

As he watched the lateen sail was hauled down. He thought the pirate was a galley, and was manoeuvring to board the other ship.

He slid down the rope stay to the deck and turned to Carter. "It's a Barbary pirate after a Frenchman, from the looks of it."

"We don't have a full crew, sir." Carter sounded a little anxious.

"They don't know that," Martin said thoughtfully. "Suppose we appear and give them a broadside." He tapped his fingers on the rail.

"But si......" Carter stopped as he realized what Martin was saying. "We could have both broadsides loaded and run out ready. They have boarded the prize, leaving a skeleton crew on the galley, with slaves at the oars."

"We give them a broadside." He hesitated. "They don't know we are here! If we drift a boat down to her, we could board and release the slaves. The carpenter would bring his tools. Once we had the ship you could bring this ship close and give them a gun. I would hoist our own flag on the pirate."

"Sir, that is madness. There may be enough men on the pirate to stop you. Even in all the confusion it will never work."

"You are probably right. So first, get the guns loaded, bow chasers with ball, broadside with canister, and run out quietly, I will take the carpenter with me and we will drift down to the pirate on a rope tied to the small boat. Keep the ship up wind, but close the other ships. In this racket, they probably wouldn't see or hear you anyway.

"If it is possible, I will board through the stern windows and see if we can release the slaves. If we can, I'll show a light. Once they are released, we will take the galley, using the freed slaves. At that point I'll show two lights. You can then show yourselves and fire a single gun. That should get their attention. If they don't surrender tickle them up with the canister."

Carter looked at Martin in astonishment. He could not believe this boy would suggest such a foolhardy plan. "But sir!"

"The guns, Carter. They are the key." Martin turned and called the carpenter over. "Bring your tools. We will need to break the chains to release the slaves."

The carpenter shrugged and went to fetch his tools. His long experience at sea had taught him, that you don't argue with officers, even if they are still fourteen years old.

Carter got the men to work on the guns. There was still firing going on between the two embattled ships.

Martin and Adams, the carpenter, paid out the rope from their boat tossing up and down on the violent sea. Both were tied to the thwarts, in case the boat was upturned.

They came into the lee of the galley as they heard the crash when the two ships clashed, suddenly they were fending off from the carved stern of the ship.

The boat rose and fell, rising above the windows in the stern. There was a small gallery across the stern and Martin timed the rise of the boat and jumped catching the gallery rail and hauling himself aboard. The carpenter's tool bag hit him in the chest as it arrived, followed by Adams who collapsed in a heap beside him on the gallery.

The window was not locked and the two men climbed into the stern cabin. The fighting seemed to be half on and half off the ship. Feet still pounded the deck, to and fro overhead.

Martin opened the cabin door. Men were fighting at the starboard bulwark where the two ships were held together by a series of grapnel lines. The stair to the slave deck was clear and the two men crept down the steps. Martin unbound the oilskin from his pistol, and loosened the sword, then drew it quietly. With pistol in one hand and sword in the other he went down the last few stairs to the galley deck. The stench was horrific.

Right in front of Martin, only five feet away, stood a big man stripped to the waist, he wore a loin cloth and a turban. Otherwise he was naked. Adams stepped past Martin and, lifting the small sledgehammer, hit the man over the head. The iron skullcap concealed by the turban rang with the impact. So the man did not die immediately. But he collapsed satisfactorily to the deck and exposed the view of the crowded benches. At the far end of the row of oars another man started forward lifting a massive curved sword. Martin lifted the pistol and shot him. The sound of the shot loud in the foetid air below decks but unheard amid the noise of battle above. Martin called "Any British here?"

"Will they fight?" Martin indicated the slaves in general. A chorus of voices answered from the benches. "Give us the chance." The reply was reassuring.

Adams was at work at the clamps for the long chains running the full length of the galley benches. As he loosed the bolts retaining the chain the slaves pulled it through, allowing them to stand. Free from all but the chain between their wrists. The first row of men released went to the unconscious man felled by Adams. One wrapped his chains round the man's neck and snapped it tight, nearly severing the head from his body. He released his chain, satisfied that the man was dead and turned to Martin for orders.

"Weapons?" Martin asked. The nearest man turned and indicated the rear bulkhead of the long cabin. The rack there contained pikes and swords. He strode down and smashed the crude lock with the iron wrist band of his chains. Another man was using a cold chisel and an iron bar to break the rivet holding the wristband of his companion's chains. As soon as Adams cleared the second full length chain, he joined the other man, breaking the wristbands loose, releasing the men completely. The released men took weapons from the racks and stood waiting for orders. Martin remembered the light. "Adams, show the two lights to the ship." Adams gave the tools to another man to carry on releasing the slaves and went into the rear cabin to show the lights.

Martin looked at the long chain. He turned to one of the British slaves. "Get them to bring the chain, we might be able to use it on the bastards."

The man nodded and called to some of the others. "I'm Billy, sir. Billy Briggs."

"Right, Billy. Let's go and kill pirates." He turned and went up the stairs to the main deck. There was still a melee of bloody fighting. There were obviously a lot of men on the French ship, though they were losing the battle. The fighting men surged forward as Martin watched. The growing group of freed slaves, anxious to gain revenge for their enslavement, surged forward attacking the rear of the pirate force, hacking and screaming as they tore at the men who had kept them at the oars with whips and scourges.

The chain was used to trap and bind several of the pirates. Martin did not see the men bound with the chain driven overboard, to drown screaming in the heaving water.

The fighting men seemed not to notice that the slaves were loose, until the cannon from the brig fired. There was a lull in the battle, but it soon restarted. Martin called to his band of men to fall back. He grabbed Billy. "Call them back and lie down. CANISTER." He shouted.

Billy shouted in the tongue of the slaves, a sort of lingua franca of the benches. Many of the men heard and drew back. Others were deaf to his call.

The crash of the guns came again, and this time the whistle of the deadly load of pistol balls, swept the deck of the ships. Death came suddenly, and impartially, killing men from both sides, though the pirates took the worst of the losses, shielding their opponents with their bodies.

Chapter Four

Decisions

Through the ensuing hush came the voice. "Drop your weapons!"

The loom of the ship appeared out of the spray, the guns run out and apparently ready to fire.

Martin held his breath. The pirates had been reduced in number by the terrible destruction of the blast of canister among them. Bodies were strewn over the deck of the French ship, which Martin now realized was a corvette. He could see the torn French Tricolor, still flying from the forestay and the uniforms of the few survivors still on their feet.

He called to Billy, "Round them all up, Briggs." Separate the French from the pirates, but disarm them all."

"Aye, aye, sir." Billy called and started shouting instructions to the men. Four of the French were still standing, though several were wounded, and dead were spread all over the deck. The surviving officer said there was a doctor below deck tending the wounded. Those wounded on deck were carried below. The senior French officer was a cavalry Lieutenant. All the ship's officers were dead, as were most of the crew.

The ship *Le Ramier* had been crowded with wounded from Corsica, where there was a revolt of the local people against the Republic. They had been driven south, round Sardinia, by the British ships barring them from the French coast. The weather had made their situation worse, and the encounter with the pirates had taken them by surprise. It had cost them a high proportion of the crew, and most of the walking wounded, who had come up to fight for the ship and their lives. The exhausted Hussar handed over his sword to Martin. Hardly able to stay on his feet, he was grateful to escape capture by the pirates.

The Captain and leader of the Barbary pirates, was one of the captives. Though wounded, he would have survived had he remained captive. At least as Billy observed he might have lived long enough to hang. As it was, Martin understood that the man had attempted to escape by jumping overboard. He suspected, that he was assisted, and probably dead before he hit the water.

Back on board *Le Corbeau* Martin went to report to a now conscious Lieutenant Wales. "So you see, sir. I had to try and do what I thought you would have done in the circumstances."

Carter, who was standing by the door, smiled to himself. "This lad would make a good officer, after all. What was Mr. Wales going to say to that? *I wouldn't have attacked the pirates and taken two ships as prizes, added to the crew by nearly 100 men, and put a comfortable amount of golden guineas in my pocket.'* Carter did not think so.

Martin stood waiting to hear his fate,

When Wales spoke, it was after considerable thought. "You should not have taken action like that, but I cannot condemn you for taking the risk as you did. After all it is our duty to attack pirates wherever we find them. I will make that clear to the Captain when we arrive, and well done, Martin. Now, have me carried up to the deck where I can see to my duties. You will have to be my legs while this damn leg anchors me."

Relieved, Martin saluted. "Aye, aye, sir."

Carter spoke, "I'll get the carpenter and some men to set up a place on the quarterdeck, sir." He turned and disappeared, shouting for the carpenter.

The harbor at Gibraltar was busy, with small craft darting between the various ships moored there. The three ships sailed in, all three showing the union flag over the two French Tricolors and the strange tattered rag which was all that remained of the Algerian banner.

The harbor cutter met the ships as they came to anchor. The Commander standing in the stern-sheets called the deck. Martin saluted and answered since Lieutenant Wales was still unable to walk.

Martin called out, "Three prizes taken by *HMS Arun,* sir. Lieutenant Wales in command, currently injured and unable to walk, sir."

On the deck of the corvette Martin waited anxiously for orders. *Le Corbeau* was having her mast refitted in the dockyard. The repairs to the corvette were much easier to carry out, mostly consisting of work that could be undertaken by the ship's carpenter. The *Arun's* prize crew were finishing off the repairs, the rigging being braced to Carter's satisfaction. The hammering from below testified to the efforts of the carpenter in tidying up the damage that still remained from action of the previous weeks.

Lieutenant Wales was now in the hospital ashore, and Martin had been ordered to join the corvette *Le Ramier* with his prize crew while the Admiral arranged for her purchase and allocation as an addition to the fleet.

Billy Briggs approached and reported, Sir; boat approaching."

Martin was startled out of his reverie by the words. "Oh! Thank you, Briggs. How are you settling in?"

"I'm pleased to be out of that bloody rowing boat, begging your pardon, sir. I'll do well enough just now. You have a good crew on this ship." He stood and waited to be dismissed.

Martin commented, "We won't be on this ship much longer, I'm afraid." He nodded at the boat drawing alongside. "Man the side, Bosun." He called to Carter, having spotted the officer seated under the awning in the stern of the pinnace.

The officer who appeared was a man, perhaps thirty years old. He was followed by a younger man, a lieutenant scarcely older than Martin.

The pipes sounded and Martin saluted the two officers. "Midshipmen Forest, sir."

"Commander Avery, reporting to assume command. This is Lieutenant Marsh. Take me below if you please, Mr. Forest. Mr. Marsh, I suggest you familiarize yourself with the ship."

In the Captain's cabin, now clear of all signs of its former occupant, with the exception of the former Captain's boxed sextant, chronometer, and telescope, which was still lying on the sideboard, survivors of the action that had cost the former captain his ship.

The Commander seated himself at the table in the cabin and opened his orders. "I am instructed to assume command of *HMS Pigeon* (*La Ramier*), which ship has been brought into service with His Majesty's navy. I am also charged with taking in a crew and returning to Eastern

Mediterranean waters to join Captain Bowers in *HMS Arun,* under his command. You, Mr.. Forest, and the prize crew are to be carried along to be returned to *HMS Arun* along with Lieutenant Marsh, who is taking over the position of Lieutenant Wales.

"I will be coming aboard with my officers and crew in the forenoon in three days' time. That is Saturday. By that time I will expect the complete list of stores ordered to be taken aboard. In view of the shortage of men at your disposal the ship will be warped alongside the quay, immediately the powder barges have been brought alongside. Any questions, Mr. Forest?"

Martin hesitated. "Sir, why are you passing these orders on to me? If Mr. Marsh is in command of the prize crew, should he not be here?"

"Mr. Marsh is the nephew of Admiral Marsh, currently posted to the Admiralty. His rank is not gained by, how should I put it, experience. He is a nice enough fellow, and he will benefit from service under Captain Bowers."

He leaned back in the chair. "Just a little tact during our voyage together, Mr. Forest, and I'm sure all will be well. I will read myself in when I return on Saturday. Meanwhile Mr.. Marsh will assume command. Do we understand each other Mr. Forest?"

"We do, sir," said Martin, who certainly was not looking forward to the next two days.

The new name of the ship had been barely dry, when the lighters towed *HMS Pigeon* alongside the quay. With her powder and ammunition loaded and secure in the magazine, the work of loading the stores for their voyage now lay ahead.

Martin had a crew of forty-one, with the men from the privateer plus the addition of 12 of the galley slaves selected by Billy Briggs, so the loading work went reasonably well. Mr.. Marsh was puzzled by the fact that Martin, an officer, was actually helping the men, providing an extra hand when needed, to keep the work going. To the men, his help was appreciated, but not looked for. They did in general feel that officers were not supposed to get their hands dirty, though midshipmen were not quite officers. Mr.. Forest was liked by the crew, so he was accepted.

While Mr.. Marsh strolled around the deck, seeing the stores loaded and ticking off the list, Martin verified the goods were stowed. The remainder of Mr.. Marsh's kit was loaded to the astonishment of the crew, and for that matter of, Martin. The four trunks, plus the three cases of wine, and two large boxes of meats and vegetables, seemed sufficient for the entire gunroom to Martin. Marsh seemed to regard it as adequate only. His inquiry whether he could restock in Naples was met with disbelief by Martin.

As he admitted, when he tumbled tired out into his bunk, it was lucky that Lieutenant Marsh was amiable. He just hoped he had a sense of humor. He would need it under Captain Bowers.

Commander Avery and the crew reported on board as ordered. The presence of the prize crew made the accommodation crowded, but the reputation gained by the prize crew in general, and Midshipman Forest, in particular, promised the prospect of yarning in the off watches for the men. There was a certain amount of awe, among the junior midshipmen who joined with the new Captain.

The voyage east along the Mediterranean was fairly quiet, though the new captain worked the men at gun drill every day, allowing the expenditure of powder and shot at least once each day.

Martin attended the sessions with the ship's Master, taking his part in the daily training that all midshipmen undergo. His age meant he was older than all the newcomers except one. The presence of Midshipman Hayes was a definite negative as far as Martin was concerned. From the moment he arrived, Hayes went out of his way to impress the gunroom that he was senior. Sadly, Lieutenant Marsh did not seem to notice. The younger members of the gun room walked in fear of the man. Marsh was actually berthed in the gun room, as he would be on the *Arun*. The *Pigeon* being a smaller ship had fewer deck officers and the gun room normally would be occupied by midshipmen only.

The tensions in the gunroom were relieved when the captain found Martin sparring with one of the members of the prize crew. Carter was supervising and giving advice to both of them. "Keep that fist up, Wallace. Now, sir, drop your shoulder more and you'll slip the punch completely. There that's the way."

Marsh was watching with interest. But seeing the captain approach he called on them to stop and saluted the captain.

Avery looked keenly at Martin. "You are no stranger to a mill, I think?"

"Well, I have had some training, sir."

"It shows."

"We will be celebrating midsummer tomorrow. Will you be willing to show the youngsters something of your skill? Perhaps a match with Mr.. Hayes, d'ye think?"

"If he will agree and you wish it, I should be happy to, sir."

"Good. Carry on." The captain left to stroll the full length of the gun deck, stopping to speak to the gun captains and any other man he encountered on the way.

Martin watched the Captain's progress. This was the measure of the man, his ability to talk to all and any, without seeming to be trying to curry favor, laugh with them at some quip, and commiserate where needed. Men would follow a man like that anywhere, with a will.

On midsummer's day with the empty sea around them and the sun high in the heavens, there was little to remind the men that there was a war on. The sky as clear and the air crisp as the crew set up the square ring, in preparation for later in the day. Martin was beginning to regret his haste in volunteering for the project. The skylarking began with several of the men taking turns at racing up the rigging, their supporters yelling and exchanging insults with the opposition. On watch in the morning he paced the quarter deck, cursing the impetuous impulse that placed him in this match, but at the same time looking forward to the chance to remind Midshipman Hayes that he was not cock of the walk.

When Martin came off watch, he went to the gunroom to strip ready for the bout. Hayes entered and looked at his slim smooth muscled body. He sneered as he stripped his uniform off displaying broad shoulders and muscled physique. "I will not be gentle with you, Forest. You should prepare yourself for a beating. It will perhaps take some of that starch out of your neck."

Martin smiled quietly, "I will look forward to it, Hayes." He slung the towel around his shoulders and left the man alone in the gunroom, while he joined Carter beside the improvised ring.

As Hayes appeared Carter weighed him up, then turned to Martin. "E 'as the muscle, but I reckon the wind will do him. Make him jump about and he'll be all yours." He looked at Martin and grinned, "Give him one for me and the lads. He's a nasty bastard." These last words were a whisper that only Martin could hear.

The Captain appointed Marsh to referee the bout, and the crew gathered round to watch. Quiet wagers being made as the two contestants prepared. Martin flexed his legs and swung his arms round to get the circulation going while Hayes sprawled in his corner. Hayes looked big and menacing, sneering and making comments to his second, one of the Master's Mates named Murdo, a drinking partner who had served with Hayes in the past.

Marsh called them together and checked that the both wore the thin leather gloves the Captain had insisted upon.

"First man down ends the round, no blows to be struck when a man is down. No kicking or gouging, and if I call stop, you will stop!"

The two men went to their corners and the bell was struck. Martin leapt out of his corner across the ring and punched Hayes on the nose, while the other man was getting set.

 Blood spurted and Hayes stepped back in shock. Then he shook his head went into a crouch and advanced across the ring, hands high as he looked for a chance to hit Martin.

His ear suffered next, as Martin danced round him flicking surprisingly hard punches at Hayes' head.

Hayes lifted his arms higher to protect his head and as Martin saw the chance he stepped in and, as his right foot hit the deck, his right fist hit Hayes in the abdomen.

Hayes was only half prepared for the blow and his counter punch was on the way as he doubled over, the air forced out of him. The fist he threw at Martin caught him beside the head. It felt as if he had been hit with a brick. As Hayes toppled Martin staggered back, shaking his head.

Marsh called time and Carter flung water in Martin's face. The crowd roared. Hayes was not popular with the crew, and the men enjoyed seeing him hurt, as he obviously had been.

When Marsh called them to the line the two men faced each other once more. Hayes fist was moving by the time the bell rang but Martin was not there. For a second time a fist connected with Hayes nose and broke it with the force of the blow.

For Martin there was now no suggestion of holding back, having felt the weight of Hayes fist he knew he would need to wear him down as quickly as possible. The man was strong and his punch was lethal.

For three rounds Martin peppered Hayes with punches to the head, and took every opportunity to concentrate on his midriff. Hayes face was puffed and swollen and both eyes were closing. The odd blow he landed hurt Martin, causing the second round to be over after four minutes. The third was needed for Martin to recover, as he forced his aching body to keep out of range of the heavy fists of his opponent.

Hayes was getting more and more frustrated with his elusive opponent, and his legs were getting heavier. He had not anticipated more than two battering rounds to dispose of Martin. By the fourth round he was gasping for breath. Whereas Martin was now breathing evenly, seemingly fully recovered from the blows that had put him down. Hayes had deliberately dropped to his knees to gain respite. As he rested in his corner Murdo nicked the glove on Hayes's right hand, tearing the leather. "That'll mark him. Could take his eye out."

As they toed the line, Hayes got the first punch in his right fist just catching Martin's cheek tearing the skin, and causing the blood to flow. Martin spotted the tear in the glove as the fist drew back once more and, instead of retreating, he stepped toward Hayes and punched with both fists into Hayes battered midriff. Hayes caught unprepared gasped and doubled over to meet both of Martin's rising fists.

As he straightened up Martin stepped back and measured him carefully before releasing another punch with the full weight of his body behind it. Hayes staggered. Then Martin deliberately hit him quickly to the jaw and to the stomach, before standing back and letting Hayes topple like a falling tree to the deck.

The cheer that went up surprised Martin, who was not that sprightly at the time. Murdo dragged Hayes to his corner, but there was no way he could get his man to toe the line. Lieutenant Marsh raised Martin's hand, declaring him, the winner.

The wound on his cheek stood out white against his bronzed skin as he came on deck for his watch later that day.

Captain Avery stopped beside him as he stood at the rail gazing out to port.

The words were quietly spoken for him alone to hear. "That was well done, Forest. You have shown the rest of the gunroom the way. It was all I could have asked of you. Just between us?"

"Thank you, sir. Of course, sir." Martin murmured back. "He did ask for it," he added, but the Captain had gone.

The wind got up that evening, and the ship joined *HMS Arun* at dawn.

Captain Bowers looked keenly at Martin when he returned to duty on *HMS Arun.* The wound was healing but the scar remained. "So, Mr. Forest, what have you to report since you left this ship, and what have you done with Mr. Wales?"

"Sir, I have to report that Mr. Wales broke his leg and was concussed during the bad storm we encountered off Sardinia. I had to take command. When we cleared the damage in the storm we encountered a Barbary pirate attacking a French corvette. They were close encountered when we arrived and my first thought was to run. But I saw the opportunity to intervene to our advantage. We assaulted the galley and released the slaves, who joined us in the attack on the pirate boarding party who had just about defeated the French ship, which was undermanned, carrying casualties. The remains of the pirates were defeated by my combined men and the French survivors surrendered to me." Martin paused collecting his thoughts, while the Captain sat patiently.

"The galley and the French ship were taken as prizes. Many of the freed slaves had been captured from British ships and they joined us. I reported to Mr. Wales and we conducted the two prizes to Gibraltar. Commander Avery was given command of *HMS Pigeon,* the French corvette that was bought in to the Navy by the court in Gibraltar."

"Mr. Forest, I am pleased to receive the extra men you have brought along with Mr. Marsh, but I cannot help noticing that they had been written in as part of the prize crew detached from my ship. By what sleight of hand, did you convert a crew of fifteen men into forty? Have I missed something?"

"Sir, the crew of our prize, *The Pigeon,* was composed mainly of Sardinian fishermen who had lost their families and disliked their French captors, two are Corsican loyalists, wanted as rebels by the French authorities. All of the men assisted us with repairing the ship and also volunteered to join into the assault on the galley. So they were signed in as members of the crew at that time."

"I see. Thank you for the explanation, Mr. Forest." The Captain lifted the paper he had at his right hand. "I have here a report from Lieutenant Wales that states that, despite the weather conditions, you captured two armed ships with the help of the prize crew only, in the proudest traditions of the service, while he was incapacitated and unable to exercise command. This will be of assistance, I believe, when we return to Gibraltar. I expect you will be called to examine for Lieutenant."

Martin was dumfounded. It had never occurred to him that he would be expected to take the examination so soon.

He was turning to leave when the Captain stopped him.

"Just one final question, Mr. Forest. How did you get that scar on your cheek?"

Martin had to think for a moment to realize that the Captain was referring to the scrape he had received in the boxing match.

"Captain Avery had a make and mend on Midsummer's day, and I was asked to give a lesson in the ring."

"How did you receive a scar, in gloves?"

"I believe my opponent's glove had a tear."

"You won, I hear."

Martin nodded.

"Midshipman Hayes?"

Martin nodded once more.

The Captain looked serious. "Martin, I know Hayes. You may have made an enemy for life. If ever you serve in the same command, watch your back." He looked at Martin seriously.

"But, sir, it was just a demonstration."

The Captain proved to be better informed than Martin realized. "So you broke his nose and two ribs. That man will never forgive."

Chapter five

Lieutenant

1794 was a year of activity for the two frigates under Captain Bowers' command. Commander Avery proved his worth on several occasions during the summer months of the year. The news of the glorious First of June and Lord Howe's defeat of the French fleet off Ushant spread thought the Mediterranean swiftly

For Martin,, now fifteen the months were for learning his trade, as he was ever conscious of the time passing. His uniform was showing the signs of his growing stature and the impending exam for Lieutenant awaited the ship's return to Gibraltar.

He had encountered Midshipman Hayes on one occasion only since the fight. They were both involved in the siege of San Fiorenzo, in Corsica, as part of the landing force under Lord Hood. The force was composed of seamen and marines from the fleet, as the soldiers under the command of General Dundas were withheld from the undertaking.

Hayes was in charge of one of the guns from *Pigeon* and Martin's company was needed to help get the gun up to the heights commanding the town. As the gun was hauled by brute force up the hill. Hayes spotted Martin lower down the hill bringing up more men. Martin was suddenly aware of a rumbling noise uphill. To his horror he realized that one of the tow ropes had snapped and the gun slipping sideways toward his men. Gravel was spattering and rocks rolling stirred by the slipping gun. Without thinking, he lunged forward, calling his men to chock the wheels to check the slipping gun. If it got away the gun could be damaged and the carriage destroyed, apart from the men in its path.

He reached the gun, and threw his weight into stopping the slide downhill. Hayes appeared on the other side of the gun, beside the single tow that was holding the gun back. He had a knife in his hand. He looked across at Martin and smiled, turning to slash at the retaining rope with the knife.

The thrown club hit him squarely in the face causing blood to spurt from his already damaged nose. He disappeared from Martin's view as he continued to strain against the slowly slipping gun. Then his men arrived and the gun was saved. A new lashing was attached and the gun continued its progress to the hilltop redoubt. Hayes was carried off by two seamen from his party and the gun was taken over by the artillery captain in command of the battery.

"Did you lose your club, Carter?" Martin asked when the gun had been delivered.

"Why, I believe I have, sir. I must have lost it on the hill."

"Somebody left this one on the slope." It seems to have some blood on it, but I am sure it will wash off."

"Thank you, sir. I should have been in trouble with the ship's bosun if I lost my weapon without some good reason." He looked at Martin innocently. "Where did you find this, one sir?"

"It was on the slope where Mr. Hayes had his accident, beside this knife." Martin held out a knife. "See if someone has lost a knife when you get the chance. It has to be from one of the seamen on the hill here."

Carter looked at the weapon handed to him by Martin. "See here, sir. It must be Mr. Hayes's knife; it is a dirk like your own." He thrust the knife out for Martin to see. "I'll pass it to one of the *Pigeon's* crew on the way back to the ship, sir."

Nothing was said about the incident, but Martin remembered the words of Captain Bowers after discussing the boxing match. A chill ran up his spine. Hayes must have had his dirk out for some reason. The weapon would not fall out of its scabbard by itself. It was held in by a strong spring. He had been standing beside the remaining rope when he, Martin, was heaving at the gun to stop it rolling off down the hill.

If the single rope had broken, Martin would have been crushed like an ant beneath the weight of the gun. It would have only taken a few strands cut, to cause the rope to go.

During the campaign Martin had cause to be ashore on several other occasions. He did not encounter Hayes again, though he worked with *Pigeon's* men on several occasions.

The return to Gibraltar did not occur until December. Martin spent the intervening time working hard at his books. He was not looking forward to the forthcoming examination. Like most young men in his situation, he was not confident that he knew enough to pass in front of the experienced board of captains.

Passing into the harbor at Gibraltar in the shadow of the rock, was nerve-wracking for Martin. It meant that now was the time for him to face his three inquisitors for the examination.

While the board sat in judgement on the three candidates examined before him, Martin sat and suffered. One of the applicants came out nearly in tears. . He had failed and judging from his age would not be considered again.

Of the other two, though both had passed, one was white-faced in shock. The other was smiling quietly, though, as Martin noticed, his linen was wet with sweat.

As the last of four applicants he waited for what seemed a long time for the call. There was one friendly face present. Captain Avery, newly promoted to Post Captain, was one of the three, the others being, Captain Masters of *HMS Stalwart*, and the senior member, Commodore Nelson. As Martin stood waiting for the grilling he had been told about, Avery said, "Mr. Forest! You were in command of a prize when you came upon a sea battle between a pirate galley and a French corvette, both armed ships, in '94?"

"Yes, sir."

"You had a prize crew of fifteen men, I understand?"

"Yes, sir." Martin was wondering where this was leading, neither of the other captains said a word.

"There was still a gale blowing and you pressed the prisoners on your ship to help load the guns, while your commander Lieutenant Wales was injured and unconscious below?"

"Yes, sir. But I...." Martin stopped.

"I understand that you attacked and defeated the pirates and also the French ship. I have the facts, do I not?"

"Yes, sir. But...."

"Gentlemen, you have both read the letters of recommendation for this officer. His record speaks for itself. I realize that, like me, you both wish to get this matter over with as quickly as possible. Can I suggest we retire and deal with it with no further delay?"

Commodore Nelson stirred in his seat. "Masters?"

Captain Masters shifted in his seat and looked at the other two board members. He growled, "Having seen the man and read the comments, I can see no need for more time wasting."

Martin's heart sank. He was not going to be tested. He had failed!

Nelson smiled. "In that case, since we are all agreed, I can tell you, young man, that your ordeal is over. Personally, I am happy to say this appointment was rubber stamped by your conduct over the past year in the Mediterranean, and I would be happy to have you under my command, if fate and their Lordships so decree. Congratulations, Lieutenant Forest."

He signed the papers in front of him with a flourish and watched while the two Captains added their signatures.

Martin was stunned. He had passed. He was promoted. He received the handshake from Captain Avery, who muttered, "Well done, lad. It's well deserved."

Commodore Nelson patted him on the shoulder and smiled up at him. "Back to your ship, lad, she'll be away without you."

Masters grunted. "Waste of time. Should have done it on the quarterdeck. Well done, lad."

He was out of the door and on his way even as he spoke.

Martin took his papers and left the great cabin of the *HMS Captain* to return to his own ship. As he reached the sally port searching for the boat, a hail from Captain Avery stopped him. "Join me in my boat, Mr. Forest. I'll drop you off on my way."

HMS Arun was running free before the freshening south-westerly wind. For Martin standing on watch on the quarter deck of the frigate it was a thrill he had feared on occasion that he would never achieve. He was not in command, but for the moment the ship was his alone to direct. The Captain and the first and second Lieutenants were all below in the great cabin discussing the fitting-out lists and the program for repairs needed before they would be sent out on their next task, in what was looking like a lengthy war. Now the Spanish had added their weight to the French fleet it seemed possible that there would be more action for the overworked frigates of His Majesty's Navy.

The ship had every sail she could carry on this course and the master, when he came on deck, had mentioned that they were making good at least 12 knots. Considering that the hull must be carrying a good quantity of weed, they were doing well.

"Sail Ho!" The call from the masthead snapped him out of his reverie.

"Where away?" He called.

"Starboard bow, about ten degrees, sir. Ship of the line, sir."

"Mr. Reed, you will advise the Captain that we have sighted the Channel Fleet, ten degrees off the starboard bow." The Midshipman, James Reed, touched his hat. "Aye, aye, sir." and ran below to inform the Captain.

Martin grinned. The Captain would have heard the exchange with the masthead, but protocol must be maintained. As the junior lieutenant in *Arun* he was aware that he was still regarded as learning his job. He had been lucky to still be here. Mr. Marsh had found life in a frigate too strenuous and had been happy to seize the opportunity to serve as Aide-de-Camp to the Gibraltar Admiral once more. As Martin had arrived on board the *Arun* having passed for Lieutenant, Lieutenant Marsh had been transferring his multiple boxes and bags to a shore boat, to take up his new position. Martin had been delighted to find that at least one of Marsh's boxes of provisions had failed to make it to the land. The gunroom had been able to celebrate in suitable fashion on the three bottles of claret which had survived the move.

Lieutenant Martin Forest rode to Eastney on a hired gelding. As he entered the grounds to the house he tried to relax, but was only partly successful. He rode round to the stable yard and tossed the reins to Will, the stable lad.

Before he could brush himself off there was a shriek. As he turned he was struck by a tornado of lace and arms as Jennifer Bowers greeted her brother, as she called him.

"Hey, give me a chance to breathe, lady." Martin cried as he swung her in his arms, all tensions gone. From the door Jane Bowers said, "Welcome home, Martin. Jennifer, do let Martin loose so that we can greet him properly."

Martin and Jennifer walked arm in arm over to the door where Jane leaned down from the step to allow him to kiss her cheek. Taking his other arm, the three walked through the doors into the house, where they found the Captain seated in the drawing room reading the newspaper. He was dressed informally.

He looked up and smiled when he saw Martin. "Found your new uniforms, I see." He put his head on one side. "Can this man be the lad that saved my family, I wonder?"

"Oh, father. Please don't tease." Jennifer scolded. "Martin has to return to Portsmouth in four days. You should be pleased he has time to come home and see us like this."

Bowers looked at the two young people in front of him. Jennifer still childish in some ways, but now taller, was showing the signs of the beauty she would become. Martin was now near six feet tall, looking more mature, the confidence in his stance confirming the way he was settling into his rank of Lieutenant. "Welcome home, Martin." hHj held out his hand to Martin. "Please do not allow these women to cosset you too much. You will find it impossible to readjust to the ship otherwise."

"Really, Charles. You would be treating the house like your quarterdeck if we allowed it. Take no notice, Martin. Come change your clothes and relax."

Martin looked at Charles Bowers who smiled and nodded. He realized that he had indeed come home.

The days passed all too fast. On his return to Portsmouth he had to concentrate on his work as the ship was being refitted for her next cruise. He felt that now he had a home once more, he would like to spend more time there if it were possible. It would be some time before the ship was ready for sea. Hopefully he would get the chance to visit again before they sailed.

The ladies came to Portsmouth when Giles arrived to re-join his ship. The Captain was unable to join them, so the party dined in the Rose Inn where the ladies were accommodated. The two young Lieutenants in uniform accompanied by the lovely Jane and Jennifer in her first grown-up gown made a cheerful family party. The summer evening was mild and still light when they rose from the table and strolled along the quay, Jane with Giles at her side, and Martin with Jennifer. As they walked and chatted a voice called a greeting. Martin turned to see a familiar face in the uniform of a Commander approaching. Uncertain at first, he realized that he did know the face, "Why, it's Lieutenant, I beg your pardon, sir. Commander Graham, is it not? From the *Victory?*"

The Commander, Robert Graham, no longer unsure said, "Forgive me, Lieutenant Forest? I have never had the chance to buy you that dinner I promised. Oh, do excuse me, Miss. I have not seen your escort since Toulon."

"May I present Miss Jennifer Bowers, Commander Robert Graham."

Graham bent over the extended hand held out by Jennifer. "I am delighted to make your acquaintance, Miss Bowers."

Jane and Giles had returned to join them. "Why, Commander Graham. How nice to see you again." Jane extended her hand to Graham. "And this is my brother, Lieutenant Giles Masters. He is passing through Portsmouth to join his ship."

Graham smiled. "I am here to find my new ship. The captured corvette, *Le Corbeau*, now renamed *HMS Racer*. I have you to thank for my new command, Martin. According to the gazette, she was one of your prizes, I believe?"

"Well I…I was there." Martin said lamely.

"According to the Gazette you were in command at the time, so you were more than just there. In my mind that means you did it, so no excuses. You can explain it all to me over the dinner I owe you." He turned to the others. "Ladies, and you two gentlemen, please accept my apologies for interrupting your promenade." He swept a bow and took his leave.

Jennifer squeezed Martin's hand. "What was that all about. I knew nothing of it. You are a hero?"

"Oh, it was no great thing. Others have done better than I." Martin said uncomfortably.

"I rather like the idea of marrying a hero." Jennifer said calmly.

"Wha…what do you mean, marrying?"

"Oh!" Fluttered Jennifer "Did mother not tell you? I decided to marry you after we first met, when you saved us on the coach." She looked at him innocently. "Of course, if you would rather not, then I will understand."

Martin looked into her laughing eyes. "Miss Jennifer Bowers, if you are not careful I will insist you carry out your threat."

She suddenly became serious. "You will be very welcome, I'm sure, Martin Forest."

Martin was suddenly conscious of the electricity between them. "We will speak again of this but meanwhile please keep this between us."

"Of course, Martin." Without warning she reached up and brushed her lips against his. And Martin realized that he was lost.

They caught up with Giles and Jane, and continued their walk back to the inn.

As Martin said goodnight, Jennifer reached up and kissed both of the young men on the cheek. Jane also, but she looked at Martin with keen interest before releasing his hand. "You will not forget your home, please?"

Martin whispered back, "How could I?"

There was a certain complication in Martin's present situation. Seated in the great cabin of the *Arun,* the hammers silent, now the shipwrights had knocked off for the night, Bowers explained to Martin.

"There are qualifications entailed in the promotion to Lieutenant that include time served.

"Like most of my colleagues I entered my son for Midshipman years ago in the expectation of our being thus blessed. Fate has decreed otherwise, though the entry remains. You have not served sufficient time to take your place in the gazette lists for four more years."

He stopped and thought for a moment then continued. "I am not trying to coerce you into doing anything against your will. But if you become a member of my family, you automatically will qualify for the service as my son, albeit adoptive, and take your place in the staff list based on the twelve years accrued since I entered my son."

He stopped and looked keenly at Martin.

"But was not the entry based on a name at the time?"

"No. We had not yet known that Jennifer was a girl, so I entered the name, James. I am, of course, aware that you have no family now, so this is what I propose. I assure you the rest of my family approve. I ask that you will join my family, legally, and become my adoptive son. It will mean the addition of James to your fore-names and Bowers to your surname. It would automatically qualify your seniority, and you need look no further for a home to which you would have a legal right." Bowers stopped at this point and poured two glasses of wine. He handed one to Martin. "You do not need to make your mind up immediately. I assure you that my house will be your home regardless of your decision today."

Martin was stunned. He sipped his wine without noticing what it was, and made no immediate reply.

After a few moments both started to speak at once. Captain Bowers lifted his hand and pointed to Martin.

"Sir, I don't know what to say. You and your family have been so kind to me. I look in the mirror and hardly recognize myself. What you propose takes my breath away. Are you sure you would want me within your family?"

"Martin, it would be difficult for me not to notice the affection with which you are regarded by my wife and my daughter. They have both urged me to do what I have proposed before I had mentioned the possibility. You are assured of an enthusiastic welcome to my family legally and physically. So, what do you say lad?"

"Then, sir. I accept wholeheartedly. I would be honored to carry the name James Bowers in addition to my own."

Charles Bowers rose to his feet and held out his hand. Martin took it in both of his, feeling his eyes smart with the emotion of the moment.

The two travelled home in the Captain's carriage. Giles had sailed the day before but he had joined in the party the night before in celebration of Martin's promotion and adoption into the Captain's family, confirmed legally in the lawyer's office the day before. The return to Eastney was for the weekend and would be the last for some months. The ship was tasked to go to the West Indies as part of the force taking the overseas colonies of the French and the Dutch.

At the house Martin was greeted by a curiously restrained Jennifer, and the welcoming arms of Jane, who smiled and said, "Martin, though I am now your adoptive mother, I would be happy to be called Jane, if you will. I think you will need to discuss matters with Jennifer privately."

Charles looked at Jane in enquiry as Martin went off to find Jennifer.

Jane said, "I fear, my love, that our daughter thinks of Martin as other than a brother. Her love for him, is as future husband I suspect."

Charles looked surprised. "But she is only fourteen, and he fifteen?"

"My darling, nearly fifteen is only just over one year before sixteen. We were wed when I was sixteen and three months. So is it so strange?"

Charles looked thoughtful for a few moments. Then reacted as Jane suspected he would. "Well, I cannot think of a better suitor for her, can you?"

Jane smiled. "He is a fine man. So, let us see. As a son-in-law, he would be welcome. Otherwise as a son he is equally welcome. Tell me, would there be any legal problem if they do wish to marry? "

"None at all. The lawyer mentioned it knowing we had a daughter."

Not knowing whether to be pleased or not, the matter was dropped for the moment between them. But Charles knew that he could depend on Jane to do the right thing, however it turned out.

Accustomed to be treated as part of the family though he was, Martin still found it just a little strange to begin with.

Because Jennifer had disappeared after their greeting on arrival, he went looking for her.

Finding her in the upstairs sun room, he went eagerly forward to take her hand, and share his joy at becoming part of the family, her brother in reality.

She was quiet and withdrawn at first, before quietly starting to cry. Devastated, he urged her to tell him what the problem was, finally getting her to explain in halting words what was upsetting her.

"If you are now my legal brother, then we cannot marry."

The simple words struck him as funny, but in time he realized that she really believed what she had said. Gravely, he said, "You realize that when you are old enough to marry, you may not wish to marry me?"

"I will. I will want to marry you. I have told you already. Nothing will change my mind. After all it is only two years to wait." She started to cry once more. He kissed her eyes.

"Stop crying, Jennifer. If what you think was true, I would not have joined the family in this way. In fact since we are not blood related we can marry if we please, and provided you still wish it, at that time we can discuss things with your... our parents. Come now, no more tears. Let us join the others and celebrate my new family properly."

He took her hand and gently pulled her to her feet. She rose and kissed him. "Oh, Martin. I do love you."

To his surprise Martin kissed her in turn and said, "And I you, Jenny. And I you."

Hand in hand they went down stairs to join the others.

Chapter six

Caribee

Lieutenant James Martin Forest-Bowers, known as Martin to his friends paced the deck of His Majesty's Ship *Arun.* The sun was high in the sky, and the water was the sort of blue only encountered in this part of the world. The dolphins keeping pace with the frigate, sliced white paths through the water. Away to starboard the two schooners attached to the command of Captain Bowers, raced along, a fine sight with all sail set.

The island of Guadeloupe lay along the horizon to port, the destination of the three ships. They were ordered to take the French frigate that was reported to be lying in the harbor at Pointe de Pitre.

The three ships approached the island from the south. The Island of Marie Galante lay to starboard beyond the two schooners. In the distance it was possible to see the buildings of the settlement at Pointe de Pitre, and as the ship approached Martin sighed with relief to see the masts of the French frigate, lying behind the shelter of the islands in the mouth of the harbor.

Captain Bowers was frustrated by the lack of movement from the Frenchman, identified as *L'Orgueil* (Proud) a frigate of 36 guns. Guessing that she was not coming out to challenge them because of the two schooners, Bowers sent them both to cruise the islands to the south.

There had still been no reaction from the French frigate. Her captain probably thought that the schooners were lurking out of sight ready to intervene as soon as he left the shelter of the harbor. It was not until the *Arun* encountered a schooner full of wine from Bordeaux bound for Guadeloupe did any reaction occur. The capture had been simple and in full sight of the watchers from the shore. The American crew were put ashore, so the word went round the island about the failure of the *L'Orgueil* in preventing the capture.

There followed signs that the French ship was coming out, and it was with grim satisfaction that Captain Bowers assembled his officers to discuss the plan of action for tackling her.

"I propose beginning the engagement as the ship clears the outer island. There is a reef extending from the island out to the south for near a quarter mile I am informed."

The Master nodded and in his deep Devon burr added, "If the tide is where we estimate it to be, he will be forced to tack to clear the reef."

The Captain resumed. "The gunner has prepared a raft with some whizz-bangs. We will position it inland of the reef itself, where we estimate he will need to tack. If it goes well it could put him off a bit at a time when he will need to be careful, could even cause him to run aground.

"He is a big frigate and I expect he will have at least 300 men. We have a smaller crew though we are better trained, so I want all guns prepared before we commence. Mr. Forest will take the long-boat and position the raft. You will set off the explosives on my signal." He looked at Martin. "With the boat crew you will have extra men, with arms in case the opportunity comes to board the ship. Otherwise you will lie off until the action is over, or a suitable chance comes to re-join this ship. Is that understood?"

The group around the table all nodded in turn.

On deck once more Martin called Carter to assemble the boat crew and select men for the boarding if the opportunity came. The carpenter reported his raft ready, and since the sea was calm, it would be good to get underway as soon as possible.

The *Arun* ran in close to the reef and on the blind side dropped the raft and boat into the water. Martin took sights on the two bearings he had been given and had the boat brought to the spot chosen. They cleared the reef with room to spare and anchored the raft as instructed.

With the boat moored alongside the raft, they sat and waited. The Frenchman seemed to take ages to reach their location, and despite the small size of the target, aimed the odd shot in their direction.

"Steady, lads." Martin said as the shots created a restless movement among the men, "You'll have the chance to get at them in good time. I think the Captain wants to soften them a little first."

His comment brought chuckles from the older hands, and reassured the younger men. Martin did not really understand how high his reputation was among the crew. His actions in taking the prizes near Sardinia were now a legend below decks. Carter had made sure of that. It meant that there were always volunteers for any action that included Lieutenant Forest-Bowers.

The signal from the ship came as the latest shot from the Frenchman splashed the boat with spray. As the Gunner's mate lit the fuses, Carter's voice was heard, "You didn't expect that did you, Wilson. A bath at the expense of Napoleon. Must be the first on this voyage; eh, lads?"

The shout of laughter at this might have been heard by the French. Wilson was known for his aversion to water in any form, drinking and washing in it was not his pleasure, and all the others knew it. He sat and glowered at his jeering mates, then grinned himself, and looked to his cutlass and the club he was armed with.

The first British guns were fired as *L'Orgueil* came near to the longboat, which was now pulling away as fast as the men could row.

The long 12 pounders of the port broadside achieved one hit which scattered splinters across the deck of the Frenchman, from the shattered fore-yard. Several of the men were suddenly struck down by the flying wood shards, and the deck reddened with spilt blood.

Then the raft exploded just as the French ship started to come round on the new tack. The shock of the explosion did the ship no real damage, but the helmsman hesitated and the ship was caught in stays. Halfway between the new course, and the old, the sails aback, and the ship drifting, all forward way lost, the tide caught it, the wind quirked and her head came round only just in time to let her draw away from the reef.

In the longboat Martin had the mast erected and hoisted the sail, paralleling the course, albeit slower, than the French frigate.

From their position it was possible to see and hear not only the running out of the guns, but the flame of the broadside as the *Arun* opened her account. The first shots bit home in the starboard bow of the French frigate, dismounting two of her broadside guns. The other seventeen guns of the enemy's broadside fired in ragged succession as they came to bear on her opponent.

There were several casualties on the *Arun,* though no one died immediately. Using his telescope Martin was able to see the rips appear in the sails following the opening shots.

On the rise of a wave he was able to see the deck of the French ship and he was heartened to see the carnage on the deck. His earlier experience gained in the Mediterranean, made him realize that appearances were deceptive. So he was not surprised at the apparent carnage, nor was he deceived into overestimating the damage done to *L'Orgueil.* She was badly out of position due to the raft explosion. Because she was still inside the confined waters running into the harbor at Pointe de Pitre, her maneuvering abilities were restricted. For the *Arun* the outgoing tide was in her favor and Captain Bowers was doing all he could to use his advantage to the full.

The ship came about with plenty of sea room, and ran down on the French frigate set to cross her bows, but the *L'Orgueil* put up her helm and brought her full starboard broadside into play. This caused the *Arun* to stagger with the impact as most of the shot hit home. Three guns were dismounted and several of the men were killed and wounded.

Watching from the other side of the reef Martin called Carter and the Gunner's mate, Tom Hughes. To the gunner he asked, "Have you any more explosions in that bag of yours?"

The gunner nodded and reached into the bag and produced a grenade. "I have four of these. My boss says if the fuse fails, throw one of these on the heap and duck."

"How do you make it go off?"

Hughes pointed to the small fuse projecting from the top of the orange shaped bomb. "I lights this, and pray I've got time to get out of the way."

"Will it cut through the rudder ropes on that frigate?"

"Close up it'll blow the pintles off."

"What do you think, Carter? When she comes over the next time, can we get within reach, d'ye think?"

"She is well taken up with the ship, sir. We take the sail down, I reckon she won't take no notice of us. If we get close enough to hook on, we should be fine."

"If we get that close I want all the men up into the stern gallery. This boat will not stay afloat in her wake."

Carter scratched his chin in thought. "You have some distraction in mind, I think."

"Well. I don't like watching while my friends run the risks. Do you?" Martin looked Carter in the eye. "Well, do you?"

"No, sir, I don't. So let us run over to the reef and drop the sail."

The long-boat sailed over to the reef as the French ship closed from the other side. With the oars out the boat surged forward, crossing the disturbed water of the reef now exposed in places. The distance between boat and ship diminished rapidly as the ship went about, showing her stern to the boat. There was no shout of warning as they grappled the gallery across the stern. All eyes were on the *Arun* approaching fast across the passage entrance. The men swarmed up the ropes to the gallery, letting the boat trail on a long rope to give it a chance to survive.

The rudder ropes were directly below the gallery running back and forth with the movements of the wheel. The gunner had two grenades joined by a halter of rope so that they could hang over either side of rudder. The rope was long enough to allow the grenades to sit opposite each other either side of the upper rudder pintle.

He had ripped up an oilskin and wrapped the explosives to stop the fuses being extinguished by the spray. When he was ready he told the others to get inside the cabin and lie down. When they were all through the windows he lit the fuses and leaning over the gallery rail, he dropped the rope halter over the top of the rudder. The bombs hung either side of the rudder blade and as he threw himself through the window of the cabin they went off with a muffled thump. The guns on the main deck fired and the sound covered the rudder explosion. The gunner ran out and hung over the gallery rail, then came back to the others.

"She'll do." He said shortly. "Pintles gone, like I said, and rudder is hanging by a thread."

As he spoke there was a loud crack from below and the ship suddenly fell off the wind.

There were shouts of alarm and men ran at the door to the main cabin where Martin and his men crouched, weapons ready, waiting for the door to be broken in. On the gallery Carter had waited to see what the chances were for getting on deck. A head appeared over the deck rail, an officer. He shouted down at Carter indicating the rudder. Carter looked up and held his arms out and shrugged. The seemed to be enough, for the officer disappeared from view.

Carter took that as a good sign and hauled himself up to the quarterdeck rail. peering over at the scene of panic that came into view. He dropped to the gallery below and called to Martin and the men inside, hauling the longboat in easily now the ship had lost way. "Come out. Quickly now." As the men came out they dropped down into the longboat once more, stumbling into their places.

Casting off, the men rowed their hearts out getting away from the stricken ship. The guns of both ships were still firing but the Frenchman was suffering now she could not steer properly. Their efforts to steer using the sails, while they tried to get some sort of rudder mounted, were causing them to suffer serious damage.

In the boat Martin stood with his telescope watching the development of the battle in front of him. During the six months in the West Indies he had filled out. Now he was full six feet tall, tanned and fit, his practice with the sword given him by Charles Bowers had made him a formidable opponent for anyone. As he stood watching he felt he should really be involved in the action that was taking place. He also knew that the men with him also wanted to join the action.

He snapped the telescope shut. "Mast up and set the sail. Set course for the Frenchman."

The men set to with a will and soon the longboat was sailing briskly back to the reef, now well marked by the breaking waters over the projecting rocks. The French frigate was now drifting with two masts broken and several guns out of action. Her sides were stained with the blood of the dead and wounded that now comprised half her crew. The Captain leaned against the rail with a bandage round his head and another round his right leg. He was professional, an unusual thing in this day and age, and though many of the crew were conscripts, he had enough real seamen to keep the ship in commission and train the conscripts among the crew.

He was desperately unhappy at the loss of his rudder. It had robbed him of his manoeuvrability and made him take damage that he could have avoided. He sighed as the British frigate sailed across the bow with the dreaded roar of the broadside guns as they fired in turn, the shot ripping down the deck of his ship. He turned and swept the horizon looking for some chance of relief for his ship. Below his men were working desperately to repair the broken rudder. Then he saw the longboat shearing in towards the stern of his ship. He turned to call for men to defend the men working below. He found he could not make a sound and looked astonished at the long wood splinter that projected from his chest. He died without a sound.

Martin's men took the workers on the rudder prisoner. Keeping them secure in the cabin, tied and gagged, he cautiously looked through the broken door. There was no one immediately outside the cabin. The stair to the main deck was unguarded. He crept to the top of the stairs and peered at the scene before him. He was in time to see the loom of the *Arun*

As she came alongside with her men poised to board the French ship, he called to Carter to bring the men up but keep them close.

The screams of the boarding party as they crossed to the other ship were answered by the cries of the defenders, now urged on by the First Lieutenant. As the two parties met Martin watched for a few minutes to see how the battle went. Then, calling on his men to follow, he ran out to tackle the officer urging his men forward. The twenty men with him streamed out after him, lashing and hacking at the backs of the men in front of them.

The battle was bloody with little quarter offered or given, but the result was inevitable Peters shinned up the remaining mast and tore the Tricolor down, replacing it with the Union flag from the longboat. The sight of the small flag fluttering at the masthead took the spirit out of the French men and the fight ended, as they started throwing down their weapons in the face of the boarders.

Martin called his men back. Three had lost their lives in the fight and another two were wounded though not mortally. For Martin himself, there was another tear in his coat and a thin bloody line where a sword tip had marked his forearm.

The *Arun* took *L'Orgueil* in tow, bringing her to anchor in a bay at the Island of Marie Galante. The island of Guadeloupe was visible just over 25 miles away. The small population on the island, though under French rule, were not a problem. The threat of the guns from the ships was sufficient for them to leave the intruders alone, and they paid for the fresh food they took.

Martin took a working party ashore to find timber for repairs, carefully paying for everything as instructed. He had been warned not to upset the people unnecessarily.

For four days the work on the ships was carried out. The wounded from the Frenchman were put ashore for treatment by the local doctor. The fit were pressed into assisting in the repair of the two ships. The captured schooner was despatched to find the other ships of Captain Bower's command. And, while the repairs were carried out, and the wounded treated, Martin was sent to practice his French and survey the island.

He found the work camp on the second day. The forest was not particularly dense, but areas had been cleared to make plantations for the planting of sugar and coffee. He came across the camp at midday on the second day of his survey. Carter, who was uncomfortably seated on the back of a mule, reported that he had heard English voices from the people working in the woodland off the road. When they investigated they came across a clearing where a large group of men was seated on the ground eating and drinking. There were six men in uniform with muskets and long bayonets lounging at a table eating their own meal. The muskets stacked beside the table.

Martin, in uniform and his party of twelve travelling in a wagon, rolled into the clearing.

The guards in uniform seeing Martin's dress rose to their feet and the sergeant-in-charge came over casually to meet them. "What is this more prisoners?" The sergeant asked.

Martin looked at him, then in his best French said, "Attention! I am an officer. Stand properly when you talk to me."

He dismounted while the sergeant was still taking this in. Martin drew his sword and pricked the sergeant in his throat. "Tell your men to stand at attention for inspection. Leave their muskets."

The sergeant snapped out the order and the men lined up for inspection. Martin's men dismounted from the wagon and collected the muskets, then took the bayonets and ammunition pouches from the dumbstruck men.

Martin turned to the group of men eating but beginning to take an interest in what was happening. "Who is English here?"

One of the seated men got to his feet. "All of us except the two maroons there, and they have been sailing with us for three years now. Who are you?"

Martin smiled. "You are prisoners?"

"Yes!"

"I am Lieutenant Martin Forest-Bowers from *HMS Arun* anchored at Grand Bourg. What is your name?"

"I am Walter Harvey, shipmaster from Jamaica."

"Right, Mr. Harvey. I will take you and your men back with me to the ship. You will be a welcome addition to the prize crew for the captured French frigate, *L'Orgueil.*"

"She was the ship that took my schooner three months ago." He turned to the other men still seated. Looks as if we've been rescued, lads. Let's get the wagon."

"Where were you kept? Do you have any things to collect?" Martin asked.

"We were locked up in the grounds of the Governor's house, here on his plantation. The slaves here had an epidemic of some coughing and we were brought in to do their work."

"Well, we will just call in and see the Governor to thank him for looking after you so well."

Following the directions given by Harvey, Martin led his group to the house of the Governor of the island. The title was honorary, in view of the size and importance of the settlement.

The house itself was big and sprawling and the design reeked money. The Palladian pillars that ranged along the front gave the house an ancient Greek look.

Martin drew up his horse at the front step and studied the man who had appeared at their approach. He was short and had a small, pointed beard and a slim moustache. His eyes darted from Martin's face to his uniform, and then back to his face.

He spoke in a sharp high voice. "Who are you? What do you want?"

Martin took time to reply. "Are you the so-called Governor of this island?"

"I am the Governor. Don't waste my time. I am a busy man. Now, what do you want?" Martin threw the reins to Carter and stepped up onto the veranda of the house. He stood and looked down on the small man in front of him, who was looking more annoyed by the minute.

"I am Lieutenant Martin Forest-Bowers of His Majesty's Ship *Arun,* currently lying at Grand Bourg. I have just encountered a party of prisoners-of-war who have been made to do work on your plantation in place of slaves who, I am told, are sick. Can you confirm this?"

"Of course. But that is no concern of yours."

"The men are not slaves. They are prisoners-of-war and should be treated as such. Therefore any work they carry out should be paid for. I have come to collect their pay for the past three months."

"How dare you address me in this way. I will have you disciplined for this."

"First the payment, 30 guineas should cover it."

"Guards, guards. To me now." He was purple with rage by now, and his words brought four soldiers running to his aid.

As they approached the clicking of musket locks could be heard. The noise and the sight of twelve muskets at the ready stopped the soldiers in their tracks. Harvey and three of his men disarmed the soldiers and stood by.

Martin said, "The money, please."

The Governor turned and stamped into the house with Martin on his heels. The lady in the dressing gown was swept aside as he entered one of the ground floor rooms, obviously an office. He knelt and opened the big safe behind the desk, and counted thirty gold coins from a bag of coins on the shelf of the safe.

He thrust them at Martin. "30 Guineas." He said ungraciously.

Martin saw to his surprise that they were English Guineas. He turned to Peters who had followed him in. "Call Mr. Harvey, please."

"Well, you have your money. Why don't go and leave us in peace."

Harvey arrived. Martin asked him, "Was there any money in your cabin when you were taken?"

Harvey looked angry, "I had 240 guineas in my safe, "T'was to buy a new ship I had my eye on. Taken me near five years to collect it."

Martin stepped round the desk to the still-open safe and retrieved the bag from the shelf. Fending off the Governor he said, "Would this be the gold?"

Harvey swore, "Dammne!" He said. "T'is my own bag. See, there is my name on it."

Martin looked and saw the name Walter Harvey, faintly written on the side of the bag.

"Count it." Martin said. All three stood and watched while Harvey counted the golden guineas, there were 30 short. Martin picked up the money from the desk where the Governor had placed it and returned it to the bag. "That's your money back, Harvey." Turning to the Governor he said, "Now the 30 guineas in payment, or its equivalent."

"How dare you....." He spluttered incoherently.

"Shall I help myself then?" Martin suggested reasonably.

The little man found some coins elsewhere in the safe and put a quantity in a bag and passed it to Martin.

"If I find you have short changed these men, I will return and take all your money." Martin said seriously. With that he turned, gestured to Harvey, and left the house.

He gave the bag of wage money to Harvey. "Pass this round to your fellows. It is some payment for the work you have all done for the past weeks."

Harvey was nearly in tears. His own bag of money returned and rescue from this cursed place was far more than he had bargained for.

He turned to Martin. "Sir. Will you hold this for me until we reach Kingston?"

Martin took the heavy bag and hung it on the high pommel of his saddle. "I'll ask the Captain to keep it in his safe-box for you."

Chapter seven

Diversions

The harbor at Kingston was busy with small craft. The collection of inter-island trading craft made navigation difficult when *HMS Arun* entered with *L'Orgueil* in company. The jury rig had survived the voyage from Guadeloupe, and the prize was sent in to shipyard hands for proper refit.

Having examined the ship Bowers was confident she would be bought by the Navy and, with the prize money from the schooner plus her valuable cargo, the officers and crew were accumulating a comfortable sum in prize money, for those who wished to save it.

Martin contemplated the account proffered to him by the Crown Agent in Kingston. He was now wealthier than his father had ever claimed to be. The moneys from the two prizes taken in the Mediterranean plus his share of the other prizes taken by the *Arun* now totalled more than £1.000 pounds. He also had the sword presented by the Marine Society for his actions in taking the galley and the French corvette, plus £100 waiting for him at his Eastney home.

He attended the reception at Government House along with his fellow officers and found himself intrigued and captivated by a young lady. His experience with women had been limited by his career at sea, and thus was only with Jane and Jennifer Bowers. This was something quite different, and the fact that the young lady in question seemed close to his own age, though in fact at least two years older, mattered little as he found himself involved in the intricate fastenings of the lady's clothing and revealing delightful areas of previously unthought-of interest.

Just over sixteen years may seem young to some, but already he was a man in stature and in presence. This night had been an education for the young man, who, for the first time, found that his experience up to now lacked the section dealing with the interaction between a man and woman, who was not a wife. He mentally corrected himself, who was not his wife. The lady concerned being the young, but by no means inexperienced, wife of a planter currently occupied with the harvest of fruit, on the other side of the island.

Martin was feeling a little guilty this morning, since the lady was married, and also because of Jennifer Bowers in Eastney, with whom he was corresponding regularly. It has to be said that the lessons he was being given by his lady friend, were so new and exciting, that little else occupied his mind for the moment.

Captain Bowers had been in the company when Martin had been selected by the lady in question. As a man of the world and knowing that the lady's interest was transient, and guessing that Martin was innocent thus far, Bowers decided that the experience would do the lad good in the long run. It did no harm to have some idea of how to carry on with a new wife, when that time came.

For three incredible nights Martin was transported by the lady, to pleasures he had never really dreamed of, though the fourth day was a sad let down as the husband reappeared. This ended Martin's introduction to the mutual delights of intercourse between man and woman.

Captain Bowers had decided to send out the schooners on independent cruises to look for pirates. For Martin it was fortuitous that a ketch had been taken and brought in for naval service. True to his promise to further Martin's education whenever it was possible, he appointed Martin to her command.

Thus, for Martin, his misery was overborne by the work entailed in the crewing and taking over command of the ketch, now designated a cutter, of eight guns. His immediate future, a period in command of *HMS Sparrow*, would give him enough to distract his mind from other matters.

Senior Midshipman John Reed from the *Arun* had been made acting Lieutenant, as Martin's second in command and Midshipman Charles Morgan had been supplied from the pool of prize crews in the dockyard. At fourteen years he had seen action and was progressing well with his studies. He did however have a problem with gambling, and the removal from the temptations of Kingston was needed to keep him alive, and out of debtor's prison. Carter was bosun. With a crew of familiar faces of men he had known for years, plus a generous contribution from the prize crew pool, Martin was apprehensive but reassured at the same time.

They sailed on a three-week cruise to patrol the Windward Passage, and the coast of Cuba and Hispaniola, both areas renowned for pirate activity.

Having safely negotiated the harbor entrance the ketch made north-eastward for their cruising area.

Midshipman Morgan was on duty on deck when Martin spoke, "Are you any relation to the former Governor of Jamaica?"

Morgan sighed. "Sir, it is the question everyone asks. All I can say is, my family come from Glamorgan, and as far as I can tell we are not related to Admiral Morgan."

"Well. Now that is cleared up we can get on with running the ship. So tell me where and how you came to be stuck in Kingston?"

"I was a member of the crew of *Agamemnon* under Captain Nelson. While here in Jamaica I was taken with the fever and placed in the hospital to recover. Sadly my ship departed before I was cured. I am thus stuck here until my ship returns, or another ship takes me back to England."

"I suspect there will be a place found for you by my Captain, who is a most reasonable man. So let us enjoy our cruise while you talk to me about the waters we are entering."

Over the next few days the crew shook down together, and got to know the sailing abilities of their craft. To Martin the cutter was a delight. It was fast and very agile. It could sail on a wet blanket, the draught less than 10 feet with the lifting keel raised. This allowed sailing in waters other ships could not reach. At 87.5 feet long and 22 feet beam, she had plenty of room to accommodate her 34 crew. Her fore and aft sail plan allowed her to sail closer to the wind than any square rigger, though she had a yard on her mainmast to take a square sail when needed. There were cut-outs between the gun ports to take the sweeps, used to move the ship in light airs. The actual sweeps, or oars, were lashed in place alongside the longboat sitting on chocks between the masts. The guns were 6 pounders and seemed small after dealing with the 12 pounders of the *Arun's* broadside. The gunner's mate had been with Martin at Guadeloupe, and he had volunteered for the cruise. Currently he was going over the guns with the designated gun captains. There was additional armament in the form of a long nine pounder in the bow, and a second in the stern, both could be swung to either side of the of the ship.

The crew was already divided into watches, and the bosun, Carter, was matching them against each other to compare their teamwork under ideal conditions. They were sailing with the wind on the starboard bow and the ketch close hauled.

The second day out *HMS Sparrow* reached the edge of the patrol area. The headland of the south western end of Hispaniola loomed on the starboard horizon. The unsettled state of the island had decreed that they would steer clear of contact.

Lieutenant Reed who had the watch turned to the Master's Mate, Ben Travers, who was gazing at the distant dark green coastline. "I understand they have plenty of problems with the maroons on Hispaniola."

"Maroons?" he paused. "Oh, the escaped slaves. I heard there are thousands there."

John Reed thought for a moment. "I believe they are getting organized into some sort of army by one of their number. This end of the island is mostly French, the other end remains Spanish."

"Is this not the place of the pirates' harbor, Tortuga?"

John Reed looked at Travers quizzically. "Tortuga Island is to the north of the island, long since cleared of the pirates that once used the place. It was also the home of the buccaneers. They were mainly stranded seamen who were marooned here. They slaughtered the wild cattle here and boucained the meat. Cured it, so that it could be kept. Many sold it to passing ships, though others stole the ships, and took to piracy."

"Education is a great thing." The voice of their Captain joined the conversation, taking both men by surprise.

Martin smiled, pleased to have caught them out. "How are we doing, Mr. Travers?"

"We are making good ten knots at present, sir. I last checked the log not ten minutes since. She sails well."

"I'm glad to hear it." Martin looked up at the spread of sail. "Perhaps we could try the topsail, the wind is right."

"Aye-aye, sir!" Stepping down the deck he called to the watch. "Hands to make sail. Set the topsail, bosun. Let's see how she draws in this wind."

Carter called the order and watched his men race up the shrouds to release the top sail from the bunt-gasket.

As the sail dropped from the yard the men on deck hauled the bunt-lines through the blocks to swing the yard and set the sail to the wind.

When he was satisfied the Master turned to Martin. "Sail set, sir."

"Very good, Mr. Travers."

After a few minutes he turned to Martin. "Sir, I think I would prefer a little extra weight at the stern. With your permission?"

"By all means, Mr. Travers, by all means."

Travers had the reefs taken out of the mizzen sail Martin noticed the easier motion of the ketch almost immediately and was well pleased. It was the duty of the Master to sail the ship as a professional mariner. It seemed that Travers had the feel of his job, the essential sympathy with the ships movement through the water.

His mental ramblings were interrupted by the call from the masthead. "Sail-Ho! Hull down on the port bow. From Cuba from the looks of things."

"What type ship? Can you see yet?"

"No, sir. She is only showing topsails. She is square rigged, more than one mast."

"Very good. Let me know when you can make her out."

Martin turned to Reed who had appeared as soon as he heard the lookout's call. "Mr. Reed, we will not take any chances. Perhaps we could exercise the guns once more before we get too close to our visitor."

Reed turned to the bosun. "Call the men to quarters, bosun."

With both watches at their action stations, the guns were run out and the gun drill exercised.

The approaching ship gradually came into view, a brig that acted in a peculiar manner.

There was no sign of evasion. Though the course it followed was downwind, it sailed with small jerking movements from side to side. The flag was tattered and appeared to be Dutch, thus highly suspect with the state of things in Europe. Through the glass Martin examined the ship carefully. There were ropes hanging down the sides, and no one seemed to be working the sails at all, despite the fact that they needed trimming. There also seemed to be no one at the wheel. The jerky motion could be explained if the wheel was lashed. The stretch in the wheel ropes would allow the rudder to jerk from side to side.

"Mr. Morgan Take the boat and board the ship and enquire if they need assistance." As Morgan turned away, he stopped him. "Arm yourselves. Take the bosun."

"Yes, sir," Morgan said and ran off calling to the bosun to launch the longboat."

Hove-to, the cutter rose and fell on the long waves that were channelled between the islands from the Atlantic. Watching the strange ship, Martin was wondering what Morgan was seeing. The sail pattern on the stranger altered as the wheel was brought up and the ship, now identified as a Snow, under Dutch colors, turned into the wind. The boarders rapidly took in the sails and the *Hilde* drifted in company, just a cable length between them.

There was a hail from the Dutch ship. The boat was returning leaving Morgan and some of his men aboard.

Carter came up the side and reported to Martin. "Sir, Mr. Morgan asks that you come across to the Dutchy. He is not sure what to do."

"Is there no one aboard? Is that the problem?"

"I can't say, sir. I was handling the sails while Mr. Morgan investigated. He told me to come here and ask you to join him."

"Very well, Mr. Reed. You have the ship in my absence. Please do not break it." These words were said with a smile that took any sting from the remark.

Aboard the Dutch ship Martin was aware of the smell of mustiness. Morgan, waiting anxiously for him, turned impatient to go below.

"This way, sir," he said, and led off through the bulkhead door and down a few stairs to the after accommodation.

The door to the captain's cabin was jammed shut, probably with the damp, Martin surmised. A strange thing in a ship in this climate. The door had to be forced open by Carter and Peters using brute force.

The interior was dark and it was difficult to see, the damp smell more apparent here in the long closed room.

Carter and Peters went to the stern windows, unlatched them and forced them open in their turn.

The sunlight burst in, illuminating the room while highlighting the mould that seemed to be everywhere. The desk in the centre was piled high with books covered in the rot that also covered the figure sprawled among them. Martin presumed it was, had been, a man.

"Out of here, everyone. Now! Carter, rig a hose, cover your nose and mouth, and clear the windows and floor of this mess. Try and avoid the books they may tell us the story of this ship. Now, Morgan, what else have you to show me. Let us see the cargo hold and other, cabins if they can be seen?"

The other cabins were not so bad, there being no other bodies within them. The hold was loaded with timber, teak lengths worth considerable money on the open market. But it was under the timber that the real find was made.

The carpenter was brought aboard to sound the well and see that the ship was seaworthy. In the bilges, the cavity below the timber cargo contained other items stored. Only these items were not meant to be found.

Having pumped the bilges as near dry as they could be, the smallest man in the ship was sent in to bring out the concealed cargo. The small figure, filthy from the bilges, dragged out box after box, case after case, filling the space in the saloon. Several of the cases had to be hauled out using block and tackle because of their weight. All of the special cargo was packed in strong metal bound boxes and had survived their incarceration intact.

The hose was used to wash the boxes down as they appeared. The air was damp still, though the atmosphere in the stern of the ship was now bearable. All the windows had been opened plus the door to the deck and roof hatches. The foc'sle had been cleared. There had been no bodies there. The body in the captain's cabin seemed to be the sole survivor.

In his cabin, among some of the books that had survived the mould and water, Martin found the log book of the *Hilde*. The last entry was made six years ago. It was in French, and when he looked back he realized that the previous pages were also in French?

The final entry was:-

I have now run out of such food as I can reach. The men have all gone. I expect God will punish them. This trap has done for me. I can see no light anywhere, when this candle dies I suppose I will too.

The treasure has done us no good. If anyone finds this they are welcome to anything my treacherous crew have missed.

God have mercy on me,
Albert Malaise, Captain   June 1787

There were a few rambling comments further but nothing more that the dying scrawl of the starving man. The reason for his entrapment became clear when the body was removed. Both of the man's legs had been broken above the knee, when he had been trapped, apparently thrust up against the desk, by some shock to the ship perhaps.

Martin sat back and considered. There was often volcanic activity in this part of the world.

He looked back at the entries prior to calamity.

Approached the coast of Cuba with caution. The bay is open and the cave is where the map shows it to be. The gentle current goes into the cave, but I will anchor here and explore by boat.

There was a hasty entry obviously made later that same day.

I have ordered the anchor raised. There is movement in the ground and the sea is rising. We are trying to claw out of the bay but the current is driving us into the cave. There are rocks moving.......

The ship is trapped and I have been injured. My cowardly crew have taken the boat to escape but I fear that they too have succumbed, to the power of the earth. I have little food and water here at my desk, so my pain will not last long. God help me.

There were no other references to the death of the captain and no explanation of the disaster that had overcome the ship and her crew. In earlier passages he read how they had come upon a treasure ship, crippled by a hurricane, survivors of her crew were clinging to the dismasted hulk. Without food or water.

They had boarded the hulk, and discovered what she was carrying. They killed all the survivors, and transferred as much of her cargo as they could manage before the treasure ship finally sank.

From this comment Martin concluded that the boxes and containers taken from the bilges probably contained some of the treasure mentioned in the log.

The *Hilde* was actually bigger that the *Sparrow* certainly at least 30 foot longer and broader in beam accordingly. The problem Martin had was dealing with the prize. His crew was too small in number to man the *Hilde* and continue with his cruise, he decided that they must return in company to Kingston, perhaps to restart his cruise after delivering the prize and her cargo of timber and treasure.

Three days later the Governor, Port Admiral, Captain Bowers and Lieutenant Forest-Bowers were all seated round the table in Government House. The fan overhead made feeble attempts to cool the humid atmosphere. Martin wished he could get back to sea where, even when it was hot, the air was clean.

The Governor, Sir Roger Makepiece, spoke, "Well. Gentlemen. It seems we have agreement. The cargo of the *Hilde* has been bid for by the dockyard and the usual prize shares distributed. As for the treasure I am almost embarrassed to say that, under the law of the land, it has been purchased by the crown. Valued at 130,540 guineas, it will be similarly distributed. The ship itself has been purchased at public auction at a further 500 guineas."

The Port Admiral, Sir Marcus Warren, was rather annoyed at being present and discussing the prize moneys being settled. Since his was a local honorary appointment, he had no claim on the wealth on the table.

The distribution of moneys went to the Admiral in command West Indies Squadron, under whose flag the *HMS Arun* and *HMS Sparrow* sailed. Though he was not even in the area his portion was assured. Captain Bower's share was also assured, as was Martin's. The crew of the *Sparrow* were well placed since there were no other naval ships in sight when the prize was taken. This meant they would receive their full shares, and in many cases there would be more money than they were ever likely to receive in their lifetime.

As Captain Bowers and Martin returned through the busy Kingston streets, Bowers said to Martin, "Well, lad. You have made me richer. You, yourself, must now be considered a wealthy man. Have you any idea what you will do with your good fortune?"

"Why, no. sir. I confess I have monies from the earlier prizes, but all remain with the Crown Agents at present. Apart from transferring the funds to Messrs Cox's Bank, I confess I have made no effort to do anything with it. My life at present is the Navy, and for that I need little."

"Well said, lad. You are yet young for such matters. I fear I am apt to regard you by your stature and achievement, forgetting that you are just sixteen years. Forgive me, please."

"I have nothing to forgive. I am complemented by your remarks, sir."

The pair made the rest of the way to the port, in companionable silence.

HMS Sparrow sailed with the dawn back to her patrol of the Windward Passage. The first of several such patrols during the year. In view of the problems with manning the prize on that first cruise the crew numbers were increased to fifty. Extra space in what was once the hold of the ketch allowed room for the extra men to sling their hammocks. Also it allowed all the guns to be manned in the event of action.

Martin had managed to keep the log book of the *Hilde*. Her new owner had changed the name to something more British, and since the log had been written in French no-one else could read it anyway. All the pages had now been separated and Martin had now read it and checked the entries with the charts, so it was now possible for him to trace the voyages of the ship with fair accuracy.

It was fortuitous, for on their final cruise before returning to England, Martin found himself sailing at night in the midst of a group of French ships, any one of which could have blown the *Sparrow* out of the water with a single broadside.

The storm had blown up with a suddenness that was typical in Caribbean waters. The evening darkened dramatically and the waves grew in size as the wind rose. Martin called for all hands to shorten sail. The crew, well drilled by this time, managed the task swiftly and efficiently. Having got the ship riding as well as possible, the night and the storm closed in around them.

During the long night, odd lights were seen in the area. Apart from those reflections of the lightning that flashed intermittently throughout the night, there were several identified as ship lights, from several different ships.

The only group of ships to be found in this area were likely to be enemy. As the coast of Cuba loomed close Martin was lucky enough to identify the inlet mentioned by the ill-fated captain of the *Hilde* to the east of Guantanamo Bay, where he presumed the other ships were bound.

He ordered the course change to weather the point at the entrance to the bay. The other ships were beginning to appear in the grey light of the dawn. The storm had abated slightly but the wind and waves were still enough to make navigation difficult, and The *Sparrow* was being tossed about by the wild weather.

One of the other ships had turned toward them and a signal was being flown. Martin ignored it and sighed with relief as they passed between the two headlands and entered the calmer waters of the bay within. The nosey ship, as Reed called it, seemed to lose interest as it was seen to resume her course toward Guantanamo Bay.

Martin was curious, as he quickly began to identify the various landmarks that had been detailed in the old log book. The large cave opening in the cliffs on the eastern side of the bay answered the description given in the log book. Martin ordered the helmsman to steer for the cave, and at the same time ordered the boat to be lowered to check the soundings through the entrance. Reed took the boat and, despite the size of the waves, had no real problem carrying out his task. He entered the cave and was gone for nearly an hour before he returned to report.

"The cave extends near four cables length into the hill behind. The height of the roof rises for half that distance. There is a sizeable rock fall that I think might be the remains of the earthquake that trapped the *Hilde*. There are more modern signs of rockfalls that probably released the ship to drift out to the point where we encountered her.

"We can sail in and keep out of sight until this storm is over then?" Martin asked.

"Better to tow and row her in. There is room to turn the ship inside, out of sight of the bay."

The storm subsided and the water within the cave settled down to near dead calm. Martin was almost overcome by the feeling of apprehension he experienced when they entered the cave. He dismissed his foreboding and ventured out in the longboat to explore the cave. The searchers found an opening high up in the side of the cave. There were traces of the remains of people whom he presumed were the surviving crew members of the *Hilde.* There were several bags, at the spot where the area had been cleared beside a spring of fresh water that came from within the rock into a pool. The scattered bones indicated that either they had been attacked or had fallen out between themselves, possibly over their booty. The scattered remains had clearly been tidied up by the local scavengers.

The bags contained gold coins of various sizes, mainly Spanish. The fact that they were still here suggested that Martin's theory was probably correct.

They brought the bags to the ship where Martin logged the find, estimating a total of 2000 coins between the fourteen bags located.

He sent watchers to the hilltop nearest to Guantanamo Bay to report on the ships which they had left when they entered the bay.

When they signalled the departure of the convoy, Martin, still feeling the apprehension he had felt since entering the cave, sailed the ship out. He did not lose the feeling of impending doom until they were once more out on the open sea.

Chapter eight

Return

1796 October

The last cruise was sad for Martin as it signalled his
return to *Arun,* relinquishing his independent command
after a period of several months. For him command had
been a worry and a delight. By the time he handed *HMS
Sparrow* over to his successor—a locally based
Commander with his own local crew—he was comfortable
in the post. The new frigate, *HMS York,* sailed into
Kingston harbor as *HMS Arun* prepared to leave. That
night there was a reception for the new arrivals and the
departing ships. The convoy had been assembled ready to
sail the following day under the protection of the frigate
and two sloops.

The occasion was one of the outstanding balls of the
year in Jamaica. There were few enough chances for the
young people of the upper class, to display their finery, and
the young, unmarried ladies were all paraded, in the hopes
of finding a husband among the collection of young
officers who came with the relieving ships.

The other, less publicised option of these occasions,
was for the wives whose husbands were away to find
dalliance with the probably more virile officers on parade

at these events. Martin was now in a position to watch, with a wry smile, the lady who had tutored him in the art of lovemaking, so called, at the time of his own recent arrival. She was currently working her wiles on a young lieutenant from the newly arrived frigate. For Martin there was no real interest in the colorful gathering. His thoughts had turned homeward. It was as he stood in the window with the darkness behind him, that he was startled by the soft voice from behind his shoulder.

"Please, don't move, sir. I would be most embarrassed to be exposed in this condition."

Without moving away from his place he swung round, to confront the person who had spoken. The young woman was trying to secure her torn gown over her shoulder, to thus prevent her right breast from being exposed.

"Why, what has happened? Your dress....?"

"The young gentleman,(the savagery that was invested in the words made Martin think of dripping acid,) was no gentleman. He appeared to mistake me for one of the prostitutes from the harbor."

The irate young lady was pretty and possibly sixteen.

"How can I help?" Martin's practical question stopped the possible tirade and brought her back to earth.

"I need to get back to my room."

"Where are you staying?" Martin thought the question a reasonable one.

She looked at him oddly. "Where else but here in the mansion? I am, after all, the Governor's daughter."

"I do beg your pardon. I have spent several months of my stay here at sea, and I have not had the pleasure..."

"Well, that did not seem to trouble my earlier escort. So if you will, sir, escort me to my room I would deem it a favor."

"Of course, Miss. My name is Martin Forest-Bowers, Lieutenant RN."

"And I am Lady Sarah Makepeace. How do you do? Shall we go?"

"At your service, Milady." And as she took his offered arm, he escorted her around the house to the servant's entrance, where they made their way up the back stairs, to the upper rooms of the house. There they entered her private room closing the door behind them. She turned and careless of her now exposed breast turned the key in the lock.

Turning on the startled man behind her, she said. "Now. Sir, I will need your help, for I cannot get into or out of these clothes without the help of another."

Trying to avoid looking at the delightful breast exposed to his view, he said, "But you must have a maid. Shall I call her?"

"She gossips to everyone. I have no secrets while she is about, and I would rather my father did not learn of this episode. So you will have to help me. Now undo the buttons down my back. Quickly now."

She turned and flung open the wardrobe. "I suppose it should be similar color to this." She lifted the skirt of her dress exposing a length of bare leg to Martin's gaze as he struggled to undo the tiny buttons down the back of the elaborate dress.

As he progressed down her back her bare skin was exposed down to below her waist. At that point she grasped the skirt of her dress and called him to help her lift it over her head.

Between them they managed, carefully avoiding disturbing her elaborate hair arrangement. The torn dress was deposited on a chair beside the bed.

The lady was now stark naked and was revealed as a beautifully formed woman, pretty faced, and with an infectious smile that lit up her face as she saw Martin's blushes.

"Am I not pretty, Martin Forest-Bowers?" She turned around in front of him. "Would I qualify for your bed, sir?" She asked wickedly."

"You would indeed qualify for anyone's bed, looking as you do, Miss."

"Now, sir. I see you are suffering from this oppressive heat. You must at least remove that jacket before you expire from our efforts." She darted forward and was undoing the buttons of his uniform jacket even as she spoke. With the jacket removed Martin felt much better, but his companion was not pleased with the state of the shirt he was wearing. She had that off over his head, while he was still recovering from her first assault.

Sarah stood back and looked approvingly at his body thus exposed.

For Martin the breath of cooler air from the open windows was blessed relief. He was now certain that his current temperature was not from the climate alone by any means. When Sarah declared that it was unfair for him to be clothed while she was not, his token resistance to her attack on his breeches, quite uncomfortable in their restriction of his now obvious manhood, ended with relieved cooperation in the task.

Suddenly, everything slowed down as the two young people looked at each other on that hot tropic night. Then Sarah took his hand and led Martin to the bed that had been in the background since they had entered the room. She sat down on the edge and still holding his hand she drew him down to join her.

The ships of the convoy spread over a square mile of sea, all eight sailing well in the steady breeze. It had taken most of the morning to reassemble the full complement, as their captains all had individual ideas about maintaining their positions during the dark hours. Despite each ship carrying a stern lantern, two of the merchantmen had managed to collide. The noise of the collision had startled all the other cargo carriers into changing course, away from trouble. *HMS Arun* and her schooners had ranged far to regain contact with their flock. All the escorts were weary of what they saw as the amateurish blundering of the ships in their charge.

While *Arun* kept to windward of the little armada, with the sloops *HMS Fox* ranged on the leeward side, and *HMS Heron* bringing up the rear.

For Captain Bowers, there was another problem. The biggest of the convoy ships was a former East Indiaman named the *Earl Warwick*. Her owner was aboard with his family. His son was a Midshipman serving in the *Fox*. Timothy Watson had no wish to indulge his family by being amongst them on this voyage. His position in the navy was at his own request. There was more excitement being part of the crew of the sloop than could be enjoyed as passenger with his family on the long voyage to England.

As an important man in Jamaica, Sir Marcus Watson demanded what he regarded as his rightful consideration on this voyage to England. He felt that the Royal Navy was servant to the needs of the nobility. His title having been passed down by his father for services to the crown, in providing money and rum to the cause, meant that his rights to nobility were satisfied thus.

Unfortunately, he was beginning to realize that his interpretation of due rights was not shared by Captain Bowers, who commanded the convoy. While Captain Bowers was prepared, during a period of dead calm to allow some intercourse between ships for socializing, he was not prepared to transfer Midshipman Watson to the *Earl Warwick* to act as aide to Sir Marcus, and allow Lady Watson to spend time with her son.

Timothy Watson was mortified by his father's posturing, as was his sister Marina, a pretty 15 year old blond who was enjoying the attention of the officers and crew. There was no way she wanted her brother there to poke his nose into her affairs. He was too bossy by far.

There was a fair amount of socializing during the period of calm. For the warships all had boats in the water, all ostensibly to assist in the passage of people between ships. In addition Captain Bowers had privately conveyed to the merchantmen, that they should also use the opportunity to launch their own boats, just in case it became necessary to tow their ships into a more favorable position, if they were attacked whilst still becalmed.

The competition between the ships in rowing races passed the time for the men and wagers were won and lost between the rival crews. However the escorts sighed with relief when the first flirt of breeze was felt and the drifting ships were once more able to make way on their journey home.

Martin's seventeenth birthday had been celebrated in the Caribbean, but as they entered the English Channel he suggested, since the crew would be split up, they use the special stores saved from that occasion for a farewell party, rather than wasting them. The weather was kind, and knowing that four of the ships were leaving the convoy off Falmouth, and the remainder, with the exception of the *Earl Warwick,* at Plymouth, there was a light-heartedness about the celebration, that combined with the close proximity of their home port, made the party go well. The ship was due for a refit in the dockyard for several weeks. Most of the officers and crew would be moved on to other ships. The officers certainly would receive a week or so break, and the opportunity to get to know their families again, before departing on their next assignment.

The Navy was enjoying considerable popularity at the time. The victory over the Spanish at Cape St Vincent had seen Admiral Sir John Jervis elevated to the peerage as Earl St Vincent.

Commodore Nelson was appointed Knight of the Bath, closely followed by promotion to Rear-Admiral for his actions in command of *HMS Captain* in the defeat of the Spanish fleet. Now blind in one eye from his action at Calvi in Sardinia, and short an arm from his wound from grape shot received in action at Tenerife, he was recovering in London with the nation praying for his swift return to health.

For Captain Bowers there would be a new ship. The orders arrived while they were off Falmouth, seeing the first of the convoy off. Impatient at the delay, the *Earl Warwick* decided to leave the convoy and make her own way up-channel to her destination port at Southampton.

With a flurry of farewell signals she left the remainder of the convoy and was a distant patch of sail by the time the remaining ships had sorted themselves out.

HMS *Arun* arrived in Portsmouth in August, with the sun shining and small ceremony.

Lieutenant Powers would be standing by the ship for her refitting, and acting Lieutenant John Reed would join him. Their orders meant that they would remain with *Arun* under her new captain.

Captain Bowers was ordered to report to the Admiralty, as was Lieutenant John Martin Forest-Bowers. There would be no chance to get home before departing for London, so Charles had sent a note to Jane from Falmouth, to come to London and meet there at the apartments they retained in the new area of Knightsbridge.

As the Captain and Martin arrived ashore they were met by servants from the house with the extra baggage for their stay in London. There was little conversation on the journey as both men were tired, having boarded the post-coach in the early evening, neither bothered to try staying awake. Both accustomed to sleeping through bad weather both were asleep before the coach left the city.

The two men—while not fresh—were at least rested when they pulled into the yard of the Cock Inn. Servants came out to meet the coach and conduct the two men to a room where they could bathe, shave, and change into clean linen. Their dress uniforms had been sponged down by the time they were ready to dress. As they examined their appearance in the pier glass there was a commotion at the door and female voices demanded entry. Jane and Jennifer swept into the room, followed by the innkeeper who had not realized who they were. Martin found himself holding Jennifer in his arms her lips seeking his determinedly.

When he came up for breath, he found the Captain and Jane regarding them both with interest.

Jane came over as Jennifer relinquished her hold on Martin. "Welcome home, Martin." Jane kissed him on both cheeks and hugged him. "You are most welcome indeed. You look very handsome. I am proud of both of my men. How about you, Jennifer?"

Jennifer, who had kissed her father rather more chastely, agreed wholeheartedly."We have decided to accompany you both to the Admiralty; where we will leave you and go shopping. If you are free to do so you are welcome to join us for luncheon at Simpsons about midday. Otherwise we will meet tonight at the apartments. All is arranged there for you both."

At the Admiralty they were greeted by a languid-looking man in civilian dress who seemed to find the whole business of dealing with naval officers an incredible bore. In the ante-room a row of chairs were set out, with several officers seated waiting their fate.

Captain Bowers was called as soon as they arrived. Martin was told to wait. As he turned to go through and take a seat, Admiral Nelson walked in. The bored receptionist leapt to his feet to greet him. But Nelson saw Martin and called a greeting. "Martin Forest, you are here already. Well met, young man." He put his good arm round Martins' shoulder and said, "You are here to join a party I am helping to organize." He ushered Martin though a door at the back of the room, leaving the assembly of waiting officers wondering just who this friend of Nelson was.

Nelson continued down the corridor still talking. "I understand you have continued as you set out. Three more prizes and the loot from a treasure ship, I hear?"

"I have been lucky, sir."

"I agree with the European monster. I understand he was quoted as saying that he would rather have lucky Generals, than experts."

They stopped outside the door of a room at the rear of the building and Nelson turned the handle. Inside the room there was a long table and several maps on the walls.

Martin recognized Commander Graham, who saw him and nodded, though he did not speak.

Nelson said, "I saw my young friend here waiting in the ante room. I thought it would save time and trouble if I just brought him with me. One of yours, I believe, Graham."

"Indeed, sir. I have just been so informed. You are welcome, Mr. Forest-Bowers."

The Admiral standing beside the table spoke. "Now we are all here, shall we proceed?" He paused to allow the others to see what he was indicating on the chart. "Admiral Nelson, you will be returning to Gibraltar in *HMS Racer* with all despatch. You take over command of *HMS Vanguard*. You will be joining Admiral Jervis. It seems that things are not going well in the Mediterranean at present. We may yet need to evacuate Elba."

The civilian who had been seated listening spoke quietly. "I understand *HMS Racer* will be attached to the Gibraltar command. Since I will need to discuss certain matters with Lieutenant Forest-Bowers, and I believe having just returned from the Indies he had had no chance to see his family, may I suggest that he travel to Gibraltar in the Sloop *Rocket* in two weeks' time? This will allow me to brief Mr. Forest adequately and give his family time to see him without seriously impairing the efficiency of his ship, or the operations of the current plans."

The Admiral looked as if he would like to tell this impudent civilian exactly what to do with his suggestions. But a cough from his aide reminded him who the civilian was.

To Martin the entire incident was baffling.

Nelson broke the spell with a laugh. "He has you there, Canning. We old men forget that life is a little different for the youngsters. After a two-year tour in the West Indies, a man needs to relax a little here in civilization, before departing once more in the service of our King." He slapped Martin's shoulder and looked at the seated man. "Tomorrow at ten, at the Foreign office?" At the man's nod, he said, "Off you go, lad, and kiss her for me. I'll see you in Gibraltar, no doubt."

Chapter Nine

HMS Racer

Martin left the room and the Admiralty, and made his way to Simpsons to meet the ladies for lunch.

He had to confess that the morning had been a bewildering procession of events. Though certain things stood out: the feel of Jennifer's lips against his, the warmth of Jane's welcome and Admiral Nelsons' friendly greeting in the Admiralty. The rest of the morning was a succession of events. For the moment, he cast them from his mind to concentrate on being with the two most important women in his life. He felt a twinge of guilt over the events in Jamaica, but he managed to push them to the back of his mind in the company of Jane and Jennifer. What he had not realized was the wide circulation of the Gazette. As the three entered the dining room there was a sudden murmur of interest among the diners, and as soon as they were seated, two of the ladies on the next table started whispering hurriedly to each other.

"What is the interest?" Martin asked of Jane.

"Why? You are, Martin, dear. Did you not know that you are a major topic of conversation in London at present?"

"Why on earth should that be?" I am just a simple Lieutenant in the Navy. I am nobody."

"Oh, mother. Martin has just arrived in London for the first time. He is not aware of the interest taken in the latest reports in the Gazette." She turned to Martin and took his hand. "You, my dear brother, are famous, because two years ago you, at barely fifteen years of age, captured two prizes with a fifteen man crew. Because of that you became instantly well off. Then, during this last two years, you have captured prizes, and taken the Dutch ship, *Hilde,* with Spanish treasure aboard. You are now rich in the eyes of London, and a hero to boot. We will receive invitations here in London from people we do not know, but who wish to know us because we know you."

Martin looked at Jane. She nodded in agreement. As they studied the menu there was a flurry of activity at the door, and Captain Bowers appeared accompanied by Admiral Nelson.

At this the clientele started clapping hands, and Nelson graciously waved and bowed before accompanying Captain Bowers to the table where he bowed over Jane and Jennifer's hands before seating himself alongside Jane.

Charles Bowers was amused at the performance. But he explained that he had been leaving the Admiralty when the Admiral had come out and joined him, waiting for a carriage to be called. He had invited him to share his carriage and join them for lunch, if it would please him.

Nelson said, "I was interested to meet the young lady who exerted so much influence over Martin here, that he defied the Admiral and insisted that he delay his departure for Gibraltar for two weeks." The twinkle in his eye as he told this blatant lie had them all laughing. The ice thus broken, the party enjoyed their lunch together with lively conversation between the courses."

In the apartment that evening with the family seated relaxing, Jane commented, "That man is certainly a most entertaining person. I swear the entire room at Simpsons was listening to his every word."

There was silence for a few moments. The spell of the encounter at lunch had still not quite dissipated.

Charles Bowers broke the silence. "I understand you are due to sail with Commander Graham in *Racer* based in Gibraltar?"

"Yes, sir. Though, thanks to Nelson, I will join at Gibraltar. I sail in two weeks' time in the sloop, *Rocket,,* from Portsmouth, though I believe…."

There was a knock on the door and the manservant came in with an envelope. "For Master Martin, sir." He handed Martin the envelope and waited while he opened it. It was headed. "The Foreign Office."

The scribbled note said, *'Room 41, 10.00 am 12th March 1797'*. The signature was illegible.

He handed the note to the Captain. He read it "Typical F.O. nonsense. Everything is a mystery. They have spies everywhere, they would have you believe. In fact, if you needed such a person you would find that they were all busy elsewhere."

The Captain handed the note to Martin and turning to the manservant said, "Ah, Miller. There will be no answer. Mr. Martin will be there."

Charles Bowers sat back. "Things never change." He looked at Jane as he spoke, acknowledging her part in keeping their home and marriage together despite the calls made on them in the cause of duty.

The manservant withdrew.

"This Foreign Office business is a little worrying." Charles volunteered, "Do you have any idea what they want?"

"I'm afraid not, sir. The first I knew of it was at the Admiralty, when we were with the Admiral. It had something to do with the civilian in the room when the Admiral was explaining things about the Mediterranean. You recall he it was, insisted I had two weeks before I left for the Rock."

"It was well done, though it is not like the Navy to concern themselves over the private life of a lieutenant. Whatever the job they have in mind, be careful. They employ spies and they have a habit of being caught and executed! So take care of yourself, son."

Martin felt a surge of affection for the big kind man who had taken him in as the son he never had. It was the first time the Captain had called him 'son', and it sounded right to him.

With Jane it was more difficult. She was younger and so very beautiful it was difficult to think of her as mother. Perhaps aunt, though easier, as just a woman.

Jennifer sitting next to him squeezed his hand, pressing it against her thigh, soft through the folds of the summer dress. He felt the excitement, the quickening feeling of arousal. He turned his head and looked at her, almost sixteen and already the softened outlines of the beauty she had promised as a young girl.

He had realized that she was the woman he wanted as his wife. He had sufficient wealth to support a wife with money to spare. He was happy to see that she had not changed her mind since they first met, nearly four years ago.

The following morning the meeting at the Foreign office went off well. His knowledge of French had improved during his service in the Indies. He was now fluent, albeit with a slight accent of the Caribbean. This was an acceptable quirk since the French colonies there produced many young people who came to France to study and earn their fortune.

He would be expected to interpret where needed, and occasionally would be sent ashore to collect information, and pass messages. He would receive an allowance separate from his naval pay of £200.00 per annum, and, where required, he could draw upon expenses if needed. He was ordered to return tomorrow for further instruction. His contact said, "For future reference, you may refer to me as merely Mr. Smith.

He called upon Cox's, the banker with whom he had deposited his prize money. The bank had been highly recommended by the Captain. Thus far Martin had few complaints. It seemed that they were happy to increase his investment without any apparent risk. With over £20,000 on deposit, he was a valued client.

He and Jennifer met by arrangement. They strolled through the gardens to the tea rooms where Martin suggested, that if they were to wed, they should really find a home to live in. "I suggest we look here in London. I am advised that whilst property is a little more expensive here, it will increase in value."

Jennifer smiled. "So you have realized that I was not joking when I mentioned that we would marry. That is good and I accept your formal proposal, though I would rather you had spoken in some more private place. What do you suggest we do about this house?"

Martin smiled. "The apartments used by the Captain and Jane are leased, I believe?"

At Jennifer's nod he continued. "I have enquired, through my bank, of the owners of the building that includes the apartment. My bankers inform me that the owner wishes to sell so that they can purchase other property elsewhere.

"I considered the suitability of converting the building into one dwelling, where we would live. The size of the house would allow ample room for the parents and Giles to stay as and when they wished, without the extra expense for the lease. Since the neighbouring property is already on the market, but recently vacated, I thought to purchase that as an investment and a place to live while the other house is being altered. How does that sound?"

"I think we should survey the property forthwith, since it will require my supervision in your absence."

Martin smiled, and called for his account.

They walked from the gardens across the street into the avenue beyond, the tall new row of houses formed an elegant parade down to the square beyond. New houses were being built on the other side of the gardens which were already laid out in the centre of the square. The clever use of the formerly wooded area had left mature trees in autumn colors, spaced by the sensitive thinning of the trees between.

The apartments were in the corner house of the row, with windows on two sides. The next house had a sign offering for sale and it was to this house the couple went. Martin had been provided with a key and together they entered the house.

It was clean and obviously well maintained. Much of the furniture was still in place. Martin had been told that if they wished, the furniture of their choice could remain for their use, as all the things still here were to be disposed of.

The upper rooms were divided into bedrooms, with a drawing room, used as a sitting room by the mother of the owner. This was still fully furnished, as was the main bedroom and the guest bedroom. Jennifer was racing from room to room delighted with the house and the things they found there. Martin followed her about and lost her. He finally caught up with her in the guest bedroom. She was looking out of the window. As he entered the room she turned and walked over to meet him. She had removed her coat when they had entered the house. The weather being warm and the house, having been closed was also holding the heat of the day.

She reached him and held out her arms to be embraced and kissed. Unwatched and undisturbed, the kiss went on and they sat on the bed still close. Martin moved his lips over her face and down to her neck. Jennifer moved beneath him turning to let him kiss the mounds of her breasts. It was going to happen—they both knew it—and as he undid the fastenings of her dress she opened his shirt. Eventually they lay, each looking wonderingly at the other's body. "Oh, Martin. I have dreamed of this."

"As have I my love."

Chapter Ten

The Med

Standing on the deck of *HMS Rocket,* Lieutenant John Martin Forest-Bowers enjoyed the early morning sun, delighted to feel the rise and fall of a deck beneath his feet once more. The Spanish coast was visible off to port, the sea inshore flecked with the sails of the fishermen working the inshore waters. The sloop was a fine fast craft, well named for her speed, and used accordingly by the fleet as a message carrier and occasionally as a scout.

The cheerful voice of the captain of the sloop Lieutenant Henry Watson interrupted his thoughts. "See! That's Cape Trafalgar over there." He pointed at the headland coming abeam of the ship. "We will be in Gibraltar by this evening."

At the time, he was not aware of the significance the point coming up ahead would have on his future.

HMS Rocket dropped her anchor as promised, albeit delayed a little by the contrary winds within the straits, which required a long tack almost to the African coast to ensure they cleared the entrance to the famous harbor.

Martin was relieved to see the graceful lines of *HMS Racer* anchored inshore of the sloop. It would mean that he could report aboard immediately rather than be kept hanging about awaiting her return.

Lieutenant Watson appeared by his side. "I will drop you off on my way to the flagship. Your gear is being loaded into the boat now if you are ready."

"You are most kind, sir. I am at your service now." He descended the side of the sloop and was seated in the boat when James boarded.

On boarding *Racer* he reported to Captain Graham, passing over the orders he had been given on leaving Portsmouth.

Graham greeted him amiably. "You will have much to do tomorrow. My first Lieutenant is currently with a prize and you will be the senior until he returns. It will be good experience for you. I'm sure you will manage. I am pleased to have you aboard." He put his hand on Martin's shoulder and accompanied him to the door.

For Martin, almost eighteen now, having his own cabin on board ship was a luxury he had never really experienced under command of another. His detached duty in the West Indies, where he actually commanded the vessel did not really count, since it was a temporary situation as he had well known. Here—despite its small size—was his own space, a place where he could leave his own things, without worrying about losing them for a joke, or having them borrowed, and sometimes never returned. Also there was no one else here to bicker and fight with, a place in fact to call his own, for the length of this commission at least.

The ship was due to sail at noon. The bosun's mate was newly appointed and not very bright. So it was with a sigh of relief when the shore boat came alongside with their newly appointed bosun on board. As he heaved his sea bag over the side and turned to salute the tall, acting First

Lieutenant, a broad grin spread over his homely face. Carter, promoted bosun, was as happy to see Martin, as Martin was to see him.

"I thought you were going to buy an inn with your prize money," Martin said

"I got my brother to do that. He can run it until the salt runs out of my blood. I found I had no sooner got home than I was ready to be off again."

"Right, stow your gear. You are needed here, no mistake. I'll inform the Captain you are here. We are due to sail shortly."

"Aye, aye, sir." Carter called a seaman to take his bag below and went to speak with the bosun's mate who was looking relieved to see him.

The voice of the Captain as he came on deck reminded him of his duties. He stepped forward to report the arrival of the new bosun, and the readiness of the ship for sea.

"You will please me by being my guest for dinner tonight, you also Midshipman...... Brown, is it not?"

"Indeed, sir, it is. Thank you, sir."

Martin heard the hail "Anchors aweigh" called from foc'sle.

"Set the mainsail. Haul taut the headsails. Watch the helm there. Bring her round gently now. The ship came round onto her course for the harbor entrance. The anchor was brought home and lashed in position. With her sails drawing, the ship moved rapidly through the water, the Master called for the sails to be trimmed to his satisfaction. Finally all things being in order, Martin set course for their first destination, Port Mahon in Minorca.

That evening the Captain's table was the scene of a merry party. In addition to Martin and young Brown, the ship's Master, Jared Holmes, and the Doctor, William Abbot attended. The Master had been around the world during his career and had many a tale to tell. The Doctor said little but was polite, and listened with interest to the conversation around him.

At the end of the meal the Master excused himself to take a look at the course, and the set of the sails. The Doctor and Midshipman Brown followed soon after. Martin was waved back to his seat when he made to leave.

"Martin, I may call you Martin, here between us, may I not?"

"Of course, sir."

"We have not had time to discuss the orders I have been given, since the time was short before our departure from Gibraltar. I would like to take some time to explain them now.

"First, do not expect to be relieved before this voyage is over. The man you are relieving has been detached for a reason. Happily we took a prize that is being convoyed to Falmouth and that gave me the excuse to remove him without damaging his career."

Martin was watching him with a puzzled expression on his face. He made to say something but the Captain held his hand up to stop him. "It will become clear shortly.

"Our orders do not include joining the fleet here in the Mediterranean, or anywhere else at present. We will contact the fleet at Port Mahon, but we do not stay. Having dropped off messages there, we travel on to Naples, or the location of the King, wherever he may be. Based on what we learn on our travels, we will carry on to the region of Alexandria. There, we have reason to believe, there will be French ships about, because of the army they have in Egypt. Your knowledge of French will be needed, and we will have to make contact with agents in the area, as well as evade capture. Because we are a corvette with French lines, it is hoped that we will be able keep clear of trouble. I am afraid if we are found out, we will need all the speed we can make. It is another reason for parting with Lieutenant Fairbrother, my former First Lieutenant. I swear he was older than me, though he claimed to be younger. Enough to say I needed someone who can think on his feet."

"I must say I am flattered, sir, at your faith in me."

"Don't be. I expect that you will reward my selection, since you have shown in your career so far the very qualities I am seeking."

Graham smiled at Martin's embarrassment. "Don't worry. I don't expect miracles, just your best efforts. So now off you go. What I have told you is between you and me, no one else."

Martin stood up. "Thank you, sir. I will do my best to justify your faith in me."

He left the cabin and went up on deck, happily feeling the cooler wind in his face after the rather stuffy air in the cabin.

They made good progress despite the indifferent weather. The second lieutenant, Will James, greeted Martin as he came on deck, shrugging into a waterproof. "What happened to the wine-dark seas Homer speaks of." He waved at the grey waters through which they were making way.

"In the same place that the blond-haired warriors and the thousand ships are. In his imagination, or a long way from here."

"You really think so, sir?"

"If you look at our knowledge of the history of the times, how could you believe anyone would go to war over a woman? We already know there were not one thousand ships to be had here in the Mediterranean. At the time, it was bronze-age I believe. There could be war over copper, or zinc, even iron, but there is no copper here. Further north perhaps, there where you would find blond haired men."

"That never occurred to me, sir. But surely, I think I have read about the search for Troy in the Levant somewhere."

"I also was taught that in my Greek lessons, but my own logic tells me that it is based on the nationality of the author rather than any consideration of geography. That's enough of the history. What is our present position?"

"We are passing the Spanish port of Cartagena to port at about forty miles, our next landfall will be Formentera, the southernmost of the Balearic Islands tomorrow in the forenoon."

"An inspired guess, Mr. James? Perhaps you would like to check the position on the chart and verify your forecast."

As James hesitated, Martin said, "Now would be a good time, Mr. James. I believe the Captain will be joining us shortly."

At this, Midshipman James jerked into action and ran below to check the chart.

"Really, Mr. Forest-Bowers. I do believe you are guilty of pulling Mr. James's leg?"

Martin smiled as he turned to Captain Graham. "I do believe I am, sir."

They contacted the fleet to the north of the island of Minorca. The despatches were passed over and the course renewed for Naples on the coast of Italy, via Cape Spartivento at the southern end of the island of Sardinia.

Twelve hours after parting from the flagship they encountered *HMS Archer,* a brig/sloop escorting two prizes to Gibraltar. She was able to confirm that the King of Naples was currently in Sicily, the French having already overrun Naples.

Accordingly, *HMS Racer* adjusted her course, now making for the closer port of Palermo. *Archer* also reported that there were French ships reported operating from Livorno in the Tyrrhenian Sea.

They parted company with the Gibraltar-bound brig and continued their progress to the south-east, to weather Cape Spartivento. They encountered the two French frigates the following day.

The report from the masthead identified them approaching from the north, Captain Graham, when called, looked long and carefully at the tiny rags of white that were appearing for longer and longer periods. He turned to Martin. "What do you think? Will they catch us, or not?"

Martin having made the same mental calculations said. "Do we want them to, or not? If we wish to evade them, then I suggest we crack on more canvas and see just how fast our ship is." He looked his Captain directly in the eye, waiting.

Graham smiled, "I think this time, discretion. Let's see how she flies."

Martin cupped his hands and called, "All hands make sail. Set royals and skysails. Shake the reefs from the topgallants. Make her fly, Mr. James."

The rush of feet on the deck ceased as the men flung themselves at the rigging, racing each other to get their sails set before the others. The white canvas snapped and bellied as the sails appeared like magic to the mast-heads. The ship heeled to the wind and seemed to leap forward with the pressure of the extra spread of canvas.

Captain Graham lifted his glass once more. With a satisfied grunt he handed it to Martin. "That should do it." He said and returned to his cabin to finish the meal that was disturbed by the report of the French ships.

A watch was kept on the distant sail until they finally disappeared from the view of the masthead lookout.

The afternoon of the next day saw them shortening sail to enter Palermo harbor. The royal flag confirmed the presence of the King of Naples in the Sicilian capital. The guns fired the Royal salute in succession, as they passed the fortress at the harbor mouth.

They lay in the harbor of Palermo for two weeks, the court of the King providing a round of entertainments which the officers were invited to attend. The British Ambassador, Lord Hamilton, was a most affable man who ensured that there was no lack of company. Many of the ladies of the court, having been separated from their men by the skirmishes with the French army, were delighted to entertain the new arrivals. Thus at all the gatherings there was a varied assortment of these unattended ladies to greet in their turn. Fortunately the presence of two ships of the line, provided sufficient rivals to make the duties of the officers of *Racer* less taxing than might have been the case. When the time came for the ship to sail, there were several of the ladies sad to see them go. Though on the ship, there was a feeling of relief, for the present at least.

They had collected no less than three agents to carry to the Levant at the eastern end of the Mediterranean. The region was once the home of the Phoenicians, whose trading ships had operated throughout the civilised world in the west, from Jaffa to pre-Roman Britain, from the seas of the Baltic, to the Atlantic coasts of Northern Africa.

In more recent years the lands had been riven with warfare, the sects and tribes that lived there quarrelling still, following the vast expansion and disintegration of the Roman Empire. Now, with Napoleon's armies deep into Egypt, the entire area was even more in turmoil.

For Martin, the feelings of guilt following their sojourn in Palermo, kept him in a restrained, introspective mood for some time. The attentions of the seventeen-year-old Contessa Di Bari had been exhausting to say the least. The lady in question had, despite her lack of years, an expertise and ingenuity in sexual athletics that astonished him and appalled him. Her seventy-year old husband, having married to produce an heir, had apparently left it to her to decide who would be the actual father.

Martin discovered that his own efforts followed the failure of several others to achieve this end. It had become a matter of curiosity in the court, and it must be said, of wager on the result of her efforts.

Mr. James approached Martin to take over the watch, with a wary eye for Martin's mood. "Any problems for me to worry about, sir?" He asked tentatively.

"The ship is yours, Mr. James." The words were calm, the tone even. William James decided to chance it. "Did you enjoy our stay in Palermo, sir?"

Martin looked at him sharply searching for some hint of innuendo. Detecting none he replied. "I really did, I suppose, a most educational period that I would rather not repeat too often. I seriously doubt my constitution could stand too much more of the pace of life there."

"Well, I do have to say that entertainment on the scale we have enjoyed must become a trial." The voice of Captain Graham interrupted the two officers as they stood beside the stern rail in the morning sunshine. Both turned to greet the Captain who had approached unseen.

"So, a beautiful morning, gentlemen. All the cobwebs blown away. I trust. Our passengers have designated a landing in the vicinity of Alexandria, if it is possible."

"Who are these people, sir? Are we to meet?"

"They are, I understand, all trained agents of our Foreign Service: two gentlemen and a lady."

"Lady?"

"Why, yes. A lady who sounds very French!" The Captain sounded surprised at this. But he carried on. "She is a person of quality, from what I observe, and quite pretty. That is according to Mr. Williams, who is, I understand, a connoisseur of beautiful women."

Both the others laughed at the Captain's comment, but each was curious to see the lady in question.

She appeared on deck later that day, and satisfied their curiosity. Mr. Williams certainly proved his credentials as connoisseur. The lady, when she appeared, stopped the work on deck instantly. Known only as Alouette, her name was neither given, nor requested, as her position as an agent might be compromised.

The lady in question approached the tall figure of Martin Forest-Bowers and spoke. Caught by surprise, Martin turned and faced the lady with an apology. "I beg your pardon, Madam. I did not quite hear you."

"It was my fault, lieutenant. I asked if you could tell me where we are."

"Of course, Madam. We are 150 miles off the coast of Egypt, closing the shore for a landing in the vicinity of Alexandria." He looked around the horizon before indicating the location of their destination. "We should reach the rendezvous by tomorrow evening, if the wind holds."

"Parfait," She murmured almost under her breath.

Looking at her—without thinking—Martin said aloud, "Parfait. Vraiment."

Alouette looked at him and realized what he said. She blushed, then, "You speak French also, M'siu Martin?"

"I confess I do, Madam."

"Then, please. I am not madam. Duchesse on occasion, Mademoiselle on others. But here and now to you, sir, I am Alouette." She gave a little curtsey and walked off down the deck to commiserate with one of her companions, who was not enjoying the sea voyage.

"Watch out for singed fingers there,, Mr. Bowers." The dry voice of the Captain brought him out of his daydream with a start.

"That lady is dangerous!"

"How so sir?"

"Every man on this ship, including me, would happily take her to his bed. But I would wager that the only man to succeed would be the one she selected, for her own reasons, unlikely to be romantic. Ah," he sighed. "So are we all made fools of by our imagination and ego."

The Captain took a walk across the deck, and when he returned he said, "I hope you did not resent what I just said." He looked Martin in the eye.

Martin blushed. "Sir, I bow to your superior wisdom and experience."

"Exercise the guns, I think, Mr. Bowers." The moment passed. The Captain was all business.

"Aye, aye, sir" Turning, Martin called the orders to exercise the guns. The rush of men to their positions soon cleared the cobwebs from his mind, and the serious business of ship handling became his focus once more.

The three agents were invited to share the meal with the Captain and Martin that evening. The presence of Alouette—the only one of the three in condition to accept the invitation—seemed awkward to start with, but her easy manner and ready wit soon had both men entranced and relaxed to the extent that both were completely comfortable exchanging repartee with their guest.

The short twilight was over, darkness fell like a curtain over the sea. The lights of Alexandria were visible over the water ahead of the ship, as she ghosted closer to the shoal waters, off the Nile Delta.

The jolly boat had been swung out ready to launch, and the three agents were on deck with their baggage, ready to transfer to the hostile shore.

"Do the honors, please, Mr. Bowers. In and out as quickly as possible. I wish to leave this particular shore before the first blink of dawn."

"Aye, sir." Martin followed the three spies down into the boat and took his place at the helm. "Cast off. Give way port. Together now, port and starboard, handsomely there."

The boat rode the waves, swooping down the face, and receiving spatters of spray as the bows rose to the next wave. It took five minutes to reach the point where the bowman jumped over into the shallows to haul the boat to the beach. Martin carried Alouette ashore while the others struggled with the luggage.

`Alouette thanked Martin prettily for his assistance, then ran over to join the other two beside the pile of luggage.

"Quietly now. Back in the boat." Martin gathered his men and the boat pulled off the beach for the journey back to the ship. He turned as they left the small group standing there, and lifted his hand in farewell. Alouette noticed and waved back. Then they were gone.

Back alongside, they hooked on fore and aft. The boat was lifted out of the water and onto the deck, with the rowers still stowing the oars.

Chapter eleven

Beat to quarters

"What do you see there?" Captain Graham called to the masthead lookout.

"Two ships, sir, one ship rigged. The other, schooner rig. Both wearing French colors.

"Clear for action, Mr. Forest-Bowers, if you please."

"Sir! All hands, clear for action."

The call was followed by the pound of feet, as the crew raced to their stations for going into action.

The three ships were closing, and it was with some surprise that Graham noticed that the French ships were making no attempt to evade the more heavily armed *Racer*.

The French corvette was showing her teeth, the row of open ports, all now showing the wicked shapes of the guns. The schooner was not well handled, and she had got herself in an awkward situation when coming about. Martin called to the Captain, "Sir, she is in irons."

"Helm alee!" The Captain called. "Starboard broadside steady. Fire as you bear."

The guns down the starboard side fired in turn bringing the three masts of the schooner down with a raffle of gear and smothering her battery of guns beneath the fallen sails.

The Captain was already concerned with the corvette. He called for starboard helm to bring the port broadside to bear on the corvette.

The corvette was right on the edge as she fired her first gun. The recoil was enough to cause her head to fall off exposing her bow to the guns of the *Racer.*

Graham did not need another invitation. He called, "Guns, as you bear." The roar of the broadside guns as they fired, one by one, smashed the French ship, wounding her almost without response.

"Stand by boarding party, Mr. Forest-Bowers."

The two ships came together. The grapnels flew, securing one to the other. With a roar the boarding party climbed over the piled hammocks at the bulwarks, and down onto the deck of the French ship.

The crew were scattered but they quickly came to oppose the boarders, and the fighting was savage. Martin found he was fighting for his life, the cutlass he had taken heavy in his hand. His clothing was spattered with blood from friend and foe alike. The battle raged back and forth, neither side seeming to be able to prevail. The impasse was broken when more men burst from below deck and joined the battle wielding broken pieces of wood as clubs, and captured weapons from the many dead and wounded on deck. Martin though at first that all was lost, until he realized that the men were attacking the French.

"Come on, *Racers,* we have them now." They attacked with renewed vigour. The other men took up the cry *Racer* and pressed forward. The French seemed to lose heart and began backing off, throwing down their weapons. The Tricolor was pulled down. With a cheer the boarders celebrated the victory.

Martin returned to his ship and reported to the Captain. "It was close ,sir The prisoners held by the French made the difference."

"Well done, Martin. What was the butcher bill? Do you know?"

"We lost twelve killed and twenty-two wounded. The surgeon thinks we will lose nine of the wounded. The recovered prisoners lost four men, but there were thirty of them with just the odd minor cuts and scratches. The corvette is the *Hermione.*"

"I've sent a party over to the schooner under Mr. Holmes. I would like you to join him and report the condition of the ship as soon as possible."

"Aye, aye, sir." Martin touched his hat and called for the crew of the jollyboat to take him over to the schooner.

The *Oriele* was a ship that had been obtained from the Americans. She had been pierced for ten guns, and used as a privateer. Despite the loss of her masts, she was otherwise quite seaworthy. When Martin boarded the Master had already started the crew on fishing the first of the masts to the stump of the foremast.

The contents of the hold were of interest. The ship had obviously taken a valuable prize. There was, apart from several barrels of wine, a box of treasure in the form of jewellery and gold ornaments and a stack of silver bars. The remaining space was taken up with bales of cloth of varying quality.

When Martin reported to the Captain, the decision was taken to move the silver and valuables to *HMS Racer.* The remainder was left in the *Oriele's* hold.

It was no great surprise for Martin to find himself in command of one of the prizes. He was given the *Hermione* of 28 guns and normally a crew of at least one hundred and thirty.

With just sixty men the ship was a lot to handle, but once the damage to the fore end had been patched, the ship was in condition to sail at least.

Captain Graham decided to take the two prizes under his protection back to Palermo. There he could either gain more men, or at least get his own crew back. And it was with some relief that the three ships made it safely to harbor.

They found considerable help in the form of repairs to the prizes, but were ordered by the port captain to carry the prizes to Gibraltar, as there was no arrangement for the disposal of such craft in the port. The prisoners were taken off however. For once there were replacement seamen to fill out the crews for the two prizes. The loss of a ship of the line due to gun damage, had exposed concealed rot in her main timbers, this meant the entire crew had been thrown on the beach, awaiting repatriation.

The senior officers of the condemned ship were all gone. Though there were lieutenants senior to Martin ashore, Captain Graham selected juniors only, preferring his own people to retain command until the ships were delivered. Thus Martin found himself with two junior lieutenants and two midshipmen and a full crew of seamen. His nucleus from the *Racer* soon had them organized into watches. Neither of the lieutenants had had serious responsibility before in the hierarchy of the 74 gun ship they had served.

While the repairs to both prizes were carried out, Martin had his crew practice working together with their new divisional officers. This allowed both young men to learn a little of what they would be required to do in the cramped confines of the corvette. He himself met James Cameron and Will Cope for the first time, two men who would became his close friends thereafter.

By the end of the two weeks refitting the *Hermione*, the crew were working together and all four of the new occupants of the gunroom, and the afterguard, were comfortable in the confines of the small frigate.

The trio of ships left Naples with despatches for Gibraltar, and a recommendation for the inclusion of the 28 gun ship and the schooner in the fleet.

For Captain Graham there was a certain pride in leading his own small command through hazardous waters. It was with certain hopes, that they sailed in a wide line abreast to cover as much of the sea as possible, in the search for enemy sail.

It was two days before they spotted sail. The *Oriole*, sailing on the starboard of the line, spotted topsails, ahead on her starboard bow. Her signals brought the others to join her in the chase though it had to be said that *Oriole* had the legs of both other ships.

When the chase was brought into view, it appeared to be more than the three could seriously bring to battle. Their quarry was a 36gun frigate with a convoy of twelve merchantmen, all under the Tricolor.

The signal went out to the *Oriole* pass to the other side of the convoy, and cut out as many ships as possible. To *Hermione* it was to keep the wind over the frigate. Martin called for the guns to be manned and run out. The rumble of the iron wheels on the decks reverberated through the ship. Below in the orlop the surgeon prepared his instruments, while his assistant scrubbed the table, borrowed from the officer's quarters for his purpose.

The French frigate cleared for action, the sound of the drum beating to quarters came across the water, as she tried to manoeuvre into the windward position.

Captain Graham took the *Racer* across the stern of the Frenchman. The name of the ship *Niobe* was picked out in gold, among the elaborate carved and gilded frame, beneath the stern windows. The guns of the British frigate spoke in turn as she crossed behind the Frenchman. Graham felt a certain regret as the elaborate gilded stern carving was shattered and torn by the broadside guns of *Racer* as she passed. The guns of *Hermione* joined the action, as she clawed upwind to hold her place to windward of the French frigate.

Now the guns of the *Niobe* joined the chorus, adding their noise to the sounds of battle.

The other side of the convoy *Oriole* was cutting out merchantmen. She fired a gun to emphasise her instructions to a recalcitrant captain. The six ships already under her control were now sailing a divergent course to the remainder of the convoy.

Hermione with guns reloaded and run out, was causing the *Niobe* a lot of trouble. Her speed and agility were keeping the frigate distracted. So *Racer* diverted and chased four more ships from the convoy under the threat of her guns.

Oriole was now herding her six captive ships back on the eastward course, with *Racer* encouraging his four to join her. The midshipman, handling signals, called Martin's attention to the flag flying at the peak from the *Racer*. It was the agreed recall. Martin studied the position of the

French frigate and his own situation. Making his decision he called to change course. As the ship's head swung round towards the frigate, the Frenchman reacted, turning to bring his broadside to bear. Martin waited, watching the relative movements of the two ships until. "All hands, ready to come about! Lee ho....! Wheel to port, handsomely there. Bring her round. Starboard broadside, as you bear. Fire!" The ship, making her final turn to break off the action, gave the frigate one last sting.

The *Hermione* rapidly caught the escaping convoy and her two consorts. She joined them in shepherding the merchantmen toward Gibraltar, while the French frigate licked her wounds and made do with her two remaining ships.

In discussion at a later date, Captain Graham suggested that the *Niobe* had been commanded by a hurriedly promoted junior officer, to replace a Royalist Captain. They had the good fortune to be able to take advantage of the Captain's inexperience.

In Gibraltar the convoy and the two prizes created a sensation. As anticipated, the corvette and the schooner were both bought in by the Navy. The merchantmen were mainly purchased by private traders, and their cargoes were auctioned in the traditional manner.

Martin, already aware of his increasing financial status, was richer by a considerable amount. His share of the prize money, according to his agent had increased his wealth to a sum he could never have dreamed of as a boy. Now approaching his eighteenth birthday, he still had difficulty taking it all in. The real prize had been the silver bullion, and treasure chest of gold and jewellery. When added to the prizes taken earlier, his fortune was now over £25,000. The agent for Cox's in Gibraltar, having collected his share, assured him that the funds would be available wherever he needed to draw upon them.

Being honest with himself, Martin did not really appreciate what his wealth meant in terms of his shore life. Thus he disregarded the wealth he had acquired, grateful that he could afford new uniforms, and some small extra things that made life a little less spartan. The fact was that his body had filled out on what had been a rather bony frame. His clothes it seemed, had shrunk accordingly.

He did note that his credit was accepted by Gieves in Gibraltar with alacrity. The attention given to the fit and cut of his new uniforms was surprising in view of his lowly rank.

The command of *HMS Hermione* went to a favored senior Lieutenant on the staff of the Admiral. For Martin, the experience of command, in addition to his earlier stint, had given him a maturity beyond his years.

Lieutenant Carrington had been given command of the schooner. Now *HMS Oriole,* she was detached to carry despatches to Portsmouth. *HMS Racer* returned to her duties in the eastern Mediterranean, where, after reporting to Palermo, she was ordered to collect the agents dropped off at the start of her commission in the area.

There were reports of French shipping in the area, so the lookouts were increased for the journey to the Egyptian coast. As it happened there were no contacts made on the outward journey.

The boat approached the land, aiming for the glimmer of a signal lantern shaded on the shore side.

As the keel scraped across the sand, Martin jumped ashore barefoot, pistol in one hand, the painter in the other. Four crew members followed him, hauling the boat quietly further up the beach.

Martin cautiously approached the lantern, which was about fifty yards along the shore to the right of the boat landing spot. As he neared the lantern, he made out the dark group of people, behind the signal. As he got nearer on silent bare feet, he was aware of the people talking, among them the voice of Alouette. He stopped, listening. She was speaking in slow French. She was saying was there was no point in all this silly cloak and dagger business. She was not a spy, nor were her friends, being held in the hut at the top of the beach.

Martin stopped and retreated back to the boat. There were twelve men in the boat and all carried arms. He called them out of the boat and had them all prepare to use their knives. It was imperative that they did not warn the other party of their presence.

He then led the men to the top of the beach and scouted along to find the hut mentioned by the woman. He was convinced that the comment had been a warning.

He found the hut, and his men scattered surrounding the small building to ensure there was no ambush. Martin approached the doorway that showed up as a darker patch on the wall of the building.

He tapped on the door.

"Qui est là?"

"C'est moi" Martin replied.

The door opened quietly and Martin stepped into the small hut. There was a dim light in the corner and two men were seated beneath the dim glow.

Another man was standing behind the door. As Martin stepped in, he moved. The knife in Martin's hand pricked him in the throat. "Make no sound or you are dead."

The bosun, Carter, stepped over to the other man, who had frozen on hearing Martin's voice. He had noted the immediate compliance by his companion. The thud of the club in Carter's hand hitting the head of the Frenchman was followed by the lowering of the man's slack body to the ground.

"Take this one, Carter." Martin ordered, and went to the two men tied and gagged beneath the lamp. "Are you all right?" He asked.

"Yes, but Alouette...!"

"We will fetch her now." Martin reassured him.

"Bosun, have the men take this pair to the boat, with the prisoners. Bring four men back to collect the lady."

Carter grinned, "Aye, aye, sir. Wallace, Grimes, Pierce and Toby, you're with me. Quiet now!

"Andrews take these two gentlemen and the prisoners to the boat."

"What do I do then, bosun?" Andrews asked.

"Bloody wait for us."

Martin smiled quietly and moved off silently over the sand. The party beside the lamp was getting impatient. Alouette could be heard saying, "I told you there was nothing here."

There was the sound of a slap, and a small cry. Then four men and the drooping figure of the woman appeared out of the darkness.

The four seamen did not hesitate, Martin caught Alouette as she fell from the grip of the man, who appeared to be in charge of the group.

"Take him." Martin ordered, indicating the man. The others were all dead. Picking up the woman in his arms, Martin carried her back to the boat where the others waited.

He climbed in and settled in the stern with the woman on his knee, her head against his shoulder.

"Back to the ship." he ordered.

Alouette recovered on the way back to the ship. She woke, feeling the fabric of Martin's coat against her cheek. She did not move while she worked out where she was and that she was safe. Then she relaxed and smiled to herself snuggling slightly in Martin's embrace, safe and secure once more.

Chapter twelve

Command

1798 February

The ship rose easily on the long swell. A storm at the other end of the inland sea, making itself felt 2000 miles away. As the ship rose on the next crest the voice of the lookout at the masthead called. "Sail ho! Fine on the starboard bow."

"Mr. Brown, take my telescope to the masthead and tell me what you see."

"Aye, aye, sir." Looping the strap of the leather holder around his shoulder he leapt on to the standing rigging shrouds and made his way up to the main mast head. There he braced himself against the sway of the ship, and took out the telescope focussing it on the scrap of white on the horizon, just to starboard of the bowsprit.

For some minutes he studied the appearing and disappearing scrap. Then he closed the telescope and put it away. "It is the French Frigate, *Niobe,* sir, the ship with the convoy."

The Captain nodded thoughtfully. "Martin, I am feeling it it's time for the crew to get some real exercise. I am fed up wasting powder in practice. So how say you?"

"Why I say, yes. It is a good time to fight, and a good day for it too."

"Call the men aft."

Martin was surprised. Captain Graham was not the sort of captain that liked to stir the men to effort. He always expected it to be forthcoming regardless.

With the men gathered aft Graham said, "You may recall we took a convoy on our way to Gibraltar. Well, we have in sight the frigate that was escorting those ships. She is a little bigger than us, though I believe we have the legs of her. I also think we can give two broadsides to her one. She will make a prize worth taking. So let us teach them how we do things in Britain.

The men cheered. Their Captain was popular, and they knew they could depend on him.

The distance between the two ships reduced. Both ships slowed, as they approached each other, manoeuvring to get the advantage of the up-wind position. The first gun was fired four hours after the ships first sighted each other. The action finished three hours later, in the fast falling night. Both ships had suffered, but the Frenchman had come off worse. Her foremast was lying at an angle across the foc'sle, and the first three guns of her port broadside were impossible to serve, her anchor was hanging down into the water and there were runnels of blood down her side showing the list she had, from taking in water. The clank of the pumps was loud across the gap between the two ships.

On the *HMS Racer* things were not so bad. Even as the smoke cleared from between the two ships, the men on the *Racer* were serving the guns ready for the next attack.

Captain Graham stood looking across at the battered French ship. "Helm a'lee" He called and the ship came round, the shot holes in the sails not helping but there was enough wind to keep steerage way.

As they approached the *Niobe* from the stern quarter, the bow man called "She has struck her colors, sir."

"By God, Martin. So she has. I knew we had the measure of her. Did I not say?"

"You certainly did, sir, and you were right. Shall I call away the longboat?"

"If you please, Mr. Bowers. I believe I will attend myself." The Captain went below to don his best coat while the longboat was pulled in alongside from its place astern while the action was being fought.

The boat pulled over to the captured ship with the Captain and a party of Marines on board.

For some reason Martin was uneasy about this. He turned to the Master, Jared Troop, "Swing her head round. I don't trust this man. I want our guns on him."

"Aye, aye, sir. I'm uneasy too." He turned to the helmsman. "Bring her head round. Get her under our guns."

The head swung slowly round until the guns could cover the French ship.

The longboat came alongside the *Niobe* and the bowman hooked on. On the deck there was a flurry of activity and several men appeared overlooking the longboat. They heaved several cannon balls over to drop and smash through the boat's bottom. Martin watched in horror as the longboat broke apart and the men were flung into the water.

"Jolly boat away. Mr. Brown, arm yourself. Guns at the bulwarks 1, 2, and 3, fire as you bear."

While the jolly boat was still being hauled in, the guns fired and the bulwarks of the *Niobe* dissolved in a lethal shower of splinters, the screams and cries from the French ship testified to the effect of the salvo. "Boarding party, get ready, starboard side." Martin called.

Both ships had cleared the struggling survivors in the water, and the *Racer* slipped alongside the French ship, grapnels flying across to secure her. With sword drawn, Martin led the boarders on to the decks of the enemy ship to find the deck strewn with bodies and few men on their feet who cast aside their weapons as soon as they saw the boarders.

On the quarter-deck the Captain was propped against the stern rail using his sword as a prop to stop himself falling.

Martin strode over to him angrily, still furious at the treacherous smashing of his Captain's boat.

The French Captain pushed himself off the rail and presented his sword to Martin then sank back against the rail. He was bleeding from more than one wound.

In halting English he said, "I apologise for my men. They were unhappy at my poor efforts at fighting this ship. Your answer to their treachery was enough. He waved vaguely at the bloody mess on the main deck. Then he collapsed.

Martin called for the doctor. When Abbot arrived he looked briefly at the Captain then shook his head. "He will be dead soon. There is nothing I can do for him, except make him a little more comfortable, perhaps in his cabin?"

Martin considered for a moment then nodded.

The jollyboat returned with seven survivors out of eighteen. The Captain lay on a board across the boat. He was white-faced and in considerable pain. Of the other survivors only one was injured badly, his foot had been smashed by one of the cannon balls. The doctor had them taken back to *Racer*, while Martin made arrangements for the safety of the *Niobe.*

Later, having left the prize in the hands of Lieut James, Martin visited the Captain in his cabin. The sound of hammering and rumbling resounded through the ship, and across the waters separating the two ships the sounds of the repairs being made to the other ship added to the noise.

Captain Graham was on his bed, still white-faced, when Martin entered. His eyes opened after a few moments.

"So, Martin, the ship is yours now. I know you will look after her."

"Why no, sir. You are still my Captain….." He broke off distressed at the look of pain that was accompanied by a gasp from the man on the bed.

As he turned to call the doctor, Graham spoke. "No, he has enough to do with the living, I will be gone soon enough." With an effort his voice strengthened. "My orders are in the desk there. Take them and read them. It is up to you to finish what we have started. I have a broken back and will soon be gone." He shook his head at Martin's start of protest. "I cannot feel my legs, and I have a bleed within that Abbot cannot stem. In my desk there is a letter to my parents, please deliver it. Happily, there is no wife to console. I never seemed to have the time to marry." He was speaking slowly, and Martin had to lean forward to hear him, as his voice faded. He looked into the eyes of his Captain and saw the life leave him.

He left the cabin and muttered, "He's gone," to the Captain's servant waiting outside the door. Back on deck amid the chaos of the repair work, he straightened up and took command once more.

That night they lay hove-to, while the necessary repairs to both ships, were carried out. Martin could not sleep, and so spent time on deck, watching waiting and thinking. He was sad at the death of Captain Graham. He had proved to be a good friend.

He became aware that he had company when he felt a small hand slip into his and squeeze lightly. Alouette said "I could not sleep either, so I came to keep you company."

Martin felt guilty once more. He had been striding up and down on the quarterdeck, forgetting that the cabin below his feet was occupied by the lady.

"I am sorry." He said. "I should have remembered that your cabin was below the deck here."

She put her finger to her lips "Hush, sir. You have no need to apologise. You are the Captain of your own ship. I am but a passenger, perhaps guest."

She slipped her arm through his and walked with him, up and down the deck for some little amount of time in companionable silence. She yawned. "I confess I am tired perhaps you are ready to sleep, too. It had been a long and busy day, and tomorrow will probably bring more events. Come. Escort me below and get some rest yourself." She giggled quietly and teasingly said. "If you are below, you will not disturb my rest."

"One moment, please." He called the Master. "Mr. Troop, I am going below. You have the deck. Call me if you need me."

"Aye, sir. I will." To himself Jared Troop thought, "Poor bugger, got the weight of the world on his shoulders." He thought for a moment then a smile crossed his face. "She'll do him some good, I reckon."

The passage was dark below deck and Martin escorted the lady to her door. Before he realized she had slipped into his arms. Her warm breath warned him of the kiss she gave him. He felt the soft body pressed to his and he lifted her in his arms, and carried her through the door to the cabin. He set her on the bed and found her helping to remove his clothes as he removed her robe to discover her nakedness beneath.

The two ships were making good headway, despite the shortage of men to crew them. Martin commanded *HMS Racer*, with Lieut James in command of her larger prize, *Niobe.*

Both ships had been repaired as well as the limited resources allowed, and though the pumps were needed in both, they were able to maintain reasonable headway.

One week after the action, Martin was able to breathe a sigh of relief. The mountains of Sicily hove into sight.

When they reached Palermo and dropped anchor, it seemed the weight of the world suddenly slid off his shoulders. It had been lodged there since the death of his Captain.

He reported to the Admiral, who listened to his verbal report with great interest. Admiral Nelson had not been aware of the secret orders regarding the agents, and their dropping and recovery. The arrangements for the repairs to *HMS Racer* were put in hand immediately, and a temporary skeleton crew found for *Niobe,* while she waited her turn for the dockyard's attention. Admiral Nelson was saddened by the news of the death of Captain Graham. "He was a fine young man with a great career ahead of him. To die as a result of such treachery is such a waste. He served with me in the *Agamemnon* at Toulon, you know"

"Yes, sir. I met him in the harbor at Toulon."

"Why, so you did, I recall. Well, there is nothing to be done, I'm afraid. You will remain in command until a suitable Captain is found." He looked keenly at Martin, "Are you happy with that?"

"Of course, sir."

Nelson seemed satisfied and shortly afterward sent Martin back to his ship with the assurance of a favorable report.

Alouette had gone ashore with her fellow agents to report to Sir Anthony Watts, a man who occupied a vaguely ambiguous position in the Embassy. Martin while still nominally Captain of *Racer* was lodged ashore while the repairs were undertaken to the ship. He had been aware that he would not retain the position, as he was too junior, but meanwhile he worked at the position as best he could.

Chapter Thirteen

Spy Games

Alouette called upon him to pass a message from Sir Anthony Watts. The knock at his apartment door was a surprise. The door was answered by his servant, Peters. The topman had adopted him since that first action where he had commanded the prize when part of the crew of *HMS Arun.*

"It's the French lady, sir!" Peters announced.

Shocked, he had risen to his feet and straightened his coat by the time Alouette came in. Peters retreated discreetly.

Alone, Alouette stepped up to Martin and swiftly kissed him on the lips.

"Bonjour, Cheri. How are you, Martin. Is all well?"

"All is fine, Alouette. But this is a little indiscreet."

"There is no problem. I have a message from Sir Anthony. He wishes to see you in his lodgings this evening."

As Martin started to protest, she put her fingers against his mouth. "No, Cheri. He is a powerful man. You cannot afford to refuse to meet him at least. Come, now. He is waiting."

Sir Anthony Watts did not stint himself as far as lodgings were concerned. The tall elegant rooms were furnished with taste and style.

He greeted Martin courteously, and put him at ease with a glass of good wine. Alouette, duty done, disappeared leaving the two men alone.

"So, Lieutenant Forest-Bowers. Is it Martin?" The question was innocent and Martin could not take offence. Sir Anthony was middle-aged, of slender build but not unfit by any means. He carried himself with unconscious grace, a reflection of a well-trained body.

He had a slight accent that Martin thought may well be Irish or from south west Scotland.

The purpose of the meeting was swiftly approached with a directness that Martin would learn was typical of the man. "So, Martin. I understand that you speak French?"

"True, sir, though I am told I have the accent of Martinique rather than metropolitan France."

Sir Anthony lapsed into colloquial French. "Alouette tells me that you have no difficulty in the use of the language, as do many of our countrymen."

Martin replied in French. "My instructors insisted that I learned to think in French. Luckily, I seem able to do so."

"Good, because I have at my disposal a ship. I believe that it is what is called, a schooner 75 feet in length?"

"That sounds right, sir."

"I wish that you take command of the craft for an excursion to Corsica, and the French coast. You would need to carry a group of agents to drop off and collect over the next six weeks. I can tell you that your ship will not be complete for two months. We have a current shortage of timber of the correct type. If you are agreeable, I understand from Lord Nelson that you can be available for this task. Before you decide, I must stress that it is important that the boat be commanded by a French speaker, and the mission will be extremely dangerous. If you are captured you will be treated as spies, and it will be the guillotine for all of you."

Martin sat and considered for a few minutes. His host showed no impatience. Finally "What of the crew of the schooner. Do I choose them or are they supplied?"

"The ship is of the Navy. The crew will be your concern."

"May I see the craft before I give my decision?"

"I see no reason why not. I can take you to see her now if that would suit?"

"All would need to be volunteers!" Martin said.

"Of course, sir." The bosun, Carter, said," Only volunteers, I understand, sir. I'll have the men assembled on deck so that you can address them, sir."

Bosun Jacob Carter addressed his selected men in the 'tween decks. He had selected them carefully. All the men who joined from Corsica and Sardinia were there plus the pick of the crew of the *Racer*. "Now, as you know, Mr. Forest-Bowers is a good officer. He's learnt well as many of us know, and he looks after us well. This is our chance to watch out for him. You'll recall the French lady from Egypt. She will be coming too. You are all supposed to be volunteers. I told Mr. Forest-Bowers that you had all volunteered. Are there any objections? Anyone wish to make a liar of me?"

Nobody dared say a word.

"Good lads. I knew you would have jumped at the chance for a bit of sport with our Martin. The ship needs tidying up but that's only for inside. On deck she has to look like a Froggie, so don't forget to bring your old clothes with you."

The *Perle* heeled to a brisk breeze, the dirty sails full. Martin adjusted his balance and walked along the sloping deck past the lashed-down guns, five each side of the broad deck. He thought that the six-pounder guns would do little to stop a real warship, but perhaps would scare something of their own size.

Midshipmen Brown approached escorting Alouette, who much to his delight rested her hand on his arm for support on the sloping deck.

Martin smiled to himself. She was as capable of maintaining her balance on this deck as Brown was himself, but it was second nature to her, politesse, earning the adoration of the young man. He touched his hat in greeting to Alouette, who had in fact shared her bed with him, maintaining the fiction of their first meeting of the day. "Good morning, M'selle. You slept well?"

"Certainly, Captain. Thank you, the cabin is quite comfortable, and the weather fine." The smile that accompanied this comment gave nothing away. Martin was reminded of the comment by Captain Graham.

"Every man on this ship, including me, would happily take her to his bed, but I would wager that the only man to succeed would be the one she selected, and for her own reasons, unlikely to be romantic.

Taking her arm, he escorted her to the chair placed on the deck in the shade of the mainsail. Peters, his servant, brought her coffee as Martin resumed his walk along the flush deck of the coastal schooner. Recalling Graham's words brought a sad smile to his face. Being used by the lady was not the worst thing to happen, and it did not change his love for Jennifer Bowers.

The Tricolor flew out stiffly, and he caught a glimpse of it as he turned. He was not happy about sailing under false colors, but he recognized the need in the circumstances.

At present there were several other coastal ships in view. This close to the French coast it was to be expected. His ship was one of the larger ships in view at present. Most of the others were ketches and sloops, with one or two square-sail barges used for carrying salt from the salt pans of the Camargue.

A xebec was the biggest of the other boats in sight and it was surprising that she appeared to be very clean and fast for a trader of her type. She also seemed to be taking an interest in the *Perle.*

As Martin walked back to the wheel at the stern of his command, he said to bosun Carter. "That xebec is a little too interested in us. Make sure we are ready to greet him if he gets too friendly."

"Aye, aye, sir. I'll have a welcome waiting for him."

Through the morning the xebec closed in on the schooner. Martin was not keen to let the other ship know just how fast the schooner was.

On the deck the ropes were cast off the cannon Loading was undertaken, though the ports were not opened nor were the guns run out.

Midshipman Brown watched the approaching ship through a telescope. "She is pierced for ten guns. Though all the ports are still closed, there is activity on deck."

"Thank you, Mr. Brown." Martin acknowledged the information, still uncertain about what action to take.

The problem was solved when the approaching ship unfurled a long banner with an emblem of a scimitar in gold on a red background. Her gun ports opened and a bow gun fired a shot across the bows of the *Perle.*

"Take the lady below and clear for action. Gun ports open. Port helm, Mr. Troop. Ease her now. Steady. Port broadside, fire as you bear.

One by one the port side guns fired at the xebec. Her guns were firing also, though the aimed cannon balls from the *Perle* could be seen doing damage. The lateen rig of the xebec allowed it to sail close to the wind as did the fore and aft rig of the schooner. Martin called for the topsail to be furled as it interfered with her ability to sail as close to the wind.

The speed of the sail change plus the response from the guns must have upset the Captain of the attacking ship. Perhaps he realized that this was not the slovenly trader he had anticipated, for she hesitated, a slight jink in her course, noticed by the master, Jared Troop. "She is going about!" He called.

"Ready about. Starboard guns stand to. Lee ho!" Martin had not hesitated, the ship spun round onto the other tack while the xebec was still starting her turn. "Starboard broadside, as you bear." Midshipman Brown's voice had broken, but it was still high pitched with the excitement of the moment.

The gunfire caught the xebec in stays, halfway round her turn. The bow bore the brunt of the damage. The foremast was shattered at the base and fell forward taking the top section of the main mast with it. The stem was weakened and planks were sprung either side of the bow. The sea brought the ship to a halt, sinking her by the bow. There was a commotion at the after end and a wailing sound. Several small boats appeared with masts being raised as the crew apparently abandoned the ship and others to their fate.

Martin realized immediately that the xebec had oars as well as the sails and was probably carrying slaves.

"Bring her alongside, quickly now. Carpenter, get your chisels. There are slaves aboard. bosun, boarders away. Mr. Troop, see if you can grapple her bow to slow her sinking while we get the slaves out."

The boarding party cleared out the remaining pirates. A succession of gunshots and cries ended hostilities swiftly and efficiently. The clank of the carpenter's chisel being hammered through the link of the retaining chain announced the first of the stream of forty-two surviving slaves from the benches below deck. They were quickly taken on board the schooner while the bosun searched the ship as best he could.

Several boxes were sent over, followed by the bosun and his men loaded down with arms. With the bows held up the rest of the ship was filling with water and now she was level with the surface of the sea.

"Cast off, Mr. Troop. Cut her loose."

The *Perle* straightened up rocking sharply from side to side as she was relieved of the weight of the xebec. As the two ships drifted apart the xebec wallowed deeper and deeper until, still almost level, her hull disappeared and the broken masts were left sinking slowly in isolation until they too finally sank beneath the waves.

Of the galley slaves there were 14 English, 4 Irish, 12 French, 3Nubian and 7 Scandinavian. The French were puzzled by the Tricolor at the masthead, and appeared afraid to say too much until they realized that it was a

British ship which had rescued them. It seemed that they had been royalists in a yacht escaping from the terror. Taken two years ago, they had been held, and employed in Algiers, before being taken to man the benches of the xebec.

All of the rescued slaves were happy to be free. Alouette and her colleagues had questioned the French and were satisfied they were who they claimed to be. Three had volunteered to join the spies in their tasks and had been accepted. The others asked to be delivered to the other Bourbonnais in the community in Sicily when the ship returned. Meanwhile they cheerfully joined into the working of the ship with the others.

The journey continued as they followed the coastline.

The sound of gunfire ahead made Martin take a more cautious approach to the small port of St Maxine. The larger town of Nice, which they were passing now, would be a good place for the agents to gather information. It would be where they would travel once ashore. St Maxine was a commercial place, with trade in and out. The *Perle* would be just another coaster amongst the many.

As they approached it was possible to see the source of the gunfire. There were two ships firing on the harbor forts. The reply to the ships was badly aimed and plainly the guns were poorly served. One of the rescued slaves said, "Damn. They are from Algiers. They are slavers raiding."

Without thinking, Martin gave orders for the guns to be cleared for action. "Port and starboard batteries, load and run out." To Alouette, he said, "Prepare your party for landing. We will be back in ten days."

She looked at him steady eyed. "Look after yourself, and I'll see you then."

"We will drop the boats as usual as we go into action. Your boat will break adrift. You look after yourself, and we will hopefully have an enjoyable passage back to Palermo once more."

A touch of her hand and she was gone to prepare for leaving the ship. For Martin, he was already contemplating his action against the two slave ships.

The larger of the two had turned to engage the *Perle* as she approached the gun battle. The fire from the fort increased as the *Perle* came into view. The speed of the schooner and her ability to sail close to the wind gave her an advantage in normal circumstances, but the slaver had a bank of oars to be used if needed. This meant that she was more manoeuvrable than the average sailing ship. But the oars were only now coming out, and Martin was already swinging to bring the starboard guns to bear.

As the slaver frantically prepared to use her oars, the first broadside from the *Perle* crashed out. The guns, aimed low, smashed and splintered the side along the line of ports from which the oars were protruding.

The slaver swung wildly round to present her other side, where the oars were already in the water. But they made the situation worse for their captain. His control of the ship was lost to the uneven rowing of the two sides of the ship.

Coming about with the starboard guns reloading, the port guns were firing as the ship crossed ahead of the slaver, the balls sweeping the deck of the enemy, leaving bloody trails from bow to stern along the flush deck.

The ship was filling with water through the terrible wounds she had received in the first broadside, the screams of the chained slaves clearly heard across the blood-stained sea.

Martin sailed on to tackle the other ship, which had now ceased bombarding the fort and had now turned toward the battle with *Perle*. Seeing the schooner bearing down on her obviously decided the captain, who turned his ship and made off toward the south. Martin turned the schooner and followed the slaver south-ward until they were out of sight of the port. He then changed course to close the shores of Corsica where the first of the agents had been landed. They closed the shore at night and collected the agents from the rendezvous as arranged.

The reaction to the campaign by the British naval force on the island during the previous years was interesting. Despite the island being the birthplace of Napoleon, he was not held in reverence as he was in other parts of France. The fierce independence of the people was the ruling factor of life on the island, a rule that did not take that into account would be endlessly troubled by the disputes of the people. The habit of vendetta as a method of achieving justice would not be broken overnight. As long as it existed government would always be a precarious tiptoe through the warring families.

For Martin it was interesting to talk to the returning agents, who found nothing strange about discussing their findings on this type of fishing expedition.

They made their way back to St Maxine to collect Alouette and her party. They were met by one of the new recruits who had bad news. It seems that Alouette had been recognized by one of the visiting group of Deputies, passing en-Route to Nice. She had been placed in the local lock-up and expected to be sent to the guillotine in Nice in two days' time. The other agents had gone to ground.

"Where is the prison? What sort of building is it?"

The agent thought for a moment, then spoke. "The prison is the old butcher's shop on the corner of Rue de Lorraine. There is a barracks on the other corner.

"Mr. Brown, I will be going ashore with Jean Paul." He indicated the Bourbonnais who had brought the news. "You will come inshore tonight to meet us. He indicated a position on the chart. If we are not here, come tomorrow at the same time. If I need more men I will send Jean Paul with a message to meet you. Bosun Carter and ten men ready to come ashore with cutlass and muskets. Is all that clear?"

"Yes, sir. Of course, sir."

"You will be in command. Do you understand?"

"Yes, sir. Indeed, sir." The excitement of the Midshipman was almost painful to watch. Martin was busy arranging for the jollyboat to have the mast stepped and calling for Peters to crew for him,

The small boat sailed off, leaving the schooner sailing offshore out of sight of the town.

Their boat was one of many in the harbor. They pulled in with the oars and Jean Paul pointed out the corner building just behind the first row of buildings. There was a soldier leaning on the wall outside the door. Martin walked over, stuffing tobacco in a clay pipe. He stopped by the soldier. "M'sieu, you have a light perhaps?"

The soldier shrugged then reached into his tunic pocket, for a small tinder box.

"Perfect!" Martin said, "Sir, would you join me?" He held out his tobacco tin.

"Merci, M'sieu." The soldier leaned his musket against the wall, and pulled out a stubby pipe and stuffed it with Martin's tobacco.

"You have a prisoner?" Martin asked nodding at the musket.

"Oui, M'sieu. A lady."

"Dangereuse?"

"Non, non, she is a perfect lady. Sadly, she is an aristo'. She was recognized." He shrugged.

"Pretty, is she?" Martin nudged the man in the ribs with a smile.

"Certainly, she is pretty; though not for us I think."

"Can I see her? Just take a look, I mean."

The soldier started to shake his head. Martin puffed his pipe and the smoke wafted past the soldier's nose.

Martin said, "Ah, well." He drew a bottle of Cognac from his pocket. "Perhaps a little taste to keep the tubes open. You will join me?"

The soldier looked at him as if he was daft, and reached for the bottle. He took a swig and his mood improved immediately. He took pity on his new friend. "Just a quick look," he said.

"Indeed!" Martin said "I would not like to make any trouble for you."

"I would not get any trouble. I am in charge here. Come" He looked around to see if anyone was watching and he took Martin to the door. The key looked as if it belonged to the Tower of London. It was a big clumsy lump of iron, though the lock turned easily.

"Round the door, she is in the barred area at the back. Quickly now." He pushed Martin in and closed the door though he did not lock it.

Inside Martin looked around and located the cage at the end of the room. Alouette sat calmly on a chair in the cage. She said, "Have you come to gloat, M'sieu?"

"Why would I do that?" Martin asked.

"Martin, is that you?" She sounded worried.

"Just visiting, but I will be back soon. Can you hang on for that much longer?"

Her hand touched his through the bars, "I was not considering going anywhere."

He bent and kissed her hand. "I'll be back," he said. "Expect me later this evening. He touched her cheek, turned and went back to the door. The soldier was outside the door looking anxious. He hastily locked the door.

Martin said, "She is indeed beautiful. What a waste! Thank you, my friend. I must go now but I may see you later. Perhaps we can finish the bottle then?"

"Good night, M'sieu. For the tobacco and the brandy, thanks."

Martin left him at his lonely post, and returned to Peters and Jean Paul at the boat.

To Peters he said, "Take Jean Paul to the ship." To Jean Paul, "I want the bosun and his men here tonight as soon as possible. I will be here. No muskets. Swords, clubs and pistols only!"

The next hours were lonely for Martin. In an alien place with the possibility of discovery at any moment, he remained in the vicinity waiting. He found a bar within view of the door of the prison and had a meal while he waited.

It was a relieved Jean Paul who appeared in the street later that night. Martin signalled him over to the ally he was standing in. "All ready?" he asked.

"The men are with the boat."

"Good. Fetch them over. I will go see my friend, the guard."

Jean Paul nodded and returned to the sea wall for the men. Martin took a sip of brandy and, slightly unsteadily, wandered over to the soldier on guard at the door to Alouette's prison.

"See, my friend, I return. And the bottle is not yet empty."

The soldier stirred and set his musket aside, while he rubbed his hands together to get rid of the stiffness. "I fear I am getting old," he said. "I find standing around is becoming very tiring."

"This will ease the pain a little." Martin held up the bottle, passing it to the weary soldier,

He took it with a grateful sigh. As he raised it to his lips, Martin saw the familiar figure of bosun Carter ambling up the road.

"Perhaps I can have another look, just to take to bed with me. My wife has many qualities, but a beauty she is not."

The soldier leered at him, "You think she may have undressed, heh?"

Martin shrugged, "Perhaps a little final fling, maybe?"

The soldier laughed, "Why not! I will look after the brandy while you see what you can do." His sudden roar of laughter at this caused Martin to look around to see if anyone was taking an interest. Apart from Carter and three of the men, scattered along the road there was no one about at this time of night.

The soldier produced the key, "Be my guest, my friend. I think she may be a cold one, but with tomorrow nearly here, who knows?"

Martin entered the room and made his way to the cage. "Are you ready to travel?" He asked quietly.

"Nothing is broken as far as I know. There is just the cage door."

Back at the front door the soldier was sitting senseless, the bottle still in his hand. Carter , club in hand, said "Everything alright sir?"

"Just a lock, bosun. Bring his bayonet. That should do it."

He turned back to the cage as Carter entered with the bayonet, Studying the padlock briefly in the reflected light from the street flambeau that came through the small window. He inserted the blade of the bayonet and twisted it in the hasp. The blade broke but the hasp had sprung loose. The cage was opened.

Alouette came out and into Martin's arms. "Thank you, my love. Now we must hurry, the magistrate will come soon with the priest."

They locked the door and returned the bayonet to the soldier's scabbard. They left him the brandy as consolation and returned to the sea wall and the longboat, which had brought Carter and the men.

As they rowed out of the harbor to the open sea once more, Martin released his pent up breath, realizing he had been holding it in. Beside him he felt Alouette shiver in the night air. Taking his boat cloak off he wrapped it round her, holding her close to keep her warm.

Alouette remained with him for two days after their arrival in Palermo. On the third day she was gone, off on another mission for her mysterious master.

Chapter fourteen

Inheritance and Wedding

Still in Palermo, for Martin the time passed slowly, awaiting the final repairs to *HMS Racer*. Her new Captain was newly promoted and full of enthusiasm, though he was not so happy to find that his ship required repair that could not be carried out in the local dockyard. The voyage would therefore be to dockyard in Portsmouth for two cracked keel ribs to be replaced. The working of these ribs would mean the pumps would be operating for most of the way. Nelson decreed that extra crew from the pool of recovered seamen currently in Palermo would be of more use in England and authorized spare hands to the *Racer's* crew, to help with the work of the pumps.

Martin travelled as courier, seconded as aide to Admiral Nelson. He was carried as passenger for the voyage home. He had not realized how much time he would have on his hands. So, he volunteered to stand a watch for the journey home, an offer that was gracefully received. He was surprised to find he was much in demand at the Captain's table and in the officer's accommodation. He took great pleasure in coaching the midshipmen under the command of former Midshipman now junior Lieutenant Brown, who had regaled the gun-room with stories about the episodes under the command of Lieutenant Forest-Bowers, and of course the activities of the beautiful Alouette, whom he was proud to call friend.

James Martin Forest-Bowers stood braced on the deck of *HMS Racer* as she raced to enter the Falmouth roads to deliver the reports and documents from Sicily to London.

He pictured the post chaise racing along the road to London. The documents would be in the Admiralty by tomorrow, and the ship would be in Portsmouth by tomorrow evening.

Martin was troubled over his infidelity, but he was practical enough to know that at the same time the experience had probably assured a happy commencement to the married life which faced him on his return home.

The welcome at the Hall was as expected, the warm welcome from Jane with a hug and a kiss on the cheek, and the restrained welcome from Jennifer impatient for the long arranged wedding to her hero husband-to-be.

At dinner that evening the Commodore, now Sir Charles Bowers, informed them that the wedding should take place as soon as possible. "Though we have this time at present, the war with France is still with us, and I see it lasting for a long time. Thus, all of us will be needed at sea." He smiled at the delighted couple at the other side of the table then, turning to Jane, he asked "Did you speak to the Vicar?"

"I hope you don't think me too forward?" She looked at the Martin, then Jennifer. "But realizing how patient you have both been, I spoke with the Vicar. He will call the final banns this Sunday. It will be possible for the wedding to be arranged for next week if that is agreeable?"

Martin looked at Jennifer, who was looking a little shocked. "So soon!" She said, "But my dress? I have no time...."

"We are going to London tomorrow." Jane said. "Martin has an appointment to keep in Eynsham before joining us in London?" She looked at Martin enquiringly.

"Of course, I will need to open the house in Knightsbridge, and it would be an honor to entertain you all. I will send a note to the housekeeper to prepare for guests."

Sir Charles smiled. "I have been taking advantage of your invitation to use the apartment at the house for the past few days. I warned the housekeeper that there would be guests for the next two weeks and she has prepared the house in anticipation. I do hope you don't mind, Martin?"

"So we should have time for everything to be done in time." Jane said. "The invitations have been out for over a week and I expect there will be a gathering who will understand the need for haste when a naval officer marries." She hesitated. I shall miss you both. Jennifer for her company here, and Martin because we have only just got you back. It is sure that you will not be allowed to stay here on land for long."

After the discussion of the night before, there was little Martin could contribute to the wedding arrangements so he made his way north in the Post coach via Winchester and Newbury. Having spent the night at Abingdon, he hired a horse to ride the remaining few miles to Eynsham. No-one recognized him as he crossed the Thames on the ferry at Swinford. When he walked into the Talbot Inn, though he recognized the landlord, it was not until he made himself known that the landlord remembered him and his father.

In the back room, Tom Ledbury, the inn keeper, brought him up to date with the local situation. Jethro Woods was still living at the Hall with Martin's stepmother, though it was said that he was also seeing a woman in Cassington. "There is talk that the place is to be sold, though as far as I know it is doing well with the farm and the rental property. I suggest you have a word with a lawyer. It is reckoned that Jethro has no right to anything at the Hall. Tis rumoured that they never wed."

Martin nodded thoughtfully. "Tom, I thank you. I believe it is time for me to claim my heritage." He stood up, brushed his uniform coat down, donned his cocked hat, and hooked on his sword. Shaking hands with Tom Ledbury, he left the inn and mounted his horse once more.

Riding up to the Hall brought the memories flooding back. The sight of the house itself brought a lump to his throat, with memories of his father taking him shooting game in the woodlands across the fields.

At the house he dismounted, tethered the horse to the tie rail outside, and strode up to the front door. The bell was the same, thought the brass knocker had been changed. He jerked the bell-pull. He could hear the bell ring within the house.

The door was answered by a young girl who looked frightened when she saw his uniform. "Yes, sir?" The girl asked in a local accent.

"I wish to speak with the mistress of the house!" Martin said firmly.

The girl bobbed a curtsey. "Who shall I say is calling, sir?"

"Of course. I am Martin Forrest." He answered with a smile.

Leaving the door ajar the maid disappeared within. She returned followed closely by Meredith Forrest, Martin's stepmother.

She looked at the tall man standing in his uniform at the door and stopped suddenly. "Martin?" She said, "Is that really you?"

Puzzled, Martin said, "Indeed it is. Are you ill, madam?" He said, alarmed as she swayed against the wall.

Martin stepped forward and helped the maid support her mistress to a chair.

"But Jethro said you had been killed? I thought for all these years that you were dead. Why would he say such a thing? He claimed to have attended your funeral in Hungerford just two weeks after you left home."

"I'm afraid Jethro was mistaken." Martin said. "And I have come to claim my heritage."

"What heritage? You have no claims here, sir." Meredith did not sound as sure as her words implied."

"I have a very real claim on the entire estate. As the eldest son to my father's first marriage, I stand before you in line of inheritance. By the way, did you marry Jethro?"

Meredith blushed, "No, I did not. Jethro is the factor of the estate, nothing else!"

The maid had been standing watching and listening all the time. She gasped at Meredith's words.

Meredith realized that she was still there and turned on her. "Go and make tea. Forget whatever you may have heard here or you will wish you never born."

The maid fled and Meredith rose to her feet regaining her composure. She indicated that they should go into the drawing room.

There she turned on Martin, very much now the old Meredith. "Do not threaten me young man. You are not yet 21 years. You cannot claim anything. Since I am your Guardian I will see that you are represented at the correct time, though there will be little enough I fear."

"You may have noticed, Madam, that I am a commissioned officer in the Navy. As such I have the rights of a grown man in law. You therefore have no rights over me. In addition, since I was abandoned and driven out as a child, I was legally adopted by Captain Sir Charles Bowers Bt RN and I am, accordingly, now Lieutenant the Honorable Martin Forest-Bowers RN. Where is Jethro? I wish to speak with him."

"You cheeky young pup. I am right here. How dare you walk in here and upset my wife like this?"

Martin turned. Jethro now stood eye to eye with him, heavier, but still quite fit looking, the same arrogant face and aggressive manner.

Marin looked pointedly at the dishevelled clothing of the man. "Ah, Jethro. Did I get you out of bed?"

Jethro growled, "You cocky bastard." He lunged forward, aiming a punch at Martin's face. Martin eased his head aside, causing Jethro to stumble off balance and fall to the carpeted floor.

"You will need to do better than that, man. Get up. Sit down and shut up!"

To everyone's surprise Jethro Woods did exactly that.

The maid was standing at the door with a tea tray in her hands, looking agape with astonishment at Jethro's discomfiture.

Meredith broke the silence. "Put the tray down. Go to the kitchen and wait until you are called!"

The maid put the tray on a table and left hurriedly.

"In the terms of my father's will, I inherit the estate on condition that I make a home available to Mrs. Forest. As far as you are concerned, Mr. Woods, you have no place here. I want you out today.

Woods leapt to his feet. "You have no right to throw me out!"

"I have and I am." Martin replied. "Get off the estate or I will have you thrown off.!"

Jethro turned and ran at Martin, ramming him back against the wall. Martin gasped as the breath was driven out of him. He lifted his clasped hands and slammed them down on the other man's neck. Jethro stumbled back, shaking his head to clear it, while Martin regained his breath and moved forward fists up. Jethro smiled and put his fists up in reply, confident in his ability to teach the young puppy a lesson.

Five minutes later his confidence had been sadly eroded. The blood from his broken nose testified to his misjudgement of the young man before him. As he reeled on his feet, the relentless fists of his opponent found targets in his abdomen and his sorely broken nose once more. The uppercut that floored him for the final time seemed to come out of nowhere.

He awoke with the touch of the wet cloth bathing his face. Meredith, on her knees beside him, was cleaning his face. It was then he realized, that the man he could see through his one unblocked eye, was the advocate from Oxford who had attended Mr. Forest's funeral.

The lawyer was speaking to Meredith. "You may stay in the gatehouse if you wish, but I am afraid you must vacate the Hall by the day's end." Turning to Jethro, he said, "You must leave the estate and you may not return without the personal permission of Lieutenant Forest-Bowers. That does mean you may not stay in the gatehouse with Mrs. Forest. Have I made myself clear?" He beckoned to two big men who had accompanied him to the house. To the bigger of the men, he said, "Robin, did you hear that? Nothing may be removed from the house that is not the personal possessions of the lady, or the man here." He indicated the recumbent figure of Jethro, still lying on the floor where Martin's fists had placed him.

The two big men were in no mood for any arguments from the man or woman. They helped load the possessions of the two people on the cart provided. Then they accompanied them to the gate where they watched them disappear down the road to the village.

Martin then returned to London, having arranged for the house to be cleaned and for servants to be hired to look after the property.

In London Martin rejoined his family and explained the measures he had taken secure his inheritance. Jennifer decided that, after they were married and Martin was once more at sea, she would make a point of travelling to Eynsham and becoming acquainted with her husband's childhood home.

As it happened there was time to spare for the wedding. For the local people of Eastney it was an occasion where they were entertained to a row of trestle tables groaning with the weight of food. Also the two barrels, one of beer the other of cider, ensured the party went with a swing. Several of the senior crew members from ships under repair in the dockyards attended.

Giles was away in the Caribbean at the time, but Doctor Abbot and Jared Holmes attended along with bosun

Carter. Peters was at the house looking after Martin anyway as were a sprinkling of Sir Charles's friends from the Admiralty. For Martin the day passed in a succession of images. The gift of flatware that arrived from Commodore Nelson, the canteen of silver cutlery from the officers and crew of *Arun,* standing on a table laden with gifts from people he had never heard of.

Jennifer looked stunning in virginal white standing beside him, excited and glowing, whilst he, in dress uniform with his presentation 100 guinea sword at his side, took the vows in his turn.

Afterwards the dining and dancing and at last alone together, helping Jennifer out of the elaborate dress, and she undoing buttons impatiently and finally the pair of them naked and in each other's arms in the big bed.

"At last, my love, I am yours." Jennifer breathed the words into his ear.

"And I am yours." Martin replied a little breathless from the exertion of their marital lovemaking. She snuggled up close to him, enjoying the warmth of his hands on her body.

There was time, Jennifer discovered, to travel a little before Martin was called away once more, and her first visit to Eynsham came in company with her husband.

Martin was pleased with the efforts made under the supervision of the housekeeper found for him by his Oxford lawyer. Mrs. Applegate was of middle years with a trim figure and at first sight a rather severe face. Jennifer was a little overawed at that first meeting until Dorothea Applegate smiled. The forbidding look disappeared as her face lit up in welcome to the young couple.

"Well, Sir and Madam," she indicated the other members of staff lined up at the door. "We have been looking forward to congratulating you upon your marriage, and welcoming you to this house. I pray you find our efforts to your satisfaction."

She then proceeded to introduce the other members of staff, the cook, Mrs. Smith, the housemaid, whom Martin recognized though looking a little better fed and less tired than before. She was followed by the scullery maid, the gardener and the gamekeeper. The lands of the estate had been extended by the addition of the meadow lands along the river.

Jennifer thought the house was charming, and Martin was pleasantly surprised at the improvements the agent appointed by the lawyer had suggested. The redecoration already done had been the major change. The horses in the stable had been added-to by the carriage horses, making the stable accommodation insufficient. So Jennifer set about the redesign of the barn to make it suitable for the accommodation of extra horses to allow for guests as and when needed.

It was while they were still at Walton Manor, that Martin received orders to report to the Admiralty.

London was hot and sticky Martin concluded, especially after the clear country air he had been enjoying. The Mail coach had deposited him at Lombard Street in the city, and the hackney carriage had dropped him a short walk from the Admiralty building.

Inside there was a different welcome from that of his first visit. The clerk at the reception table rose to his feet and called him by name. "Lieutenant Forrest-Bowers, please come this way." He led Martin to a private waiting room at the end of a corridor. Having seated him he enquired if he would like a glass of wine or perhaps coffee while he waited.

Martin asked, "Well, who am I waiting for? Can you tell me?"

The clerk looked baffled for a moment then he said, "It is your father, sir, the Commodore."

Settled with coffee Martin waited for his adoptive father to appear, mystified and intrigued, since they had last spoken only two days ago.

The Commodore came into the waiting room, drying his hands on a cloth. "Martin, my apologies. I have kept you waiting far too long. Do come through to my room and I'll tell you all about the project I have in mind. I would have spoken to you earlier, before you departed for Eynsham but the plan was just an idea at the time. I did not know how long it would take to get things going.

Seated at his desk Sir Charles looked searchingly at Martin. "I understand that when you were in the Mediterranean you were involved with landing, and collecting, agents on French territory?"

Martin nodded, "I speak French as you know. Sir Anthony Watts called upon me to take a cutter and drop off agents, to collect them later. It did entail me landing in France on occasion."

"Well, I'm afraid the wretched Watts fellow has asked for you again since you are not as yet posted to a ship. What he has requested is that you be given a command of a ship that is capable of defending itself against the average smuggling vessel, but not so big as to be immediately presumed to be a warship. I have found just such a ship, a schooner, American built. She is fast and handy I'm told, carries ten six pounder guns, and two long nines, bow and stern. She will take a crew of up to fifty men, though she will handle comfortably with thirty five, I am informed that the call for volunteers from *HMS Racer* to crew the schooner produced nearly the entire complement.

"Lieutenant Brown and the Master Jared Troop have both requested they be considered. That, of course, is up to you. You will be ranked as acting-Commander for the commission and depending on its outcome I am assured that you will probably be confirmed in that rank."

The Commodore leaned back in his chair and looked at Martin with raised eyebrow. "I have suggested you accept Lieutenant Charles Morgan as first, I understand he served under you in the West Indies, and you reported well on his conduct."

Martin remembered Morgan, who was not related to the former Pirate and Governor of Jamaica. He nodded his acceptance of the man.

"Do I take it you will accept this commission?"

Martin started out of his trance, "Of course, sir. I will be happy to accept. How soon would I need to take command of ...of...I'm afraid I do not know the name of the ship I am given?"

"That is because I have not mentioned it. I was asked to keep it secret until I had your acceptance of the post. She is named *HMS Bangor* and lying at Dover. You will be expected to repair on board in ten days' time. I will inform Lt Morgan and the Master to select the crew, if that will be satisfactory."

"That would be acceptable to me." Martin replied. "Meanwhile I presume that I will be told what is required of me in detail by the Foreign Office."

"In fact you will not! Your orders will come through this office. By issuing orders from here, we will ensure that you are not tasked to do anything which unfairly places you, and your command, in hazard." As Martin went to interject, Sir Charles held up his hand to stop him. "Wait. I do not mean that you will not be asked to risk your ship and your life, as all naval officers are from time to time required. It is the ridiculous we are guarding against. Sailing inshore into shoal waters because some clerk decides that, according to his map, the location would save a half-hour walk. We undertake the responsibility of separating the impossible from the possible, without you needing to weather the wrath of some mandarin from the Foreign Office and blighting your career."

Martin sat back at this explanation satisfied, and in fact, secretly pleased that he would in effect sail under the Admiralty rather than the Foreign office.

Sir Charles rose to his feet. Martin rose also. The commodore came around the desk and put his arm round Martin's shoulder. "I'm proud of you, lad. Happy that you bear my name and are wed to Jennifer. We, Jane and I, feel blessed that we have gained a family."

Martin left the Admiralty pleased that he had a command, but unsure just what he would be expected to do. One thing he fully intended doing was to take the next mail coach to Dover and see the ship he would be commanding.

At eight that evening the mail coach left Lombard Street en route to Dover. Martin was seated with six others for the uncomfortable trip.

In the Fleet Inn next morning after a wash and a shave he ate breakfast before going down to the harbor to find *HMS Bangor* among the ships moored there.

He travelled back to Eynsham two days later to rejoin Jennifer, having acquainted himself with his new ship. She had meantime created turmoil in the house, with all the alterations required to make the country home she had decided she wanted.

Importantly, Dorothea Applegate had approved of the alterations she had introduced, and both women had worked out a cooperative working arrangement between them.

It was then Martin understood that whatever his position at sea may be, in the house his voice only carried the authority that his wife allowed, however diplomatically the situation was disguised.

Chapter fourteen

Playing the cat

1800 The Channel

The wind blew spray into the face of the young Midshipman standing his watch on the deck of the heeling schooner. The thrill of being in command of this splendid ship, however temporarily, filled him with pride. The thought that one day he might well have such a command of his own was what made the day even more enjoyable.

The sound of steps on the companion ladder brought him back to earth with a start, as he searched his mind for anything he may have forgotten to include in his report to the Captain when he arrived on deck.

Commander James Martin Forest-Bowers RN stepped onto the quarter deck of his command with his own private thoughts. This was his first real command, an Admiralty appointment, in fact gazetted as Acting Master and Commander. Provided he performed his task and obeyed orders, he might continue to command for the rest of his naval career. Another wind-borne sheet of spray brought him back to reality and he ruefully wiped his face with the thought that the sea made no distinctions between Midshipmen and Captains.

Midshipman William Smart lifted his hat to his Captain and reported the course and the weather to him as he had been instructed.

Martin smiled at the high-pitched voice of the young man and acknowledged the report. "Carry on, Mr. Smart. Watch the trim."

"Aye, aye, sir." Smart replied briskly and, feeling two feet taller, turned to the helmsman. "Keep her close there. Watch her head."

The helmsman answered briskly, "Keep her close. aye, aye, sir." He smiled quietly, well aware that he knew more about the trim of the ship than the lad, but he was popular with the crew and keen.

Martin heard the exchange and smiled to himself. The boy was learning.

"Keep me informed if we sight any other ship, Mr. Smart. I will be below!" He turned and returned to his cabin where he was preparing a report for the Admiral. The cruise had been without result for the past week and he was now considering the option of trailing his coat along the coast of Normandy, or perhaps returning up channel to see if there was any action toward the Straits of Dover.

The cry from the masthead lookout solved his dilemma. "Sail ho! On the port quarter, running free, hull up from behind the Ile de France."

Martin was on deck immediately. "Up helm. Take a tack, Mr. Brown. Let us get out of his sight. We do not wish to scare him off."

"Aye, aye, sir!" Midshipman Brown passed the orders, as Lieutenant Morgan and the Jared Jones arrived on deck. The ship settled on a tack that diverged from the course of the quarry.

"When you are ready, Mr. Morgan and Mister Holmes. My cabin, if you will."

He descended to the stern cabin, now his sole domain, and called to his steward for coffee for himself and his two guests.

The three men seated themselves in the comfortable cabin and, as Martin brought out his orders and opened them, both Morgan and Jared Holmes could not resist leaning forward to see what was being revealed.

In many ways it was a disappointing sight, a chart and a single sheet of paper covered in script.

Martin lifted the single sheet and read it through. His brow creased as he read and, when he was done, he read the whole sheet again.

Turning to his two companions, he said, "Gentlemen, we have here an order which is a request disguised as an order, or the other way about perhaps. Whatever, it's substance is that we give chase to the sail we spotted this morning. Without allowing him to know who we are, find out his purpose before capturing him and bring the whole ship and her contents and crew to the Fal, specifically St Mawes. At the castle there, we are ordered to stand off and allow the entire ship and her crew and content to be examined by specialists. What they will be seeking, I know not? All I am told is to carry out the instructions to the letter."

"A strange task for the Admiralty to set." Morgan observed.

"That is not an Admiralty order, or I miss my guess." Jared Holmes, the Master interjected.

"You are right indeed, Mr. Holmes. This is from our Foreign Office masters. I fear with orders like this the opportunity to do the wrong thing is more than doubled, for there is no direct 'do' or 'don't'. This is all 'as you think fit' or 'if you decide!'"

He sat back and noticing his untasted coffee lifted it to his lips and sipped the rich brew.

The schooner caught up with the mysterious sloop from the Ile de France during the night, the lookouts on deck keeping the outline of the sloop's tall mast in sight against the lighter starlit sky. Orders were whispered and the boarders ready. Rope fenders were hanging down on the port side as they closed the other ship portside-to. The grapnels went across and the boarders followed swamping the deck with men, who secured the visible members of the other ship's crew. Lieutenant Brown led chosen men below and shortly reappeared with two gentlemen and a lady, who were all complaining vociferously. They were brought to Martin's cabin where they were seated in front of the table.

When Martin entered he was greeted by both men speaking at once. The lady stayed silent and, on seeing Martin, a small smile appeared, twitching the corner of her mouth.

Impatiently, Martin waved to the two men to be silent. Neither took notice so Martin told them to be still in no uncertain terms. The men sat open mouthed at being reprimanded in such a manner from such a young man.

Martin turned to the lady who looked at him directly and in a small voice said, "Hello, Commander Forest-Bowers. Do I find you well?"

Martin bowed over her outstretched hand and kissed it. "I am indeed well, better even for seeing you."

Not sure how to address her he elected to let her lead the way.

"I am still Alouette to my friends, "

"As I am still Martin to mine," he replied.

Seeing this exchange the two men kept quiet waiting to see what was happening.

"I have orders to see you all safe to St Mawes. Your sloop will accompany us there. From there I am afraid I have not been informed of your future movements."

Alouette turned to the two men, "I will not introduce you. I will merely say that this exercise is being carried out for our protection, and it was arranged by 'merely' Mr. Smith."

Martin smiled and Alouette laughed aloud. "Tell me, Martin, did he not say that?" In a deep voice she said, 'You may refer to me as 'merely' Mr. Smith.' Am I not correct?"

Martin nodded, "Just so."

The two men left the cabin to be entertained by Mr. James and the gunroom. Alouette remained to reminisce with Martin, after turning the key in the lock. Having been advised that Martin was now married, she insisted that he demonstrate his prowess for the benefit of a friend who had been abstemious to a degree recently.

Chapter fifteen

Russia

1801- The Baltic:

HMS Bangor made good time over the light swell, her sails full and hull heeling to the fresh breeze. She was on her way to rendezvous with a cutter out of La Rochelle. The Biscay weather was being cooperative for a change and there was no other sail in sight.

Martin leaned to compensate for the movement of the schooner and inhaled the fresh sea air, the sun was taking the sharp edge of the autumn chill and the blue sunlit sea was flecked with white caps.

He watched the porpoises leaping and playing off the bow, easily keeping pace with the ship. He was thoughtful. His orders had been as vague as ever. It was an irritation that the instructions issued by the Foreign Office were ever thus, couched in terms that allowed discretion but hinted at the penalties of overreaction.

He was carrying no passengers this trip. There was a twinge of guilt as he recalled the latest episode in his relationship with Alouette.

The delivery of the cutter and the agents involved had gone off without any problems. Alouette had been a welcome diversion for the several hours that had been needed for the delivery to St Mawes.

'Merely' Mr. Smith had waited to meet the agents when they were landed and the contents of the cutter were removed by a team of local men, who transferred barrels and cases, boxes and bales, from the hold of the cutter to several small craft which had surrounded the two ships when they moored opposite the castle.

It had seemed to Martin that the cutter had been used to import contraband. The contents of the hold had certainly looked like brandy, tobacco and such smuggled goods he was sure.

He shrugged. It was not his business to query what his lord and master did, or did not, do. In this case it was a simple question of doing what he was told.

The schooner had sailed that same early morning, her duty done. Her new task, the present one, was to meet offshore with a boat from La Rochelle.

It was mid-afternoon before the sail was spotted, and early evening before the two ships were close enough to exchange signals. It was a full dark though starlit night by the time the two ships were able to join company, and for a boat to be launched to bring papers and two people across to *HMS Bangor*.

The ships separated before dawn. The stranger made for the French coast while *HMS Bangor* turned for home.

Martin had been in command for three months, and apart from the dalliance with Alouette, was missing Jennifer, his new wife sorely. The two men he had picked up from La Rochelle were both close-mouthed and both required to be delivered personally to the hands of the Foreign Office. The ship required provisions. Having been at sea without land contact for three months, there were things the bosun and the first lieutenant required to be put to rights. It was therefore sensible for the ship to be taken to the Chatham dockyard for provisioning and to have the list of repairs and replacements attended to. This would allow Martin to deliver his charges direct to their destination.

They spoke a naval cutter in the Channel and Martin was able to send messages to the Admiralty and to Jennifer, warning them of his imminent arrival in London.

The journey up-river was tortuous after the freedom of the open sea. There were ships and small craft everywhere, but the passage was achieved with the help of the pilot.

The arrival at Chatham was a time for a frantic rush to the Post coach for the agent in charge. The more leisurely arrival and departure in the Bowers' coach, made time for the handing over of the ship to the shipwrights a more restful procedure. Martin was expected to report to the Admiralty the following morning, but the rest of the day, and the night, belonged to Jennifer and Martin.

That night Martin discovered that his wife had missed him and his attentions, as much as he had missed her.

Though he still felt guilty, he was grateful to the women he had been with. The experience had allowed him to conduct himself well enough to satisfy Jennifer's growing joy in their relations.

The following day he presented himself at the Admiralty, as instructed. Once again he was received by his adopted father.

Still carrying the rank of Commodore, Charles Bowers was looking a little less robust than usual. His situation at the Admiralty was more demanding than the quarter deck of a frigate.

"Why, Martin. It is good to see you once more." The Commodore's voice boomed in the lofty-ceilinged office. "How are you coping with the cross-channel spies? Have they been causing trouble?"

"In fact, sir, anything but! I have now delivered all three of the latest bunch to London. It was difficult to hold them back when the city came into sight. They set off in a post coach before the moorings were completed!"

"Were they, by George? There must have been a few things to pass on for them to be so hasty."

"I myself was not slow to follow. Jennifer was at the quayside with the carriage by 10 am and, I confess, we were brought to the house with commendable dispatch. Despite the short duration of my last voyage, we both felt the separation endless, and were happy to be together again."

Charles Bowers smiled. I trust you will both be able to spare Mrs. Bowers time to eat dinner tonight, for she will be expecting you both. Since you came into our lives she has made it clear that you have become the son we could not have."

"Please. My entry into the family has been the best thing that happened to me. I hold Jane next to Jennifer in my affections. Seeing and enjoying her company, will be a true pleasure."

"Hrummpf!" The Commodore appeared to sneeze into his handkerchief. Though in truth it was a cover for the pride and joy that his companion had brought into the lives of his wife and himself. "So to business, Martin. I have here the instructions of the Admiral that have recently been delivered.

Commander Martin Forest-Bowers RN strode the deck impatiently. The ship was behaving well. The tasks so far set had been accomplished as ordered with no real problems. So why was the fleet waiting? He scanned the horizon. British ships of the line seemed to be everywhere he looked, the Danish fleet beyond. From the shore the cannon of the Danish Tri Kroner fort were firing enough shots to keep the group of smaller craft, led by the frigate *HMS Amazon* under the command of Captain Edward Rou, at bay.

The force had been given the task of assaulting the fort, when the northern section of the Danish fleet had been subdued by Admiral Nelson's fleet of 12 of the shallower-draught ships allocated by Admiral Sir Hyde Parker. Nelson had transferred his flag from *HMS St George* 98 guns, to *HMS Elephant* 74 guns, for the battle. Having taken up position opposite the Danish fleet, Nelson's ships opened fire, despite the fact that three of the squadron has run aground on the central shoal, including Nelson's former command *HMS Agamemnon*.

For Martin, as always when action was called for, he became impatient with delay, and it was necessary for him to contain his impatience in the presence of the crew. He deliberately slowed his step and, when Peters appeared with his sword-belt and his fighting sword, he allowed him to place it ready to put on, before fetching coffee for his Captain and Lieutenant Morgan, The sight of the pair sipping coffee at this time was commented upon by the crew who marvelled at their officer's coolness in the face of imminent conflict.

The subsequent assault on the fort was a bloody one. Captain Rou lost his life in the fighting. The Danes certainly stood their ground without giving an inch more than they needed. The big ships' action led by Admiral Nelson in *HMS Elephant* was an equally vigorous face-off that ended in a cease-fire based on politics rather than the guns of the fleets.

For Martin the entire business left a sour taste. It seemed a betrayal to the men of the Danish fleet, who had acted as they should. The action cost them the forfeiture of a large part of their fleet, after a battle they did not actually lose.

For Martin there was, as always, another task. Frigates, big or small were the workhorses of the navy and the Admiralty resented having them lie idle. It was no real surprise that *HMS Bangor* was ordered to St Petersburg. In company with the ship-sloop *HMS Watchet* 26 guns, the two ships made good time to the waters off Russian capital.

Martin prepared to receive visitors and sorted out the despatches he carried for the British agents he was ordered to contact.

As he rightly guessed, the arrival of two ships in the vicinity caused havoc among the small craft in the area. Among the small craft, scattered as they became identified as British ships, was one that had an accident with her mainsail. It was rounded up with several others, taken to gain information about any of the ships in Neva Bay. When the people from the boat which had mainsail trouble were interviewed, Martin sat in to the interrogation. The boatman was a thin young man who was obviously unwell. He spoke

English and, once they were within the cabin with the door closed, he identified himself as the agent Martin was expecting to contact.

Known as Ivan only, Martin was able to re-assure him that his parents, who ran a silversmiths' business in London, were both well and anxious to hear from him.

Ivan smiled as Martin read the bulletin he had been given. "I am very grateful for the way Britain has played fair with my parents. As you can see, I do not expect to see them again. I am ill and I have been told I will not see the year out. If I may I will read these notes here while I am able and possibly answer at least some of the questions immediately."

"By all means, sir. Please use this cabin as you will. There are others to investigate so I will see they are dealt with elsewhere."

He rose and left Ivan with his sealed orders.

There was no move from the Russian ships anchored in Neva Bay. No challenge to *HMS Bangor* and her companion, so the two ships extracted such information as was available from the small fry they had taken, and released them. They relieved the fishermen of their cargo of fresh fish. The fishermen had no real complaint since in fact they were paid more than they would have received in St Petersburg, and they did not have to pay the tax on their takings either. Ivan departed with the rest, despite the offer from Martin to carry him back to England and his parents. He was able to pass on the fact that a substantial cargo ship was expected in the port during the next few days.

For Martin it was a decision he had not expected to make. He sent for the captain of *HMS Watchet*. Lieutenant Colin Marshall arrived promptly on board and was seated in Martin's cabin drinking coffee within the quarter hour.

"We have an interesting situation arising. The big cargo ship, mentioned by our agent, is probably French. I can only guess that it has coasted up the Baltic from Denmark using the German waters, and then Russian. The care that has gone into this ship's progress to St Petersburg is an indication that the cargo is of extreme value or importance.

"Have we no idea at all of the cargo carried by the ship? Surely someone would know here in St Petersburg." Colin Marshall was a pleasant competent seaman who handled his ship well, but Martin feared that he was not comfortable with the intrigues of international politics.

"Of course," Martin concluded. "The cargo could be human, a Duchess perhaps, but why in a French ship?"

"I think, in the light of this news we have to see if we can intercept this ship, if only to settle our own minds in this matter."

Marshall said "But what of our orders? Are we not required to return with all despatch?"

"I think in the circumstances we are justified in investigating this matter properly, in case we are witnessing a change of heart by the Russians. So we stay for a while anyway, and see what we can see."

It was three days later that the French ship hove into sight. She was an East Indiaman mounting at least 10 guns, all bigger than the armament on both British ships. When she noticed the two warships outside the harbor entrance, she turned as if to run for it.

But the two Russian frigates moved out of Neva Bay and her master changed his mind.

For Martin the movement of the Russian ships decided him and he signalled Marshall to intercept the French ship while he crossed the course of the Russians to challenge their presence.

As they closed the lead Russian ship a voice called across from her decks to stand off out of the way.

The voice spoke in French. Martin called back in English pointing at the flag clearly flying free above his head. "Do not interfere. We are intercepting an enemy ship on the high seas"

This caused considerable comment on the deck of the Russian.

An English voice then called from the Russian ship. "I am the British ambassador here in St Petersburg. My name is Hervey. I order you to clear the area and allow the cargo ship through."

Martin thought about this for several minutes then answered once more. "I command here at sea. That ship flies the flag of my country's enemies. It is my duty to stop her and secure her if I am able. Please inform your Russian Captain to withdraw, otherwise I will presume he is sailing under false colors and is actually allied to the French. In which case, I will open fire upon him and his companion."

Across the water the sound of a single gun could be heard.

The Frenchman stopped immediately, under backed topsails. The gun-ports of *HMS Watchet* were open and a curl of smoke could be seen above the still waters. Martin waited for an answer from the Ambassador. None came. Both Russian ships returned to Neva bay. The Frenchman came up with *HMS Bangor* and hove to once more.

"Mr. Morgan I will take a boarding party across to the French ship. Keep her under the guns at all times."

"Yes Sir."

The longboat commanded by Midshipman Brown reached the Frenchman quickly. A companion way was lowered to allow them to board. Martin strode across the quarter deck followed by Midshipman Evans and Peters. The bosun assembled the rest of the boarding party along the starboard bulwark.

"Commander Forest-Bowers R N. from *HMS Bangor* at your service, M'sieu. I have come to accept your surrender. Please have your passengers brought on deck and provide a manifest of your cargo."

The French Captain spoke. "Sir, I have orders to deliver my passengers to the hands of the Tsar of all Russia."

"For what purpose, pray?"

"I believe as hostage.

"Who is this hostage? Such an important person and why a French ship?"

"All I know is what I was told. The woman was collected from a a strange ship with her servants. She does not speak my language thus I know nothing of her history." He waved toward the stair to the accommodation. "See for yourself."

Martin looked at the emerging group in astonishment. He had not seen people like these before. The men were warriors, obviously. They had long slender blades in scabbards thrust through the sash they wore. They had leather over their shoulders and strange helmets, with side pieces covering their faces. The eyes were strange with a fold over their upper lids.

Behind them came two women in robes, leading a slender woman with a white face and black hair. Her eyes were more almond shaped than the men, and she stepped daintily up to the deck of the ship where she stopped and bowed to the officers standing there.

Martin bowed in turn to the lady. He spoke to her in English. "Madam, whom do I have the honor of addressing?"

The lady looked at Martin directly. "You are not like these other barbarians." Her gaze took in the group of French officers. "They would have treated us badly, had they dared."

She stepped forward brushing aside the hands if her two ladies. Close to Martin she said quietly, "I have been passed to the Tsar of Russia because his country borders on mine far to the east. We do not have war but there is no friendship between us. These French think to influence the Tsar, to have him join with them in their war against Britain and Germany."

"What do you think, Madam?"

The white face lost its impassivity. "Truly, you are not of this time, that you ask a woman for her opinion?"

Martin shrugged.

"Since you ask, I think I would be a curiosity at the Russian court until one of his drunken relations or even the Tsar himself, decides to investigate this body beneath the robes. when they discover that I am just a woman they will use me, and discard me perhaps give me to their soldiers to play with. I do not think I can be used as a trade with my father. I am a woman and of little value in my country."

"Madam, have your servants gather your baggage. You will be joining my ship for the remainder of this voyage. It will be livelier than this great tub, but the company will be more congenial, I guarantee."

The lady turned and said something to her servants. They turned and disappeared below.

Martin called Carter. "Go with them below, Carter, and make sure nobody interferes with them or steals from them."

Carter ran over to the stair and stepped smartly below. Martin turned to the French Captain. "Send two hands to assist the ladies in their task." The Captain issued the order, before he realized that Martin had spoken in English.

Martin looked at him and said, "We will have things to talk about, Captain. It will while away the hours on the long voyage home." Turning to Peters he said quietly, "Call the marines on deck. Smartly now."

Peters stepped to the starboard bulwark and leaned over. "Now, Sergeant. Bring your men on deck at the double!"

The marines had followed their captain in a second boat while the attention of the French was on the negotiations on the quarter deck. They trotted up the companion way and formed up on deck.

Martin addressed the assembled French officers. "Your weapons, gentlemen, please."

Grim-faced, the French officers surrendered their swords and pistols under the combined threat of the boarding party and the marines.

Martin gave up his cabin to the Oriental Princess. Lieutenant Morgan took command of the Frenchman, with men under a midshipman from the *Watchet* to reinforce her prize crew.

All three ships set sail for the fleet at the other end of the Baltic Sea.

The Princess joined him at the table for dinner on the first night. Martin discovered that she was well informed and very bright. They had a lively time discussing the state of the world and the situation of women in the modern world.

Her own situation was an unhappy one at present. When she returned she was aware that she would be passed to an old man as a wife or concubine. As a woman she was too old now to merit marriage to a young noble.

On the second night the subject arose once more and she mentioned that, if she had been taken by one of the Frenchmen, she would have been permitted to either stay single or marry an inferior, provided someone suitable could be found to accept a woman despoiled by a European. She bewailed the fact that she would have to accept her fate and suffer the groping of an old man since no European had taken advantage of her.

To Martin it was unbelievable that this delicate flower of womanhood should be condemned to such a cruel fate.

"Forgive me suggesting this. But do you need to be raped to qualify for this exclusion?"

"Why, no. For I can claim rape. But I must be able to prove I have been deflowered. I can claim that I protested, but I must have been penetrated to prove my words."

"Then perhaps it would be possible to solve your problem, without the violence that would come with rape."

"Why, Captain Forrest. Would I be correct in assuming that you would yourself assist me in this matter?"

Martin found himself blushing, and also extremely embarrassed.

She took pity on him. "Martin, may I call you that?" She hesitated. "Do you think you could help this plain Princess of China with this situation."

"Princess, you may be many things. Plain is not one of them. Any man would be delighted at the opportunity to enjoy the favors of such a beautiful woman."

It was her turn to blush, though it was not too easy to see through the white make-up on her face.

With great dignity she rose to her feet. "You should be aware that my name is Mai Ling. If we are to become better acquainted I see no reason why we should stand on ceremony. Would tonight be too soon for our first meeting?"

Martin leapt to his feet, he bowed. "I would be honored."

The events of later that night were engraved on his mind, and however much he rationalised his part in the events of the succeeding nights, there was no way he could deny that the close association with her beautiful body was an experience he would never forget. The delicate doll-like body had knowledge of pleasing a man that had to have been taught to her during her education as a child.

After the initial pain of their coupling, her enthusiasm grew with each opportunity they took to enjoy each other.

When they rejoined the fleet, Martin reported information to the Admiral and informed him of the Princess and her entourage, and how the French had planned to use her. The Admiral decided that the prize be sent back to England. The prisoners were transferred to a ship of the line that was returning to Portsmouth for repair, carrying other prisoners. The prize would leave under command of a wounded Captain with a crew made up of spare men from two of the fleet ships sunk during the action of the past few weeks. Martin was ordered to transfer her when the prize became ready to sail, in three days' time.

Mai Ling made her tearful farewell privately. When she appeared on deck to transfer to the prize, she was her impassive self once more, thanking Martin for his courteous treatment during her stay on board.

Chapter sixteen

Channel hopping

1802- Peace

An uneasy peace was signed between Britain and France. And despite the vociferous efforts of elements of the Government, a fatal reduction of the fleet and armed forces was averted.

For the fleet, great efforts were made to keep ships at sea wherever possible. For a twenty-two-year-old Commander there was considerable risk of being beached. So for once the association with 'merely Mr. Smith' was welcomed.

For most of the year there were agents to carry and people to rescue. This particularly applied to those people who had fled the rule of Napoleon, whose land and property had been abandoned to the mercy of the state.

The truce had guaranteed the safety of the returning émigrés, but the cynical disregard of such promises was ignored by authority. The result was abuse and violent local reaction, where the recovery of land and possessions was attempted.

The year, therefore, was passed in a depressing series of excursions across the Channel to rescue and save people who, in the opinion of many, did not deserve it.

Many of the voyages were made in the guise of smugglers, and this entailed the actual smuggling of goods that possibly, finished up in the household of 'merely Mr. Smith' himself.

For the Lieutenants under Martin's command, the experience they gained sailing in the confined waters of the channel was invaluable. As the year grew to a close the return of the war seemed inevitable. The result of this for Charles Morgan was his appointment to take over command of *HMS Bangor* while Commander Forrest-Bowers was given command of the frigate *HMS Diane* of 32 guns, a former French warship of recent construction.

He was joined by Lieutenant Reed. Carter had stood for Masters' Mate and transferred at his request. He was greeted by the newly rated bosun Patrick Peters whom he had known since his first voyage on *HMS Arun*. More recently on *HMS Bangor* Peters had been bosun's mate.

"Well, Peters, a new rating. How is your mother these days?"

"She is well, sir, and now wed to the Rector and comfortable with it."

"Good to have you here, Peters. Carry on." Martin was indeed pleased to have familiar faces about him.

The uneasy peace was finally ended when Britain decided to keep Malta, an island due to be returned to France under the peace treaty.

Napoleon had been furiously preparing to recommence the war and Malta was essential if the French were to re-take Egypt. This was clearly unacceptable to Napoleon.

The impasse was resolved with the declaration of war by Britain and hostilities were resumed.

In the period of peace all sort of preparations had been made by the French for the invasion of Britain and the re-commencement of hostilities. The invasion of Germany was undertaken almost immediately. At sea the blockades were re-commenced and defences all along the southern ports were created, in many cases using worn out battle ships as floating batteries in harbor areas.

For the frigates there was always work, and despite the demands of the fleet, 'merely Mr. Smith' was able to employ Martin and *HMS Diane* on numerous excursions to and from the French coast.

The collection of Alouette, looking exhausted, from the beach at the mouth of the *Aber Vrac* near the town of Plouguerneau in the Finisterre region of France, caused Martin much concern. Apart from their physical association enjoyed over the years they had known each other, Martin had grown to like and respect her as a friend. Seated by her bunk as she rested after boarding, Martin expressed his concern at her condition.

"Dear Martin, I am but a tool in the armory of the anti-Bonaparte forces. As such I am employed wherever I can do the most good for the cause. This time it was for some time as a prisoner in the local prison. I am afraid I have been damaged more than I anticipated." She fell back against the pillows with a sigh.

Doctor Corder was not pleased when he completed his examination. His report to Martin made clear his concerns. "I am not a specialist in these matters. The fact that the mademoiselle has been beaten I can attend, but she has been abused savagely by someone and has been infected with disease." He coughed at this point, embarrassed. "I have done all I can for that damage, though it will take more expert hands than mine in future. The disease will require hospital treatment. I have given her something to make her sleep."

"Will she recover?" Martin asked anxiously.

"That, I cannot honestly promise." The young doctor was as good as any Martin had met and had been found for the ship, by Mr. Smith himself.

Martin took his words seriously, thankful that he had the services of such a well-trained man.

Dr Corder continued, "I will keep a close eye on the lady and in the meantime I have dosed her with a recently discovered remedy for her illness. But I cannot guarantee the result. I can only stress that the sooner we can reach a hospital the better."

The ship was already on course for Portsmouth and all Martin could do was to ensure that they made the fastest passage possible.

Raul Chavet had been the man who brought Alouette to the rendezvous. He could only report his own part in her rescue. "The agent who interrogated her is known to us as a savage. M'selle entered the prison to contact a person held there. There was no question of her supposed crime. It was a sentence of three days to clean and work for the keepers as punishment for being cheeky to the M'sieu le Maire when he groped her in the market. She slapped his face and earned the small punishment. She was able to contact our man in the prison, but attracted the attention of the pig, Portet.

"He called for her interrogation, we learned of it and the Maire had her released when he was told. He could do no more. Portet, the agent, carries a lot of authority in the area and with Paris. He was absent when M'selle was released."

Martin noted the name for future reference, including it in his report to Mr. Smith.

Alouette survived the journey to Portsmouth and the hospital there was able to continue the work started by Dr Corder, who accompanied her. Martin was called to London for a special meeting after the report had been sent forward.

The ship was ordered to stay in harbor for a two-week period. Martin had been able to visit the house in Eastney, where he was happily received by Jane and Jennifer, who was visiting, knowing that Martin was due to dock in Portsmouth. The Commodore was in London. It was expected that he would be given a fleet command during the next month. The rank of Rear Admiral came with the new command and both women were excited at the news. For Martin the three days he was given before his summons to London were a welcome bonus. When he called at the hospital on his way to London, he was pleased to see Alouette looking better. She said that she was recovering from her ordeal.

When Martin reported to Mr. Smith he had the situation well in mind. "Sir! This man, Portet, should be dealt with. I believe from the attitude of the other agent, Chavet, that Portet has power in the area. Certainly Chavet was scared of him. If we can remove Portet from the position he occupies it will make things much easier for our agents."

"I'm inclined to agree with you. He has been operating elsewhere, and wherever he has been, he has caused us considerable trouble. The problem seems to be how we go about it. He has a team of people around him which makes it almost impossible to get near to him."

He strode up and down in his office deep in thought.

"Any suggestions you may have would be welcome."

"I do have one, sir. I believe that there is a move afoot to destroy the invasion boats being assembled on the Channel coast. I think it might be possible to attach an extra party to one of the raiding groups with that mission in mind. I think capture would be the best solution. The man is obviously well informed and could be a source of information of the situation in Northern France.

Mr. Smith stroked his chin thinking. "If you can come up with a plan, I'll look at it, but no promises, mind. Just now I wish you would check on the preparations of the boats at Boulogne. Don't take any risks, but I would like your assessment of the capability of the boats there.

"I would expect you to spend at least two weeks on this task, giving you plenty of time. I leave it entirely to your own discretion. If you sail tomorrow, I will expect you here fourteen days later and we can then discuss the suggestion you brought tonight."

Mr. Smith turned and left the room. Martin stood staring at the picture over the mantelpiece. He thought it was typical of Mr. Smith to leave things the way he had. With a sigh he picked up his cocked hat and left the building to return to the London house where Jennifer was waiting.

Jennifer looked at her husband. At twenty-three he had done well. As Commander, the rank went with the command. He was still some way before post rank, but his association with Mr. Smith had been beneficial to his career. Of that there was no doubt, though Martin's own talent for the work had been equally helpful.

Her news was difficult to retain, but she was determined that Jane should be present when she announced it. Jane was after all her mother. Much though she wanted to tell Martin it had to wait until tonight, when the Admiral and Lady Jane would be in attendance for dinner, before the party left to attend the Ball at Lady Richmond's London home.

So it was not until the evening while seated at the table with Lady Jane and Sir Charles on either side, facing her beloved husband that she announced that she was pregnant. The stunned silence that followed this announcement may have signalled anything, but the joy of her husband's cry and obvious delight of her guests made it quite clear that her news was welcome.

As they prepared to leave for the Ball, Jennifer spoke to Martin explaining why she had waited to make the announcement. Martin looked at her smiling. "My darling, of all the women in the world, you and Jane are the important two in my life. How could I ever object to your consideration for the lady who has been mother to us both? I am delighted that you are happy, though a little concerned that I may be absent for the birth. Come, let us get this Ball over so that we can enjoy being together in the privacy of our own bed."

Jennifer giggled. "You make me blush, sir, with your comments. But let us hurry as you say, and spend as much time together as your career allows."

The departure from Portsmouth had been without ceremony. The frigate was one of many coming and going from the busy harbor, and thus *HMS Diane* slipped off to sea without creating a ripple.

The course almost due east from Selsey Bill, followed the south coast of Britain. The lights of the various towns along the coast came and went with the miles as the ship progressed on her way to the Boulogne area.

In the Captain's cabin of the *Diane* there was a discussion about ways and means being held between Martin and David Thacker, Lieutenant, currently on leave from the Prince of Wales own. The green tunic and overalls displayed his membership of the Rifle Brigade. In the corner of the cabin behind his chair was his weapon of choice, the Baker rifle, never far removed from his person.

He was on board by invitation. Having recovered from the injuries he had received in Spain he was now awaiting transport to rejoin his Regiment, apparently somewhere in Portugal.

Having become acquainted with Martin, he had agreed to lend his support and expertise to the task of abducting Albert Portet.

Both of the others were accustomed to the French mainland. Both had accompanied Martin in his excursions ashore in the Mediterranean.

They were expected to connect with the frigate *HMS Phoebe* which had brought raiding parties for the attack on the boats assembled in Boulogne for the invasion of England. She was accompanied by a gunboat, *HMS Whitby* and two captured brigs stuffed with combustibles to be used as fire-ships.

The snatch party would be carried ashore in one of the fire ships and collected just along the coast by their own longboat.

Martin, David, Paul and Pierre would have in addition the services of Carter and Raul Chavet, who had arranged transport and some diversions if needed. But most important, he had located the whereabouts of Albert Portet, the target of their undertaking.

At ten that evening they embarked on the fire-ship *Cayenne*, a schooner of 75feet length. The three man crew agreed to drop them off at the *'plage'* beside the entrance of the harbor. The longboat would collect them from the beach.

The ship was left under the command of Lieutenant Reed. It was all they could do to make sure that the purpose of their mission was disguised by the burning of the boats.

The noise had started by the time they reached the beach. The plage stretched north in the dim light cast by the town lights. In the harbor there was the crack of muskets and spurts of flame as the arsonists set to burning boats. The *Cayenne* sailed in on her last voyage, the flames appearing from her hold as she made for the two moored frigates lying beside the entry to the inner harbor.

Martin saw the strike as she hit the first of the moored ships, and rush of fire climbing the tarred rigging of the Frenchman, as the hungry flame jumped to the second ship in the rising wind.

The snatch party followed the lead of Raul Chavet as he strode briskly and openly to the street above the beach where the carriage waited. All managed to squeeze in and the carriage set off on the road to Wimereux. Just a half mile from the port the carriage stopped. Chavet got down and approached two people leaning, smoking pipes beside the sea wall.

After a short conversation he rejoined the party. To Martin, he said in French "Portet is still in his house." The carriage moved on and turned inland, stopping beside a copse of trees where there was room to conceal it in a glade screening it from the road.

"Now we wait." Chavet smiled grimly. "Check your weapons, my friends. This man is ugly and vicious. But he is not a coward and we could have a fight on our hands."

A man appeared as they dismounted from the carriage. "He comes." Was all the man said.

In the distance the noise from the raiding parties at the port could be heard and the occasional spurt of flame and smoke highlighted the area. The sound of hooves on the track could now be heard clearly. Martin placed his small group along the line of the road, then he stepped out to stand in the path of the riders.

Two men, Portet and another they did not recognize.

The two pistols Martin pointed was enough to stop the riders and the two men were quickly subdued and bundled into the carriage. Martin and Chavet rode the two horses as they made their way back to Boulogne. The town was in turmoil, the harbor full of burning boats, while musket fire was concentrating on a group a men hiding behind a stack of boxes and protecting them from the attack that was taking place. There seemed to be a lack of firing from the defence position. So Martin turned to Chavet, "Let us take the pressure off the survivors, shall we?" To David Thacker he said, "Look after our friends here. Carter stay with the lieutenant. If Portet tries to get away kill him!"

"Let's go," he said to the others and they ran quietly down the pontoon until they could see the attacking force. At least a dozen soldiers were loading and shooting at the defenders, keeping them from the boat bobbing alongside the quay across the open ground between them. Martin's men lined up and opened fire on the soldiers. Three fell immediately. Others were reloading and at least one raMr.od clattered against the stones of the quay, having been left in the barrel when the shot was fired.

Two more men fell as there was no cover from the fire of Martin's men. The others ran back down the quay away from their ambushers. "This way!" Martin called. "Let's join our friends in the boat."

Chapter seventeen

Escape

The party ran round to the waiting boat, joining the men from the raid and collecting the Lieutenant and the prisoners on the way. As they started to row their way out of the harbor a sail crossed the water at the other end of the quay. Their boat was under the command of a bosun from *HMS Phoebe*, Martin saw the sail arriving and grabbed the man whispering in his ear. "That's trouble," he said. The bosun said quietly, "Now what? We were supposed to be away long since, but I had three men adrift. Then we got pinned down by the soldiers. By the way, thank you, sir. I thought we were looking at French Prison till you came along. Who are you, sir? I don't recognize you."

"Commander Forest from *HMS Diane.* I'm here on different mission. Look, bosun we are going to have to play a game here, I think. Pull over to the quayside and tie up. Chavet, can you and Paul perhaps find some of the Tricolors that the soldiers wear?"

Chavet grinned and patted his knife. He beckoned Paul to accompany him and the pair disappeared along to the mainland end of the quay, where many of the wounded soldiers were still wailing and crying for assistance.

It would have been difficult for Martin to interpret all the sounds he heard around the moored boat but, certainly, the sounds from the soldiers diminished considerably by the time Chavet and Paul reappeared carrying several of the small flags, used by many as headscarves.

Martin gave several of the men in the boat the flags, some with the bloodstains an additional reminder of their origin.

"Now," he said. "All the men with flags take and load muskets. Oarsmen take you places. The rest of you are prisoners. Only French speakers may talk, and only then to ask me for orders. Understood?"

There was a chorus of replies from the men. The prisoners were gagged so that they could not give warning. Martin waited until the ship at the end of the quay had tied up alongside, then he quietly called, "Give way all. Silence now while we run the gauntlet."

He looked at the eighteen men and the two prisoners, then at the moored sloop at the end of the quay.

"Bosun, how many men do you think on that craft?"

"Should be thirty, sir. But I reckon they're less than that. She don't seem to be well handled, so I'd guess her crew are mainly ashore."

"That's what I thought. Let us ask them to give a hand with the prisoners. When we get to her I'll board and speak to their captain."

The bosun smiled grimly. "Take care, sir. I think it might work. I'll warn the lads."

He passed down the boat whispering to the men as he went. Then from the bows he turned and Martin made out his nod, indicating they were ready.

"Hello, *St Cloud,*" he called in French. A head appeared at the stern of the sloop.

"Permit me to come aboard to speak with your captain. I am Lieutenant Roget of the Gendarmerie.

The boarding port was opened and steps dropped into place to allow him to climb aboard the small ship. The longboat tied up alongside in the shadow of the hull of the sloop.

Martin pulled himself clumsily aboard, playing the landlubber for the benefit of the seaman waiting to assist him.

"Thank you, young man," Martin panted. "Busy night, heh?" His eyes were everywhere checking the three men on deck. "You seem a little short-handed. Everything happening at once, I suppose?"

His escort grunted and led him to the cabin at the break of the deck aft.

The captain was a scruffy sailor armed with a sword which had been acquired from some unfortunate officer. He looked about forty, with a dirty face and a permanent sneer on his face.

"What do you want, M'siu Policeman?"

Martin stared into the man's eyes. "That is Lieutenant, Sir, to you! Get on your feet when an officer addresses you."

The man looked uncertain but rose to his feet anyway. "I am captain of this ship." He said aggressively.

"In what navy? I suggest you stop playing games, and take me to your captain I wish to speak to him."

The man said "He is wounded and I am in command."

"Where is he?"

The man turned to the seaman who had escorted Martin. Take this man to the ..." Martin slammed his hand on the deck and drew his pistol. Pointing it, he said, "You take me to him now!"

The man looked at him, his eyes now scared. "This way." Martin shepherded both men in front of him into another cabin where a man lay with a bloody shoulder in the berth. No one was attending him and he was muttering in delirium.

Martin waved the two men out of the cabin. "Why is no one attending your captain?"

Before the man could answer, Martin called Chavet. "Bring the doctor and the prisoners."

The pistol stopped the comment that the so-called captain would have made. Martin had backhanded the man and the heavy metal had smashed into the sneering mouth, knocking the man to the deck.

The seaman grinned. He muttered, "Served the bastard right."

Then the bosun, Chavet and the others were swarming aboard, followed finally by Lieutenant Thacker with the prisoners.

The seaman's eyes widened at the sight of Portet, tied and gagged. Then he grinned. Portet was not a popular man in Boulogne.

There were four men aboard including the captain. The remainder of the scratch crew had been sent ashore to perform duties in dowsing fires and fighting off the attackers.

"Prisoners into the brig, and get someone to look at the captain in his cabin, he is wounded and needs attention." Martin turned to the seaman still standing beside him. "Where did he get the sword?"

"He stole it from the captain. Then he used it on him."

"Why?"

The man shrugged. "He is a thief. He was going to steal the ship. We were waiting for his men to report and take the ship out of port."

"Why did you stay?" Martin was curious.

"I needed to leave. My politics are of another kind." The man was determined and proud.

"You tell me, a member of the Gendarmerie, that you are a Royalist? "

The man laughed. "You are, I would guess, British, though you're French is excellent. You command men who have no French. I guessed that you are of the raiders and are escaping. You have that swine, Portet, as a prisoner. I am right, am I not?"

Martin smiled, "I'll see you in England. Meanwhile go with the other prisoners."

"My name is Paul Cartier, and the signal to the tower is X flag." He left and walked over to the other prisoners to be herded below.

"Get under way, bosun." Martin ordered. To Carter he said, "Check the guns. We may need them before we get away."

"Aye, sir." Carter called two of the other men to help and began examining the six gun battery on the port side.

The sails rose on their yards and the ship started to slide away from the quay. A group of men appeared at the far end.

Martin called to Carter "I believe those men are pirates bent on stealing this ship. I cannot abide pirates. See if a gun will bear before we get out of range?"

"A pleasure, sir," called Carter cheerily, and set to work on the after gun, calling for powder to go with the bag of pistol bullets that comprised grapeshot for specific use against grouped enemy. He had the gun loaded and ready by the time the ship was beginning to heel to the pressure of the sails.

"Fire when you are ready, Carter." Martin said quietly. "Let us leave with a bang."

The sound of the gun was loud and the effect satisfying scattering the pirate group into a bloody shambles. With the X flag at the masthead, the fort at the entry to the harbor, now re-occupied, ignored the *St Cloud* and she cleared the port without further trouble.

Contact was made with *HMS Phoebe* and *HMS Diane* just after dawn. *HMS Whitby,* the gunboat, had been lost getting too close to the defences the previous night. A stray shot had entered the barrel of the mortar mounted on the foredeck. The ignited shell within exploded prematurely. The explosion had been spectacular and had occurred when the raiders had been at Wimereux.

Martin resumed his command much to the relief of Lieutenant Reed.

The prize, *St Cloud* ,under command of a Midshipman was sailed to Portsmouth, in company with the *Diane* and reports sent immediately to Mr. Smith of the capture of Portet and the other prisoners. All were sent to London with Martin to be interrogated by Mr. Smith's team of specialists.

The opportunity to join Jennifer in the London house was welcome and, although they had little time, at least they were able to enjoy each other for the three days Martin was in London.

As his twenty-third birthday passed and the birth of his child approached, Martin found his chances of being at home in time to meet his child diminishing. After several excursions in the channel, Mr. Smith released the frigate and *HMS Diane* was sent to join Nelson's fleet in the Mediterranean. Later in the year the news of the birth of his daughter came by despatch with the other mail for the fleet. The time dragged through to the turn of the year and the long months of the Mediterranean winter. For the frigates there was the occasional opportunity to get away and perform detached duty, albeit short term, as the Admiral was always conscious of the need of frigates to keep his fleet in touch.

The resumption of the war had led to the renewal of the blockade of Toulon where Villeneuve and twelve French ships of the line were bottled up.

The problem of maintaining the blockade was made worse by the need to obtain fresh water and the supply and refitting of the ships where needed. This entailed a journey for the ships to the Isles of Magdalena, 200 miles away, and on occasion there were only frigates present to keep watch while the ships of the line were refitting and storing.

Since this situation was worsened by the renewed declaration of war by the Spanish Government, there was the problem of looking in two directions for the blockading ships. Bonaparte was meanwhile expanding his army in the expectation of invading England. His collection of boats for the invasion had been renewed and protected. All he now required was a diversion and the weather to produce the right conditions.

From his place on the quarterdeck of the *Diane* Martin was becoming aware that important events were occurring.

The greatest problem he was facing personally was the grinding boredom of the blockading duty. The time dragged, passing slowly for the remainder on the year, with a series of competitions between ships where weather permitted, boat races and shooting matches between the officer and fencing matches and tuition for the less experienced.

The plans for the invasion depended on the French fleets at Brest, Rochefort, and Toulon breaking out to rendezvous in the West Indies. There, in the expectation that Nelson would follow Villeneuve, they would give him the slip and return East across the Atlantic to sweep the English Channel clear and escort the French invasion fleet across, to land in England.

Bonaparte's plans went rather astray. The Brest fleet did not manage to get away from the blockade by Admiral Cornwallis. Admiral Missiessy managed to escape from Rochefort with some of his ships, during a storm. However when he reached the West Indies, and made a successful sweep through the islands raiding and gathering considerable loot, he failed to make the rendezvous with Villeneuve. The Rochefort ships returned home without encountering any British ships on the way.

Villeneuve sailed while Nelson was at Magdalena in January 1805. His ships suffered damage in a storm and they returned to Toulon. Nelson, having been warned by one of his frigates, sent Martin to search the eastern end of the Mediterranean under the mistaken impression that Villeneuve intended sailing in that direction. Unsuccessful in his search, Martin rejoined the Admiral in Palma, Majorca, where the fleet was storing and learned the Villeneuve had returned to Toulon.

In March, when Villeneuve broke out once more, Nelson was misled again, starting the search of the eastern end of the Mediterranean, until he was advised that the

French had been spotted 300 miles to the west. He gave chase. Villeneuve was joined by six Spanish ships of the line as he sailed to the west. He eluded Nelson in the West Indies and was soon on his way back to Europe.

Nelson sent a frigate to England with the warning and set off in pursuit. The ships at Rochefort were sent to Ferrol to enhance the fleet there.

Martin was sent to contact the Ferrol fleet under Sir Robert Calder, to confirm the rendezvous off Finisterre.

In foggy conditions *HMS Diane* witnessed the arrival of Villeneuve's fleet and signalled the flagship accordingly. The ships of the line engaged with the French, hampered by the foggy conditions. The British captured two of the French ships, but darkness prevented the capture of any others. For Martin, ordered to stand clear, it was frustrating, The French frigates were well clear of the big ships of the line, and initially unable to give battle to the British contingent. After a long night the fog was still present, and the frustrated Martin had to watch the French fleet make off to Vigo.

Admiral Carter joined Cornwallis off Brest.

Without the French fleet to escort and protect them, the huge assembly of boats at Boulogne was a waste of time, and the assembled troops were redistributed to the borders with Russia and Austria. The Emperor, was furious at what he saw as cowardice on the part of Villeneuve. He sent an Admiral to take over from Villeneuve, who decided that his only salvation would be to defeat the British fleet. So he set sail with his assembled fleet to give battle. He did not have the additional ships from Rochefort as the messages he sent by frigates were intercepted . The *Didon* was caught by *HMS Phoenix*, and a second, *Mistral,* encountered *Diane* which was searching for the French at the time.

For Martin the sight of the lone French frigate was a relief. After endless-seeming days of nothing but the odd fishing boat to break the monotony, the cry from the masthead lookout brought him on deck with a will.

"Where away?" Reed called.

"Downwind, fine on the starboard bow, sir. Topsails of a Frenchie."

Martin looked around the deck. The men were obviously as frustrated as he was. It looked as if the entire crew was on deck after hearing the lookout report.

"Let's trim our sails and prepare for action, Mr. Carter." The Sailing Master smiled grimly. "Aye, aye, sir. Bosun, let loose the reefs. Helmsmen, let her run full and bye."

The extra pull of the sails, and the easing of the wheel allowed the ship to slip through the sea a little easier.

"Permission to exercise the guns, sir?" The midshipman stood hopefully before his captain, eager to keep his men busy and maintain the excitement brought by the sighting of the French ship.

"As you wish, Mr. Brooks. Both watches, if you please." Martin smiled at the sight of the eager 13 year old giving his orders to bosun Roberts, 15 years older and a world wiser by then. The rumble of the guns being run-out and returned was present for the next two hours, before comparative peace was restored. By mid-day the ship was hull up, the Tricolor a splash of color at her mizzen.

"Well, Mr. Carter. What do you make of her?"

"She is the *Mistral,* sir. 32 guns, fifteen years old, I would guess,and she is trailing weed from the looks of her."

"Every little helps, Mr. Carter. Mr. Reed! Clear for action!"

"All hands clear for action, marksmen to the tops." The immediate rush of feet in response signalled the readiness of the crew for the action to come. The surgeon Henry Corder reluctantly went below to organize his space, in preparation for the inevitable surgery that would be required during the forthcoming action.

Martin looked around the decks at the men poised in place by the guns, the hammocks packed around the bulwarks, to provide cover and inhibit boarders.

"Starboard guns, run out and load, Mr. Reed."

"Aye, sir." Reed repeated the order to his gunners. The rumble of the guns on the deck recalled the earlier practice, though this was no practice. This was in earnest, and the guns were loaded with powder and shot.

"Up helm. Fire as you bear, Mr. Reed."

The voice of Lieutenant Reed could be heard calling off the forward guns on the main deck of the frigate. "Number one gun, fire; number two gun, fire." The crash of the impact of the 12lb shot was heard over the sound of the sea and wind. The *Diane* crossed the bow of the *Mistral,* her guns sending shot after shot crashing through the bulwarks and flying down the main deck causing havoc on the way. Guns were dismounted and blood sprayed everywhere where men were hurt by the flying shot and splinters of the shattered bulwarks and broken gun carriages every time the cannonballs impacted on the wood.

Thus far the French ship had not replied. Martin had the feeling that the captain was not a skilled veteran as the 18pound carronades blasted out from the end of the row. Martin prepared to wear round, taking fire to bring the port guns into action.

The starboard guns were reloaded and lashed in place, and the gun crews raced across to assist the port gunners prepare for action.

The starboard guns still working on the *Mistral,* opened fire as the *Diane* turned to port to bring her other broadside to bear. Several of the missiles impacted on the stern quarter, spraying splinters and scything down the helmsman. Carter caught the wheel to stop the ship falling off to starboard, and the two stern chasers fired into the Frenchman as she rolled with the recoil from her own broadside, the two 9 pound shots catching her low, punching holes near her waterline.

Then the *Diane* came round on a parallel course and the full portside broadside came to bear. The ship disappeared in the cloud of smoke from the guns. When the wind ripped the curtain aside it revealed a sorry sight. The mainmast of the *Mistral* toppled and fell the rigging, dragging the foremast which had snapped at the lower Fore-top. The mizzen stood alone, though swaying dangerously. The sails had smothered the men serving the guns, and several of the starboard guns were leaning at drunken angles where they had been dismounted by the fire from the British frigate. As Martin watched the colors were hauled down. With her way lost, the shattered ship wallowed in the ocean, a forlorn relic of the once proud craft.

"Away the longboat, Mr. Reed. If you please. Take a party and secure the prize. Bosun, man the jolly boat. Take a party of marines to see there is no trouble. We will secure alongside directly."

The repair parties were at work already, the carpenter checking the damage done by the French cannon. There were several men wounded by the flying splinters and the helmsman was wrapped in canvas awaiting burial.

Checking with the Doctor, Martin found him packing a bag to cross to the French ship to help attend the wounded.

"The wounded here are attended. Two will die, I believe. The others will survive with rest and time. My man can attend them while I am away." The Doctor had a wry grin, "I suspect I'll have a little more to do on the Frenchie."

"Take care, Doctor. We are coming alongside as we speak so I can assure you of an easy step to board her. As long as the weather holds, we should be able to keep close company while repairs are carried out. I will join you on board presently." He nodded and returned to the deck in time to bring his ship alongside the prize, and take her under control.

On the deck of *Mistral,* Lieutenant Reed had men clearing the raffle of ropes and canvas from the dead and wounded beneath. The French crew were working alongside their captors, separating the broken spars, salvaging what they might from the damaged rigging. The bosun had the jollyboat still in the water rowing round the ship checking for visible damage at the waterline. The *Diane* was alongside the port side of the *Mistral,* the ship's undamaged side and the French carpenter was just completing the repair, plugging the two holes made by *Diane's* stern-chase guns.

On board the Frenchman, Martin collected the papers still lying in the captain's cabin. The man himself was dead, shot by what the Doctor thought was a pistol bullet.

"Are you sure of this?" Martin asked.

Doctor Corder looked serious. "The wound is too small to be a musket, and typically was not caused by shrapnel. I'll dig the bullet out when I have finished here." He turned, his apron bloody from operating, and called the next forward from the queue of patients requiring attention.

Chapter eighteen

Trafalgar Bay

Martin returned to the deck and crossed to his own ship, The papers of the prize laid out on the desk in his cabin revealed that the ship was bound for Rochefort with orders for Admiral Missiessy to set sail and join Villeneuve to give battle to the British fleet. The orders had not been delivered and, obviously, now they would never be.

Martin returned to the deck and there he encountered Lieutenant Reed, who was on his way to report. "Sir, the hull is now sound. The bosun is rigging the mainmast to stand as the foremast. I have men bracing the mizzen and we should be able to get under way by morning."

"The papers from the ship indicate that we have intercepted instructions for the French fleet at Rochefort to come out to support Villeneuve against our fleet under Nelson. I need to get this information to the fleet as fast as possible. Can you manage with the prisoners and the men you have already. Lieutenant Ash can take over your duties, while you carry on with a middy. I would be happier with you in command here.

"The bosun's mate will stay with you. I'll take Mr. Carter and the bosun with me. I will sail straight away. I suggest you set course for Falmouth with the prize and we will rejoin whenever we may."

Martin shook Reed by the hand. When the arrangements for crew were made, the Doctor returned, "I have left the French doctor still at work, but now in a position to cope."

"Thank you, doctor. Where we are going it is possible you will be seriously employed. Mr. Ash, cast off and set all sail."

The young junior lieutenant dashed forward shouting orders. The bosun smiled at the activity and chivvied the men into action.

Aware that the fleet intended to cruise offshore in expectation of finding the combined French and Spanish fleets, Martin set course to intercept the fleet, more in hope than expectation, was prepared to make a guess when he reached the area. In fact he encountered the frigate, *HMS Phoebe,* 36 guns, now under the command of Captain Capel. In company the two frigates joined the main battle fleet on the 20th October, the day before they encountered the French-led force in Trafalgar Bay.

Martin called upon the Admiral to make his report and present the captured despatches.

"Well, young Forest-Bowers, you are looking well. I am happy to see you making progress in your career. Tell me of your lovely wife. She is well, I trust."

"She is well indeed, I am informed, as is our child who will be named Jane, after our adoptive mother." Martin was concerned. The Admiral was not looking at all well. His face was gaunt and his thin frame even thinner to Martin's eye. His manner was as ebullient as ever and he soon had Martin smiling at his comments about some of his officers.

Nelson became serious when he took time to read the translation of the messages Martin brought. "The instructions you have intercepted are a duplicate of those intercepted by *HMS Phoenix*. She met with the French frigate, *Didon*, and, having overcome her, found a similar instruction to this despatch. It seems that Admiral Villeneuve sent his instructions twice. Since we have no news that Rochefort has responded, we will pray he did not send a third copy. I will expect you and Captain Capel to dine with me this evening. I have the feeling that we will be rather busy tomorrow. It will be good to have some younger people at the table for a change."

Captain Hardy, who was at the Admiral's side at this time, looked at his Admiral in astonishment. The fact that Nelson regularly entertained the midshipmen on the *Victory* was well known throughout the fleet.

As Martin was rowed back to his ship he was thinking of the forthcoming battle. He was well aware that the frigates present would not play a big part in the battle, but there were frigates on both sides and the possibility of battles between them was ever present.

Fascinated, Martin studied the opposing fleets through his telescope. The enemy were in a scattered line and the British line was split into two sections. The flags fluttered as the signals passed between the divisions of ships. Though there were obviously plans made for the attack and defence it was difficult to make sense of them from this position. There was a group of five frigates with the French fleet, all carrying the colors of France. He looked around at the group of frigates accompanied by the schooner, *Pickle,* and the cutter, *Endeavour.*

The actions of the frigates would be controlled by the senior Captain, Captain Blackwood of the *Euralyus,* 38guns.

He thought about the entertainment last night. Nelson had been on good form. The others at table had joined in to make the evening an enjoyable one. Certainly, it would have been difficult for a stranger to believe that the men around the table were facing the prospect of desperate action and a serious prospect of death the following day.

"Signal from the leader, sir. Form line on my port beam and make sail to engage the enemy. "

"Make sail, Mr. Carter. Helmsman, steer small and come up to the leader on the port side."

Martin looked sideways at the helmsman. Noting it was a steady hand at the wheel, he left it to him to carry out the maneuver without unnecessary fuss.

"Shall I order the guns to clear for action, sir?" The voice of Lieutenant Ash asked, rather hesitantly.

Martin considered the question, not wishing to point out that they were still an hour's sailing from the enemy frigates who were themselves preparing to meet the British ships.

"It would probably be best to wait until the leader decides to clear for action. Don't you think, Mr. Ash?"

Ash blushed slightly. "Of course, sir." He retired to the rail and resumed pacing as he had seen his seniors do.

The events of the day were imprinted on Martin's memory to such an extent that Jennifer was fascinated when he described the events as he has seen them. The action he was involved in against the French frigates was all but forgotten in the shadow of the main events of the day. For the onlooker the battle of Trafalgar was noise and smoke in huge clouds. To the educated, the masts that stood above the clouds, showed success and failure as they moved with the progress of the day. They stood and fell, sails flew and burned, and men died in their hundreds, friend and foe alike. They died from the highest to the lowest, and history was made. A Nation mourned their hero who, in winning, lost his life.

The action against the frigates was going to be a victory in itself. Martin had no doubts, nor it seemed, had any of the other captains in the English squadron. The French had not been told, but their desperate action reflected their agreement of this. There was little time to study the main battle as their own battle was bitterly fought.

The surviving frigates, and their prizes, kept company with *HMS Victory* as she made her way to Gibraltar to refit, prior to her return to England with the body of the Admiral. With the repair to *HMS Victory* and the repairs needed to the *HMS Diane,* the frigate was retained to escort Nelson's flagship, carrying his body on the journey back to England, where they both arrived on the 5th December 1805. The Admiral's body was carried to Greenwich on the 6th and, after three days lying in the Painted hall in Greenwich, to St Paul's for the burial service.

The affection for the Admiral was reflected in the number of people who turned out to witness the funeral procession. There were tickets issued for the service in St Pauls as so many wished to attend.

A period of national mourning ensued.

For Martin and the Bowers family the sense of personal loss was only relieved by the joy brought to the family by the presence of Jane, the child who was a delight and lifted the air of gloom whenever she appeared. For two golden weeks Martin was able to get to know his daughter during the period of the funeral and thereafter, while their lordships at the Admiralty deliberated over his future. The actions over the past months had resulted in rewards and punishments as the developments at sea had played out. In Martin's case there were victories and the assessments of both Admiral Nelson, and the mysterious Mr. Smith to be taken into account.

Rear-Admiral Bowers had little to say in the proceedings in this case, content as he was to let Martin's own actions speak for themselves.

The Gazette recorded the latest details and the announcement of his promotion to Post Rank came as no surprise to his adoptive father, mother or wife. It was only to Martin that it came as a surprise.

The announcement was the occasion for a celebration, however subdued in the circumstances.

The orders, when they finally arrived were odd. The Admiral was surprised, but not excessively, since he saw the hand of Mr. Smith' in their drafting. It did, however, mean that Martin would be sailing East with Admiral Troubridge, who was scheduled to take command of the East India station.

Chapter nineteen

Disturbing events

1806...The Indian Ocean

The blue waters of the Indian Ocean flowed past the stark white of the wake outlining the black timbers of the 36 gun frigate, *HMS Diane*. Three merchant ships were bobbing along to leeward, a schooner and two tubby brigs, all loaded, Martin understood with rare silks and tea. He had encountered the three ships by chance. They had been part of a convoy, scattered by a violent storm to the south. Driven by the violent winds northwards, they had suffered losses of men and much of their food had spoiled.

HMS Diane was patrolling in the Indian Ocean searching for a French privateer that had been causing havoc with the trading ships from the African coast, and from South Africa.

When she encountered the three merchantmen, they were storm-battered, and far north of their course. Deciding that they were in sore need of provisions and repair, their closest port was Bombay, and Martin decided to escort them there having shared with them, water and provisions from his own stores. The weather had moderated and the little convoy was little trouble, Martin had time to relax and allow his thoughts to drift over the events of the past months.

The time had gone faster than he expected. The voyage out with the East Indiamen under the command of Sir Thomas Troubridge in *Blenheim* 74 guns had been lively, after an encounter with the enemy ships under the command of Admiral Linois. The French Admiral had broken off the action when he had suffered serious damage from the heavy guns of Blenheim.

The journey round the Cape had been adventurous due to the heavy swell, a feature of the Southern African coast. On the long reach across to the Indian coast there were attempts, on two occasions by French privateers to cut out the East Indiamen. On both occasions it had been possible to cut them off and in one case inflict heavy damage on the audacious ship. Only the sudden fall of darkness had saved her.

Now the Admiral had departed. Martin smiled when he recalled the meeting between Admirals Sir Thomas Troubridge and Sir Edward Pellew, one with orders from London to relinquish command, the other having received no orders to hand over. The two men finally resolved the problem with Troubridge departing for Cape Town. The only sorry thing about the whole matter was the condition of the *Blenheim* when she left Madras. After grounding on the way into the harbor she had been in a bad condition when she left for the Cape. The pumps were working full time as she sat at anchor before leaving. The Admiral insisted that they would be able to make the voyage.

"Sail in sight." The masthead reported. "Astern. Hull down. She looks like a cutter, sir."

"Mr. Reed, let us ease the sheets, and signal the convoy to close up once more." He looked up at the masthead. "Keep an eye on the cutter. Let me know if she signals us."

"Aye, sir," the lookout called and resumed his sweep of the horizon.

The cutter *Daisy* caught them up before night and the news was not good. *HM S Harrier* under the command of Lieutenant Troubridge, the Admiral's son, had arrived in Cape Town having lost touch while sailing in company with *HMS Blenheim* and the frigate *HMS Java* in a gale to the east of Madagascar. He feared both ships had been lost with all hands.

The cutter had brought mail for the admiral in Bombay as well as for *HMS Diane* and for Martin in particular.

With nightfall the wind dropped, so Lieutenant James Hammond, in command of the cutter, *Daisy,* dined with Martin and the Captains of two of the ships from the convoy. He was full of the gossip of the garrison at Cape Colony. The recent acquisition of the Colony from the Dutch had been accomplished with little problem. During the past few months the community had settled down to the new rule and a social scene had evolved. The lieutenant had obviously entered into the social whirl with a will and was enjoying life to the full.

The returning breeze early the following day allowed the cutter to leave the convoy behind and race off with its despatches for the Admiral, Sir Edward Pellew.

With the weather continuing fine, the convoy made good time and the ships were delivered to Bombay within the week.

For Martin there was time to read his mail at leisure, to discover with great joy that Jennifer was again with child.

Though once more he would be absent for the birth and miss getting acquainted with his new family member until his return to England.

He answered her letter immediately with a special letter expressing his delight and love.

He then began on the invitations to various social functions forming so much of the life of these outlying outposts of the Empire.

Bombay was fascinating. Hot undoubtedly, though it had been hot in the West Indies, there was the eternal scent of spice and corruption. That had been the way the Doctor had described it. Dr Corder had a way with words Martin had found. His shrewd insight had been a source of entertainment, accompanied by his talent at cards, in passing the time on the long ocean voyage they had recently undertaken.

He edited the letter he had started on the last voyage across the Indian Ocean. His last letter home had been despatched from Cape Colony. Now he was finding it difficult to concentrate. There had just occurred a bustle of movement and the sound of an impatient voice from the hallway outside the drawing room where he was trying to deal with his correspondence.

He rose to his feet and strode over to the door to find out what was happening. Before he reached it, the door burst open and a flurry of skirts announced the arrival of a youthful body surmounted by an annoyed, but pretty face, hurtling into the room and into his arms.

They, by instinct closed around the figure, allowing him to assess that the young lady was formed properly and proportionally.

He released the lady from his embrace and bowed briefly. "Excuse me, miss? I do not believe we have been introduced."

A young man arrived at that point, breathless and flustered. "Isabella, I told you. Lieutenant Troubridge has gone." He stopped, seeing Martin standing looking interestedly at the young lady. He bowed to Martin. "Your pardon for this intrusion, sir. I am Michael Lambert, sir, writer to the Governor. This is Lady Isabella Staunton. She has been up country for the past six months and was acquainted with the former occupant of this house, Lieutenant Troubridge. Your ship in the harbor convinced her that he was still here, though I did inform her that he had already left Bombay."

Martin bowed gravely to the couple. "Captain Martin Forrest-Bowers of the frigate *Diane* at your service. Since we are now introduced, can I offer you tea?" He clapped his hands. In response the servant who had followed the two young people into the house departed to arrange matters. The lady curtseyed daintily, and in a small voice said, "You are most kind, sir, especially after our rude and clumsy intrusion into your privacy."

Leading them through to the shaded veranda overlooking the Harbor and the sea beyond, he saw them seated and volunteered, "I am actually pleased to have an excuse to stop what I was doing. I confess it was duty which had me seated at this time, and I felt guilty that I felt it my duty to answer invitations at this time, having been absent for so long. Such correspondence should stem from a willing pen, don't you agree?"

Isabella smiled, "I confess, sir. It had not occurred to me. But on reflection I have to agree with you." Her blue eyes twinkled as she looked up to meet his eye.

Michael Lambert spoke up, asking how long the *Diane* expected to be in Bombay.

"That will be up to the Admiral, though I do know I am due to return to England in six months' time with the East Indian convoy," Martin said, beckoning the servant to present the tea to his guests.

"Will you be attending the Governor's Ball on Saturday?" Isabella asked.

"I have just opened an invitation," Martin said, "I confess I had not yet decided.

"Oh, you must come. Everybody will be there. It will give you the opportunity to become acquainted with local society."

"I presume you will be attending?"

"Certainly, my father and mother are hosting matters as the Governor's lady is still away up country at present. Her health is poor and the summer heat does her no good."

"I believe I will attend in that case, though my dancing skills have been neglected of late."

Michael broke in at that point. He had been feeling increasingly left out in the conversation and was jealous of the attitude of both Isabella and the Captain who seemed to have established an instant rapport. He had been unable to establish any in the past two years he had known Isabella. "Sir, what will your duties be here in the Company area?"

"I have no idea as yet. I answer to my Admiral, Sir Edward Pellew, who resides in Madras. With the departure of Wellesley and the death of Lord Cornwallis, it will be for Sir George Barlow at least until the arrival of Lord Minto to decide where I may best serve."

"Captain Forrest-Bowers, can I offer to show you a little of our city here while there is yet time?" The innocent suggestion from Isabella was a surprise. Such a suggestion in England based on such a short acquaintance would have raised eyebrows.

Martin decided that things were apparently a little more relaxed here, and he answered, "If that is acceptable, I would be flattered to be escorted by such a charming guide."

For the rest of the visit he found it difficult to ignore the effect the presence of Isabella was having on him. He was also aware on the attitude of the young man with her, who was obviously enamoured of the young woman who showed not the slightest interest in him apart from friendship.

He actually was sorry for the young man who seemed in all other aspects a likeable and, he would have thought, attractive person to others of the opposite sex, just not to Isabella.

He mentally shrugged. *That's life* he thought and put the matter from his mind.

The following day, having established that there was no matter too pressing for his attention, he accompanied Lady Isabella Staunton in her carriage on a tour of Bombay.

The busy dusty city was hot and smelly, the mass of humanity pressing and pushing, all involved in their own affairs.

The turning away from that part of the city was a relief and Martin was delighted when the carriage drew up in the shady gardens of an abandoned estate overlooking the sea. There was a breeze off the water, refreshing after the humidity of the morning. They stepped down from the carriage and Isabella led him on a tour through the abandoned garden. It had obviously belonged to a family of wealth. There was a pool shaded by trees, and the flowers still created splashes of color wherever he looked. As they wandered through the paths and secret glades among the trees, Isabella caught his hand and led his to her favorite places. "I have known this garden for some years." she said. "We swam in the pool, and played hide and seek."

"I can see it would have been a joy to young people. It is a joy to me now, especially in contrast to the city."

"Come now, we can eat." She pulled him back to the poolside where a cloth had been laid with an assortment of food and a net with bottles of wine hung into the water of the pool to keep cool. Of the driver there was no sign.

"Where is the driver?" He asked.

"He will be sleeping until I call." She said and sat daintily on the rug beside the repast. "Come, sit beside me." She patted the rug and he joined her. As they talked and ate in an easy atmosphere he relaxed, laying back after a while and enjoying just being there, smelling the perfume of the lady beside him. He was not surprised when she joined him laying down, her soft breath brushing his cheek.

Such was society in Bombay at the time, though discretion was necessary, there was a tolerance implicit in the attitudes of the members of society, owing to the weather and the demands of duty and the lack of a changing population. No official notice was taken of the blossoming relationship between Captain Forrest-Bowers and Lady Isabella Staunton. Such was their own discretion, little scandal would have been there for people to gossip about anyway.

With the needs of the ship to attend to and the succession of tasks assigned, the affair which started quietly ended quietly, without bitterness and in fact with a friendship that endured.

The arrival of the 74 gun *HMS Samphire* with its full complement of officers during an absence of *HMS Diane* chasing pirates further north along the coast provided the social scene with sufficient new faces to satisfy even the most voracious appetite. The legendary willingness of the Navy in these circumstances ensured that, upon his return to Bombay, Martin was relieved of the burden on his conscience. Lady Isabella was now rumoured to be engaged to Lord Patrick Simion, heir to an Earldom with estates on the Norfolk coast.

Impatient to get back into what he regarded as real action, Martin attended the Governor's residence with his report on the cruise. He was aware that the convoy was assembling in the harbor for the voyage to England, and was eager to ensure he was accompanying them.

In fact there was no need to worry. There was no question in the event. The arrival of two armed ships of the Bombay Marine, to assume the duties the frigate had undertaken, was anticipated and his orders were already struck.

The convoy would be under the overall command of Commodore Sir Henry Balcombe KB, in command of the 64 gun *HMS Boscombe* arriving from China with ships joining the convoy. She had with her two brig/sloops, each of twenty guns, *HMS Dido* and *HMS Pluto,* plus the 32 gun frigate, *HMS Banner,* a local-built ship also returned from the China station.

Gazing down over the harbor at the assembling convoy, Martin was astonished at the number of ships involved and the appearance of many. All were armed, many heavily, since all were merchantmen. Some of the bigger ships were painted in the fashion of naval vessels with the buff and black hulls painted to highlight the gun decks in naval pattern, with dummy ports scattered the length of the decks indistinguishable at this distance from the real.

At the time of sailing there were forty ships in the convoy, Though the departure was managed fairly smoothly, the fleet was scattered over an area of several miles by the time all ships were clear of the harbor.

HMS Diane, Martin, her captain, second in command of the convoy. Was the last to clear the land, her orders currently to chase up the stragglers so that some sort of pattern might be established before nightfall.

It took three days to get the convoy. in a state to satisfy the Commodore. By that time the temper of all the escort captains was severely frayed. The cutter, *Daisy,* arrived in Bombay as the convoy was leaving and, having delivered its despatches, had the misfortune to be seized upon its departure for the Cape, to sail with the convoy. She was thereafter condemned to act as courier between ships for the duration of the Indian Ocean voyage. Called to the flagship during the third day, Martin was conveyed to the *Boscombe* by the *Daisy*. He commiserated with young Lieutenant Hammond, her captain. "When the Commodore speaks the world stands still" He mis-quoted with a wry smile.

"And lesser beings tremble." Hammond completed the mis-quote with a tired shrug. "May I offer a glass of wine, sir. It will take at least 30 minutes to beat up to the flag."

Martin accepted gratefully. It had been a tiring time ever since leaving harbor. He sometimes thought that the merchantmen were deliberately obstructive, the way they handled their precious craft. He sighed. Perhaps obstructive was the wrong word to use though reflected the actions for the rearmost ships in the fleet.

Hammond brought the wine himself and stood with Martin watching the parade of ships as they clawed their way past toward the head of the convoy.

"I heard before I left Bombay that the beautiful Lady Isabella is to marry!" he said.

Martin looked at him sharply, suspicious that the young man was provoking him.

He relaxed the comment was just that, a comment. "I was aware there was something in the wind. I am acquainted with Lady Isabella. She was kind enough to show me about Bombay when I first arrived, why, it must be a year since?"

"Certainly a year, I recall you entertained me when we met sailing north on your way to Bombay. That was after Admiral Troubridge was lost."

"Was anything else discovered about that loss?"

"Nothing reported, though odd pieces of wreckage found could have been from either *Blenheim* or *Java.* There was no real way of telling."

The *Daisy* came abreast of the flagship and ropes, thrown from the deck of the flag, were used to secure the cutter against fenders alongside. Her sails were dropped hastily and Martin hauled himself up and through the sally-port onto the deck of the flagship. He straightened his coat and hat then raised his hat in salute to the Quarterdeck and the flag.

The Commodore's aide greeted him and escorted him to the great cabin where Commodore Balcombe was seated at his desk.

To his surprise the Commodore rose to his feet and came round the desk to greet him. "Captain Forrest-Bowers, is it not. I know your father well. We were middies together at the beginning of the American revolt in Boston. We shared the gunroom of the old *Indomitable,* 60 guns. It leaked like a sieve. The sound of the pumps will haunt me to the day I die. But we had some good times aboard her regardless. Perhaps he mentioned me?"

Martin was rather taken aback by the effusiveness of the Commodore and decided in the circumstances to humour him.

"Why, sir, I do recall your name from my boyhood, though I regret it was some time ago now."

"Of course, my boy, of course. It was long ago, he seemed to drop into a dream for a few moments. Then he woke up, walked briskly round his desk and seated himself. He picked up a paper from the desk and passed it to Martin. It was in the usual form and detailed his duties as escort to Cape Colony. It went on to say that new orders would be given at that point.

"You do understand that this convoy splits at the 15 degree north line of latitude. The China division turns south-east to clear the island of Ceylon en route to Canton, under the command of Captain Arnold in *HMS Banner,* We will to meet *HMS Juno* and *HMS Nanking* at the rendezvous. They will form the escort for the China convoy with Captain Arnold. Have I made all clear to you, Captain?"

"Perfectly clear, sir. Though I am a little surprised at the need, sir?"

The Commodore tapped his nose with his finger. "Strange things happen at sea, Captain. It is as well to be prepared."

"Quite so!" Martin agreed. "Better safe than sorry!"

The Commodore rose to his feet once more and staggered slightly, catching his balance against the desk. "Well, good bye, Captain Forrest-Bowers. Good luck and I have been happy to meet you." He turned and gazed out of the stern windows humming quietly to himself.

Martin turned and left the great cabin. On deck the First Lieutenant, acting as aide to the Commodore, approached Martin. "How is he, sir?"

Martin looked at him sharply, "Why do you ask?" He said..

The Lieutenant stood firm "Sir, I am worried. He has been acting a little oddly lately. I fear he may be ill."

"Has the doctor seen him?"

"The doctor has difficulty in seeing anything, Sir. His sojourn in China has resulted in a dependence on the opium to the extent that he is seldom conscious."

Martin looked intently at the Lieutenant. "At the rendezvous I will board and I will bring the doctor from my ship. I will decide at that point if any action is needed, and will act accordingly. Until that time you will, of course, support the Commodore to the best of your abilities!"

"I will, sir. He is a popular man with all of us, sir."

"I gathered that from the manner and attitude of the crew. Carry on now and we will meet again at the rendezvous, in two days' time."

Martin climbed down into the cutter. They cast off, leaving the flagship and dropping back to the *Diane.*

Back on board he discussed matters with the doctor. James Corder had become close friends with Martin as far as their relative positions allowed. His thoughts, reference the Commodore, were interesting. "Without seeing the man I cannot be sure. But I have the feeling that he may well be suffering from lead poisoning, or even arsenic. Both are possible and unfortunately both substances are fairly freely available.

"There is another possibility and that is worrying. Does the Commodore have any plants in his cabin?"

Martin thought about it. "Yes. He has a plant in one corner, a tall sort of cactus thing as I recall. It was still in bloom when I was there."

The doctor looked up sharply. "A cactus, you say, that has just recently bloomed?"

"Yes, it was taller than me I recall, and above the blossom was a scatter of white flecks on the bulkhead and the deckhead. It seemed as if it had exploded rather than just opened."

"Oh, my god. We must get to the flagship immediately. The Commodore is in serious danger."

"Danger?" Martin was taken aback. "What do you mean? Is this something to do with the plant?"

"Sir, we must go to him immediately."

The two men were making their way on deck as they were talking, the doctor almost running.

On deck the *Daisy* was visible still close enough to recall.

"Mr. Reed, signal the cutter to return forthwith." Martin snapped.

"What will you need, Doctor?"

"Only my bag and the services of a pair of strong arms. Once we get rid of the plant the cabin must be thoroughly scrubbed clean."

"What about the Commodore?"

"I fear it may be too late to stop the process. If the plant is what I think it is, the effects are progressive. From what you say the Commodore must have been there when the blossom bloomed. The plant is not a cactus as such. It is apparently a form of Agave, very rare. I was only aware of it when an Indian doctor showed me some spores from the plant which had been given to him by a monk from a monastery in the Himalayas. He said the spores were useful for certain conditions, but were actually toxic for people who suffered from respiratory conditions. If inhaled, they caused internal blockage because the young spores start growing within the lungs.

"My feeling is that either the plant was given in ignorance, or more seriously and possible, deliberately to dispose of someone without the threat of prosecution."

The *Daisy* came alongside. Without even waiting to tie up the two men were swung out on ropes from the main yard and lowered into the tossing boat below.

Chapter twenty

An odd situation

Lieutenant Hammond ordered all sail set and caused the cutter to fly through the water tossing spray to the sky in her efforts. The urgency of the orders made it clear that speed was of the essence.

They came up to the flagship and took the leap on the top of a wave to the ladder up the side of the ship. Both managed safely and boarded the flagship. The doctor immediately asked for the Commodore. Martin arrived and was in time to prevent the lieutenant from having the doctor either clapped in irons or thrown overboard. Martin's appearance smoothed things over and the doctor was taken to the Commodore's cabin. Sir Henry was seated on the deck his back to the desk, looking bemused.

"Assist him to the quarterdeck quickly, and get rid of that bloody cactus overboard." Martin nodded to the First Lieutenant. "Tell the men to wear cloths round their nose and mouth when they take the plant and ditch it out of the stern windows. Then have the cabin scrubbed by masked men to begin with. Get rid of all those flecks of white around the plant blossom. Once that's organized, report back to me on the quarterdeck!"

The First Lieutenant dashed off to perform his tasks. Later on the quarterdeck he reported to Martin.

"Tell me. Where did the plant from the Commodore's cabin come from?"

"As I recall he was presented with it by the Chinese Lord who was the Emperor's agent in Canton. A particular gift, I was told."

"Did the Commodore have any problems in port there?" Martin persisted.

"There was just a small matter of the concubine." He sounded doubtful.

"Explain this small matter?"

"Well the truth is, Sir Henry is Presbyterian, and inclined to rescue people, especially young women who are used and abused. There was no impropriety. Sir Henry is simply charitable. This is not always understood. It seems his misunderstanding extended even further than the normal distrust of the Chinese for the 'round eyes'."

"By giving the plant as a gift, he in effect murdered Sir Henry."

The Lieutenant watched as Doctor Corder worked over the Commodore. The sick man was half sitting on a pad on the quarterdeck. Suddenly he broke into a paroxysm of sneezing into a cloth held by the doctor.

When he stopped he fell back looking exhausted. The doctor sat Sir Henry upright. "We will repeat the treatment when he is more recovered."

Martin looked at him. "Can you give any idea?"

"In this the cure may kill him. I have to try and get the spores from within his lungs, this is the only way I can think of to do that here."

The Commodore beckoned to Martin. "Captain," he gasped, he raised his finger to the Lieutenant, to join them.

"Captain, you will find my orders in my desk. I am not able to exercise proper judgement at present, and I hear it is possible that I may be dying anyway. You," he motioned the First Lieutenant, "And you, doctor. Witness my words at this time. Bring paper and pen and if I am able, I will write my decision."

Twice more the sneezing was induced before the doctor allowed Sir Henry to rest. Sir Henry then dictated orders for Martin to assume control of the convoy.

Deciding to retain his place in *HMS Diane,* he changed the position of the ship to better control things when the convoy split. Otherwise things remained as before. At the 15th parallel they encountered the two China squadron sloops, plus two additional ships for the Cape convoy and an additional ship bound for China.

There was a certain amount of backing and filling, and two near collisions before the ships managed to divide into their appointed convoys. Finally with an exchange of signals the ships parted on their divergent courses.

Martin watched the China convoy as it disappeared over the horizon. Turning to Lieutenant Reed. "Well, Mr. Reed. We have a command once more and responsibility for twenty-four ships."

"Including a ship of the line, sir." Reed commented.

"As you say, including a ship of the line!" Martin said almost to himself. He had no real illusions, being of the opinion that Cape Colony would provide a new senior officer for the convoy, and probably a new commander for *HMS Boscombe,* the Commodore's ship.

The next few days saw little activity apart from the ongoing frustration of dealing with stubborn shipmasters, who seemed incapable of understanding the simplest of instructions on station-keeping and the need to keep riding lights at night to prevent colliding with the next in line.

The attack occurred as they drew close to Reunion Island. Having navigated their way through the Seychelles Island chain, the convoy had managed to scatter itself fairly effectively, creating considerable effort for the escorts who finally managed to gather them into some sort of order after wasting a day chasing stragglers halfway to Madagascar.

The *Daisy* really earned its captain the gratitude of the escort commander. As Martin commented to Reed, the lively little cutter was a godsend in these circumstances. The convoy was together when the French frigate appeared on the far side of the convoy. As luck would have it, the *Hampshire* was on that side of the small fleet, one of the largest and most heavily armed East-Indiamen. Her captain was an ex-naval captain who ran his ship on the same lines as his former command, with a broadside of 12 x 12 pounder guns, he ensured would be loaded and ready to run out, as soon as they were needed.

At the appearance of the frigate the fiery captain had no hesitation in turning his ship to keep the weather gauge. His flag signals would have been approved by the Admiral. They announced the presence of the frigate hull down from the direction of Reunion.

Later signals verified it was French. The raiding party manifested itself with the appearance of other sails. Smaller craft that were revealed to be an armed dhow, and an armed schooner. All three ships exhibited the Tricolor.

Martin deployed *HMS Dido,* to the support of the *Hampshire. HMS Pluto* was ordered to remain with the convoy accompanied by *HMS Daisy.*

All of the Indiamen were armed to a varying extent. The majority had an array of 9lb guns for defence against pirates. The attacking ships appeared to be French Navy. They, therefore, were a greater threat than the average pirate.

Throughout the convoy the sound of the preparations to repel the attack could be heard. The rumble of guns being run out and loaded seemed to reverberate from ship to ship. For Martin there was the threat of the frigate to be countered. *HMS Boscombe* was stationed on the weather side of the convoy. Her First Lieutenant was looking forward to action at long last. The Commodore was hanging on and the Doctor seriously hoped that he might survive providing they could reach the Cape Colony. Doctor Corder had confided to Martin that he was convinced that the sneezing therapy had given Sir Henry a real chance to recover.

Martin placed his ship to intercept the French frigate, sending Lieutenant Asquith, a young firebrand who was commanding *HMS Dido* to intercept the dhow. The schooner was reaching across the course of the convoy and would be under the guns of the *Boscombe,* which was showing no signs of her true purpose, appearing as she did to be just one of the martially-painted Indiamen. Albeit rather larger than some, she did not stand out without her flags, as several of the merchantmen were of her size.

There was a mass of ships. Surely it would be possible to collect one or two. Captain Michel Charlet strode back and forth across the quarterdeck of his ship, *Mirabelle.* His mind working on ways and means of cutting out as many of the ship with their rich cargos of trade goods for the English market.

There were no doubts in his mind that his 38 guns should overcome the smaller number of guns of the British frigate. *HMS Diane* was rated as a 32 gun frigate. In fact the number related to the former broadside guns. On the quarterdeck there were four more guns mounted on slides. These were carronades, firing 18lb balls at shorter range than the other guns in the broadside. It also did not take into account the pairs of chase guns, mounted at bow and stern. These guns fired a 9lb ball at considerable range.

All in all the weight of a broadside combined was nearly the same, though that figure diminished with distance owing to the short range of the carronades.

For the French Captain any doubts were swiftly dismissed. It was true to say that after the defeat at Trafalgar the French navy carried very little weight in the eyes of Napoleon. A spectacular success here would allow the Captain to return to France in triumph, a matter and an aim close to Captain Charlet's heart.

As Martin approached the French ship he allowed the ship to fall off the wind a little, just give his opponent the idea that the ship was a little sloppily handled.

Charlet did notice and was a trace more casual in his approach himself. Martin was watching hopefully and he saw the minute opening for his idea. "Let her fall off a little more, cox'n. Let's see if he notices. Carefully now." The bow of the French ship came up a little more in response. "Right, cox'n. Bring her up sharply. Port guns run out, Mr. Reed."

The *Diane* spun to starboard, the weight of the guns assisting her to come round. As the guns came into line with the enemy ship, Reed did not hesitate. "Port guns, on the uproll, fire!"

The smashing effect of the broadside was immediately apparent. The manoeuvre had placed the two ships broadside to broadside, at that moment. The effect of the shot had been to shatter sections of the bulwarks of the French ship and dismount four of her guns. The carronades had done dreadful damage, shattering the after deckhouse and sweeping the men on the quarter deck into a bloody mess against the starboard rail. The shattered wheel, and the pulpit on which it was mounted, were scattered in pieces among the other debris on the scarred planking. The *Mirabelle* lost her Captain and her steering at the same time, to a lucky shot from the forward port carronade, while the solid ball of its companion gun hit and shattered the deck where it joined the hull of the quarterdeck. The grapeshot loaded in the other gun, slightly lighter in weight, distributed its cargo of pistol balls like a leaden flail smashing all before it.

The ship's head fell off the wind. Without a hand at the wheel and under near full sail, it careered round before the wind, sailing in a series of jerking movements while the crew attempted to gain control of the rudder from the second position below decks.

For Martin, there was no suggestion of allowing the French ship respite. The *Diane* took up the pursuit immediately, bringing her second broadside to bear despite suffering several hits from the enemy, fire by the gun captains who saw the chance and took it. The broadside when it came was enough to cause the Tricolor to be hauled down.

On the other side of the convoy the unfortunate French schooner had encountered *Boscombe*. She was sinking by the head after suffering a 24lbs cannonball on the stem-head which had sprung the bow planking, creating a massive inflow of water.

Dido had missed its chance at the dhow. The *Hampshire* had used its preparedness to close the gap on the French ship, so had been able to fire its broadside at the dhow. A lucky shot had taken the mast of the craft, stopping it in its tracks and allowing *Hampshire* to come alongside and hold it under its guns, until *Dido* came to take over the prize.

Mirabelle, with a jury steering rig, was joined to the convoy with a prize crew. The schooner was beyond salvage, and continued its journey to the sea bed. The dhow was taken into tow while a jury mast was rigged, and the convoy resumed its progress toward the Cape of Good Hope.

There were no more attacks on the convoy for the rest of the trip to Cape Colony, though the weather deteriorated. The storm that developed caused the ships to lose two days being re-gathered into some sort of order. Repairs were needed to several damaged ships so that they could proceed to the facilities in the settlement. Certainly Martin was delighted to see the coast of South Africa loom over the horizon. As they sailed into Table Bay he at last realized just how tired he was. Having the responsibility for the convoy for most of the voyage was harder work than he had anticipated.

The arrival at Table Bay did not mean that he would be able to relax, with reports to write and the matter of the health of the Commodore to explain. As one of the most senior officers in the port at the time, the responsibility for locating a new captain for the *Boscombe* was largely his. A week passed before order was finally restored to the section of the convoy which would continue the voyage to England.

The command of the *Boscombe* was given to Lieutenant Acting Commander William Armitage of the sloop *Pluto*. The Commodore being too ill to travel, Martin was given command of the reconfigured convoy now reduced to 18 ships. The sloop, *HMS Pluto,* would sail commanded by her First Lieutenant, a Cornishman named Penrose.

The prizes were retained at the Cape. The eventual repairs would provide work for the shipyard. The dhow would be sold. The frigate, once repaired, would be taken on the colony strength. There were many stranded seamen and officers who could be appointed to sail her.

The Commodore was unhappy at having to remain in Capetown. Unfortunately there was no option. He was not fit to make the voyage by that time. Doctor Corder was pleased with his progress, but would only predict eventual recovery. The sad part was that though he might recover, the attack had, in his opinion, shortened the Commodore's life by several years.

Chapter twenty-one

Homeward bound

Summer 1807

The Privateer lay at anchor in lee of Santa Cruz de Tenerife in the Canary Islands. Her Captain, Patric Vanier, was tall dark and almost handsome, his eyes perhaps a little too close together for true good looks. In nature also his friendly smile had proved winning with the ladies, but it could very swiftly turn to a snarl as many had found out to their sorrow.

He was pacing up and down his cabin at the moment, still mulling over the news brought by a Portuguese ship bound for the Azores.

A British convoy from India was a prize worth having, especially since the French Indiamen were becoming fewer and fewer. There was of course a ship of the line and a frigate in the escort. He disregarded the two sloops and cutter as meaningless in real terms. He knew he had a fast ship in the captured French corvette which was armed with 24x12 lbs guns. All were well served by former naval gunners. His only problem was creating a distraction so that he could cut out as many of the merchantmen as possible. His lieutenant came into the cabin with a message from the island Governor.

He tore it open reading the Spanish words easily. His lieutenant looked at him anxiously.

His Captain's smile revealed that the problem might be solved. "Two French ships are approaching, so let us dress accordingly, and I will recruit them to keep the escort busy while we raid the convoy.

The *Hirondelle* now looked every inch her former self, a clean and tidy French naval craft carrying a senior French officer.

As the two frigates *Agen*, 40 guns and *Collette* 36 guns, came to anchor, their guns were still firing the salute to the French Admiral's Flag, at the masthead of the corvette at anchor. The Spanish garrison on the island were in no real position to interfere with the French ships. In fact the ships were allowed to re-store and water for the remaining part of their voyage from the West Indies. Provided they paid for their stores, the Spanish could not really afford to turn them away. The guns of the ships were sufficient incentive, so their Admiral informed them, as they all sat enjoying a glass of the local wine.

Their orders had been to make their way back to join the French fleet at Brest. They had encountered bad weather in the mid-Atlantic, and as a result had been delayed.

"Gentlemen, this is a fortunate meeting. As we speak the British East India convoy is making its way up the African coast toward us. I would have been happy to have attempted to snap up the odd ship. Now you are here there is a real chance of a coup."

He paused and waved for his servant to refill the glasses.

The Captain of the *Collette* posed the question. "Sir, with respect, our orders are to sail with all despatch to the French mainland."

"Captain Artois, if I may point out, I actually outrank the Admiral who issued those orders. Though in the circumstances, I hardly think there will be any argument raised when you turn up with a couple British East Indiamen loaded with exotic cargo."

The second Captain nodded thoughtfully. "Really, Maurice. What difference will two days make? And with such a prize?"

Captain Artois sat back, still not really happy about the idea, but in the face of the enthusiasm of the Admiral and his colleague, there was little he say or do about it, perhaps only get the job done and out of the way as soon as possible.

On the way back to their ships he asked his colleague what he knew of Admiral Vanier.

"I knew of him when he was a Captain. But it is true, that was perhaps seven years ago. As you know there are many of the Admirals we knew, who are now either dead or out of their positions. They all had to be replaced!"

Artois nodded in understanding unwilling to give up his doubts. But in the face of his companion's logic there was nothing he could say.

The two men, once back on board became the complete professionals their jobs demanded. Both individually made their preparations for the diversionary attack they had been ordered to make on the British convoy.

It had been twelve days since the convoy had taken on fresh water and fresh fruit at Bathhurst in Gambia. The merchantmen had acquired a fairly disciplined manner of operation, and the escort had sharpened its procedure. The *Hampshire* had volunteered to take a positive part in any convoy defence. The fire-eating former naval officer had offered to carry four guns from the fort at Capetown, promising that they would be delivered to the dockyard on his arrival in England. The 12pounder guns were included in the *Hampshire's* broadside. They had been too small for the battery at Capetown, which mounted 18 and 24 pounder guns. He had also offered passage to stranded seamen, of whom many were actually members of the Royal Navy, landed through injury. They included some veterans of the action during which the Cape Colony had been taken from the Dutch.

It was with some amusement that Martin observed the regular drills undertaken by the gun crews on the Indiaman, as he passed on his patrols about the convoy. It was true that all the East-Indiamen were better armed than average merchantmen. The prevalence of pirates and enemy ships was a hazard they all met. The value of the cargoes they carried compensated them for the weight of the guns and the bulk of the ordinance. Crews were recruited from ex-naval personnel for that reason, and the wages of the crew made it worth their while to serve. The additional benefit was they were exempt from being pressed back into the navy.

All the escorts were instructed to keep to strategic areas around the convoy, maintaining protection where ships were vulnerable. The *Hampshire* was placed in what appeared to be a loophole in the defensive screen. *HMS Boscombe* sailed in the centre of the convoy, which was now capable of sailing, during the day at least, in pretty close order.

Not surprisingly it was the cutter, *Daisy,* which reported the strange sail on the horizon.

The convoy had succumbed to the pressure of the weather and reached out to bypass the Canary Isles to seaward and pass through the gap between the Azores and Madeira. With the option to run into Madeira if weather or enemy action made it necessary.

The appearance of strange sail from the direction of the Canaries could mean friend or foe, so Martin decided to take no chances. Since he had the time he warned the *Hampshire,* and ordered the *HMS Boscombe* to take the lead of the convoy, to allow her to drop down on any attacker on either side of the lines of ships. They were now sailing in three lines of six with *Hampshire* in the Port line, ship number three. The heaviest armed of the other ships were all in the outer lines of the convoy.

At the warning from the cutter both sloops had taken positions on the threatened side of the convoy. Martin had placed *Diane* at the rear where she could go either side of the lines of ships. The convoy was adjusting to the increased sail which always caused a certain amount of backing and filling to accommodate the differences in sailing qualities and sail handling. By the time all was settled down, the strangers were identified and nearly hull-up.

There were three ships in all, frigates, all with the Tricolor flying. Two were making direct for the convoy, the other was sailing to pass ahead of the nodding lines of ships.

Signalling the *Boscombe* to the starboard side of the convoy Martin took the portside and sailed to meet the single frigate which was aiming to round the head of the convoy.

He heard the crash of the big guns from the *Boscombe's* broadside as he reached the head of the portside line of ships. The enemy frigate was now clear in view and through his telescope Martin could distinguish the crowded decks, a surprising number of men for a normal frigate's crew.

"Mr. Reed! Run out and load both broadsides if you please." He paused, "Every second gun grapeshot, and aimed to sweep her decks. I do believe he intends to board and cut out some of our flock."

"As you wish, sir. We could give him a real bellyache. Shall it be ball for the carronades?"

"That will do nicely!" Martin strolled along the deck calling the odd word to the men manning the guns, hands clasped together behind his back as if he was on a Sunday walk in the park.

Most of the men were by now accustomed to his coolness in the face of action and they appreciated the way his air of assurance made them feel more relaxed.

Martin was by no means assured. It took a lot of effort to maintain the casual appearance, but he knew it reassured the men, and in the same way it had an effect on him. Once the action started there was no time to feel worried or frightened. There were too many things to keep track of to allow distractions in interfere.

He looked across toward the other side of the convoy. Clouds of smoke obscured the action between the ships, but he could still see the topmasts of the *Boscombe* and the crash of the guns was re-assuring.

His own problem was approaching rapidly. Now with the wind almost directly behind him, he could make out the guns run out on both sides of the ship and guessed that the enemy had not decided which way he would attack.

"Portside broadside I believe, Mr. Reed. I am going to cross his bow and send him down to *Hampshire* for a second helping. I will hopefully come about and run through the convoy between the lines. Signal *Hampshire* to prepare a welcome."

Reed grinned as he acknowledged his Captain's order. From the sound of it he had things well in hand. "Steady, lads," Reed called. "Portside first, boys. We'll cross his bows and fire as we bear. To the Middy in command of the starboard broadside, he said, "You'll get your chance as we thread the needle!"

Confused, the middy nodded in agreement, puzzled. What did threading the needle mean?

"On my order, quarter wheel to starboard, helmsman."

At Martin's voice the helmsman tensed ready. "Quarter helm to starboard, at your order. Aye, aye, sir!"

Martin waited. He could now see the men at the guns of the French ship. Odd, there was only one man in uniform on the quarterdeck, an Admiral? Normally, there would be several formally dressed officers present, especially with an Admiral aboard.

Intrigued but not distracted, he waited until the moment was right.

His call to the helmsman was immediately answered and the ship heeled to starboard. As the head came round, the port-side guns fired in turn. The balls smashing into the starboard side of the enemy ship, the grape shot sheeting across her decks.

She staggered and jinked as the *Diane's* guns did their work. Only when they were almost clear did the Frenchman's guns start to answer, and by that time they had little effect.

Martin felt the strike of the enemy shot as he called. "Stand-bye to come about! Helm a'lee!"

HMS Diane swung hard to starboard and she completed the turn catching the wind from astern now pointing down between the two lines of her convoy. The bosun could be heard calling his men to haul the yards and trim the sails on the new course. Mr. Reed called out "Starboard broadside run out, and stand by."

The port guns were loaded by this time the crew poised waiting for the next bout.

Doctor Corder appeared at Martin's side. In a quiet voice he said, "If you would step below a moment, sir. I'll attend to this." His finger touched Martin's side where a sliver of wood had opened the cloth of his uniform and cut a line across his ribs from front to back.

Made suddenly aware that he must have been injured when the enemy shot had hit. "I did not feel it," Martin said.

"It will not take long." Doctor Corder said. "It's not serious", and he set to work. "I have two dead and six injured from the fire from the Frenchman. The wounded will survive. Your cabin has a hole in it, but apart from that no great damage." He finished strapping Martin's ribs and helped him with his coat. "That will do for now. I'll attend to it properly afterwards."

Martin returned to the deck carrying the cup of coffee his servant had produced while the Doctor was attending him.

On deck Martin turned to the man. "How did you get hot coffee? The galley fire is out."

"The watter flask wuz knocked down when that cannonball came into your cabin. It fell onto t'doctor's lantern. I went to pick it up like, and I burns me fingers on t'metal. So I thort if t'outside hot, watter inside will be too. An it wuz. So I thort, coffee for t'Capn's what I thort."

Martin looked at him in amazement. "Thank you, Harris. It's much appreciated." And he turned to survey the situation in time to see the cloud of smoke as Hampshire opened fire on the Frenchman. The enemy frigate staggered at the unexpected impact of the fourteen 12 pound cannonballs, all aimed from the deck of the *Hampshire* firing down into the Frenchman, creating havoc on her decks smashing holes and scattering splinters everywhere.

Patric Vanier was appalled. The unexpected attack from the Indiaman had created terrible damage to his beautiful ship and the British frigate was overtaking fast down between the ships in the convoy. Enough was enough! He decided this was a mistake. He called for the helmsman to steer west, away from the convoy and abandoned the other two frigates to their fate.

The *Hirondelle* flew off to starboard away from the convoy as *Diane* passed between the merchant ships in pursuit. The crew of the *Hampshire* were cheering as *HMS Diane* chased the enemy westward away from the convoy.

Martin made sure that the raider was well clear before he gave up the chase, unwilling to leave the convoy short of protection.

HMS Boscombe signalled success, and when they got back to the convoy, Martin saw the two sloops escorting one of the French frigates, which had lost a mast. The other had received one broadside from *Boscombe* and decided, that was enough and turned away and made all speed toward the African coast, leaving its compatriot to fight alone.

The French captain was brought aboard Martin's ship and presented to Martin for questioning. Maurice Artois was very upset about the abandonment by his fellow captains. He described their characters in graphic detail to Martin.

Eventually, Martin stopped the tirade. Speaking perfect French, he pointed out that he did get the message but, by the way, who was the French Admiral in the other ship.

"He called himself Admiral Patric Vanier."

"His is a new name to me. Where is he based?"

"I do not know! I only know he was once in the navy. I suspect that he is no longer and the Admiral's coat was merely window dressing to get our co-operation for this raid."

"I see, and your companion?"

"We sailed from the West Indies, Martinique, in company with orders to report to the fleet at Brest. I met him in Fort de France for the first time. Otherwise I know little of him."

"Well, Captain, you will be with us for some time it seems. If you give me your word that you will not try to escape, you may enjoy a certain freedom while we are at sea?"

Artois nodded, "You have my word, captain, and my thanks."

Chapter twenty-two

The Channel

1807-8

Gibraltar was busy. Ships were there from the Mediterranean fleet being refitted. Others were en-route to supply the British troops being landed in Portugal to oppose Napoleon's troops invading from Spain. The Spanish people were requesting the help of the allies

Napoleon had placed his brother on the Spanish throne, officially declaring Spain a part of his own domain.

Russia had signed a treaty with France and ordered Sweden and Denmark to deny their ports to British trade, and to place their fleets at the disposal of the French.

For Martin there was little time to relax. After visiting the Port Admiral he was soon back on board his ship, with the addition of a second frigate to replace *HMS Boscombe.* She had been given another captain. Commander Armitage, who had been in temporary command, was given the *Collette ,*renamed *HMS Brimpton,* currently refitting in the dockyard and due to sail to Falmouth for orders when the refit was complete.

HMS Pursuit, the frigate replacing *HMS Boscombe,* led the convoy out into the Strait to assemble and set off up the coast of Spain.

At the rear of the convoy, now with the addition of three more ships, Martin and *HMS Diane* herded the merchantmen into some sort of order. The sloops and *HMS Daisy*, Lieutenant Hammond's cutter, dashed about the clutter of ships pushing them into some sort of order for the remainder of the voyage to Falmouth, where the convoy would start to split up and make for their ports of destination.

The weather was foul for the first part of the voyage and the escorts were continuously preoccupied with keeping the ships together. The problem was that because of actions of French privateers in the channel it had been necessary to maintain the convoy system.

The weather caused damage to several of the ships so it was of nearly three weeks before the convoy started to split up at Falmouth. There they dropped three ships, a further seven departed at Southampton, three more at Portsmouth. The remainder were destined for the London river. *HMS Pluto* and *Diane* were ordered to bring them upriver, with instructions for Martin to report to the Admiralty on his arrival.

Baby Jane Forrest-Bowers was delighted to be raised up high by her father. When he tossed her into the air and caught her, her delighted chuckles were a joy for Martin to hear. Jennifer stopped him before he got too ambitious. "Please, no more, my love. She will be sick. As it is she will not go to sleep with all the excitement."

Reluctantly, Martin handed his daughter over to Jennifer, who in turn passed her to the nurse for her preparation for bed.

When the nurse had left the room Martin held Jennifer close. Kissing her tenderly he said, "I have missed you both, and this house. I fear I have been too long away from you, I doubt I will be allowed to stay for long. While this war drags on so does our time apart."

"Father and Jane are feeling it too, I fear." Jennifer said. He has to work such long hours at the Admiralty these days. For Jane it is difficult, for there are men in London who would take advantage of her, given the chance."

Martin looked at his wife sharply. "What men? Is the Admiral aware of this?"

"No, of course not. Were he to find out he would be forced to call the men out. I fear the two main offenders are skilled duellists, with sword and pistol. Jane fears for his life. I know one man has threatened to challenge the Admiral if she does not submit to his demands. The man is mad."

Martin stood back. "Who are these men? Who has threatened our father?"

Jennifer looked at Martin cautiously. She had only once seen him look so seriously determined. That was when they first met, and he had stabbed a highwayman through the hand. In a low voice she said. "Sir Paul Rowland and Michael Barrat."

"Is Jane at home here?" He indicated the house next door.

"Yes," Jennifer said. "She is hoping to see you while you are in London."

"Now will be a good time." Martin said. "This is a serious matter that must be cleared up as quickly as possible."

"But Martin….." Jennifer's protest was lost as Martin swept out of the door.

He entered through the private way between the two houses. James, the butler, met him and said, "Her ladyship has a guest."

The way he said it stopped Martin in his tracks. "A guest?" He asked.

James said "Sir Paul Rowland, sir." The way he said it said all Martin needed to hear.

James led him to the drawing room. As Martin put his hand to the door handle he heard a scuffle within.

Throwing open the door, he said softly, "Jane, my dear, I have come to call."

The man who was holding Jane by her upper arms turned to look at him. Spitting the words out he said, "You will have to wait your turn. She is mine first."

Martin stepped forward and took the man by the scruff of the neck, the tight stock constricting the man's breath. Twisting the stock, he peeled the man away from Jane who fell back onto the chair behind her.

Martin let go of the man and punched him in the stomach, followed by a punch in the face that split the man's lips. The man reached for the sword at his side. Martin clouted the man sending him reeling against the settee. "How dare you? You ignorant excuse for a man". He twitched the sword from the scabbard. It looked like a dress sword, but Martin noticed that the blade was serviceable and had wear from use. He bent with the sword and placed his foot on the blade. With a wrench he snapped it off halfway down its length. Throwing the hilt section into the corner, he dragged the fallen man to his feet and slapped him round the face, back and forth several times.

"Are you listening to me?" He said looking the bedraggled man, wig awry, facing him. The blood from his lips smeared his face, mixing with the powder from his wig and cheeks.

"I am giving you warning. If any mention of this is made by anyone, I will seek you out and kill you. If by chance I am not here, my men will drag you through the streets like the cur you are. Now get on your knees and apologixe to the lady you were assaulting. Whatever blackmail you were attempting to use forget it. If there is any hint of interference with this lady, or her husband and family, you will feel the lash, and your death will be painful."

The man crawled over to Lady Jane, on his knees, "I apologize, my lady. I was overcome by your ..." The sound of the round-arm slap from Lady Jane's right hand made Martin wince.

"Get out of my house, you crawling toad. And you may tell that apology for a man Barrat that his welcome here will be as warm as yours has been. My door is closed to you and your ilk."

James, the butler, happily hauled the battered man to his feet and bundled him off through the door. Martin went with him. "For the lady's sake, no more will be said of this. But if I hear of any attempt by you or your friends to act again in this way to anyone at all, I, or my people, will kill you without warning or mercy. Are we clear?"

Sir Paul Rowland nodded, with hatred in his eyes, but fear also.

Martin returned into the house. "Thank you, James. You heard?"

"Yes, sir. You can depend on me."

"I was sure I could." Martin said and returned to the drawing room.

Jane was on her feet and she spun round as Martin entered. He took her in his arms and she melted against him. Holding her and supporting her, he half-walked half-carried her to her sitting room, seating her on the chaise-longue, where she lay back her dress disarranged by the violence of the assault by Sir Paul. Ignoring her dishabille, she took Martin's face in both her hands and kissed him warmly on the lips. He stood up still holding Jane's hand. "Dear Jane, I would have wished for a happier homecoming, though I am delighted to be here and to see you unhurt by that dog."

"Dear Martin, thank you for rescuing me once more. The man was threatening to call Charles out in a duel. He has a deadly reputation as a duellist. You must take good care, my dear. That man is a snake."

"I will, Jane. Please do not worry. I have dealt with men like that before." He stood up and strode over to the fireplace. "Tomorrow I will ensure that Sir Paul and his friend will not bother you or our families again."

Mr. Smith listened to Martin's story with interest. It was the following day. Martin had been instructed to call at the Foreign Office the moment he landed, after delivering the convoy from India.

"Sir Paul Rowland is known to me, as is his friend Michael Barrat. You need not concern yourself with either of them." He rang a bell at his side. When a man entered, he gave him a note scribbled while he waited.

The man left and Mr. Smith then began speaking to him about the next project had in mind. Later that day Martin called upon the Admiral at the Admiralty.

Sir Charles rose to his feet to greet Martin, taking his hand. "My dear boy, I am happy to see you looking well.

The convoy arrived safely, I understand, thanks to you. Their Lordships are pleased with you, though I understand that damned Smith man has your services again."

"Now, father. Mr. Smith is not the ogre you appear to believe him to be. He has served me well in my naval career and has only asked that I work for our country in a slightly different way."

Sir Charles walked to the window, touched at Martin's calling him father, though he was only Martin's adoptive father. "Will we see something of you this time?"

"I understand that you will, sir. I am ordered to remain some weeks here in London. My ship will be sailing under my first Lieutenant, escorting a convoy to the Baltic. You will see a lot of me if you are available yourself. I understand you have been spending, as Lady Jane puts it, far too much time here. Certainly she feels a little neglected? And your granddaughter was heard to say, 'who'? The day you passed through the room on one occasion."

The Admiral looked up sharply at this comment and for as moment Martin thought he had gone too far. Then the smile spread across the tired face and Sir Charles said, "I do not believe you, sir, since it was I who explained to your daughter who you were. However you may report to her ladyship that I will be home to join my family at dinner this evening. Ah, I fear I am forgetting myself. You will need to send a message to the ladies to that effect. We have an appointment elsewhere today. You are to accompany me."

He sat smiling quietly for a moment then said, "You need not start writing. for your information we will be joined by the ladies for luncheon before we attend the reception. However, I do have some work to clear up here, so it might be a good time to take a stroll. It will give you the opportunity to purchase a present for your own wife who, it seems, has a birthday that only precedes the birthday of your daughter by two weeks."

Martin looked baffled for a moment. "Oh, my!" He looked appalled. "How could I have forgotten?" He rose to his feet and saluted. "With your permission sir."

"Don't forget to return here to accompany me to our rendezvous and the reception."

"I will not forget, sir," and Martin made a hasty exit to get the present for Jennifer.

The reception was well attended and, when Martin and Jennifer arrived with Jane and the Admiral, proceedings were already underway. Having been presented to the Prince of Wales, the party retired into the background, finding a certain peace and quiet on the terrace of the house where several groups were taking the air. The aide-de-camp found them and called them to attend on the Prince. With no warning the small party were ushered into a side room off the crowded reception room. There was an exclusive group of people, mainly service officers and their partners present. The Admiral was called forward before the Prince who was standing at the head of a strip of carpet, with an aide beside him holding a plush pillow on which lay a decoration. Sir Charles approached the Prince. With some ceremony he was formally presented with the title of Baron, for his services to the country, especially to the Royal Navy during his period at the Admiralty. His promotion to Rear Admiral had already been promulgated in the Gazette due out the next day.

The Prince was graciously introduced to Lady Jane Burrows, with whom he was already acquainted.

It was with some trepidation that Martin discovered he was now addressed as Captain, the Honorable Martin Forrest-Burrows RN. A title he felt uncomfortable wearing though Lord Charles, as he was now known, would have been disappointed if he had not adopted the honorific.

The occasion of the birthday of his wife and the celebration of the elevation of Sir Charles was an opportunity for a party. Jennifer and Lady Jane threw themselves into the preparation with enthusiasm. Lady Jane, with the weight of the blackmail threats lifted from her shoulders, was looking and feeling happier. Jennifer was happy for her and was delighted with the gift from her husband. The emerald necklace was one of the spoils from the Dutch prize in the Caribbean, purchased on his instruction by his prize agent. It had been intended as a 21st birthday present, but in his absence the moment had passed. On this occasion his own forgetfulness, thankfully remedied by the reminder from Sir, no, Lord Charles, made its availability the easy option, rather than rushing around shopping at the last minute.

The occasion was an opportunity to repay hospitality. It did entail the entertainment of several of the officers from the ships of the Admiral and of Martin. Giles was happily back from the far east and had brought with him the bride he had found in Bombay during the extended return voyage from his service in Canton. His ship had been delayed for two months during the monsoon season. The meeting with Lady Isabella Staunton had been dramatic, and the fortuitous. Giles had been travelling the same road, his party had split up when some members decided to accept the hospitality of the Rajah of the small province they had passed two days earlier.

They had made good time with the reduction of their numbers and Giles with his cox'n and servant, were within hearing when the dacoits had challenged the party ahead around the bend. Giles stopped his horse and swung down to approach the bend. He saw the group stopped in the road by six men armed with tulwars, the curved blades glinting in the evening sunlight. Giles looked at his two men. Benson, the cox'n, and Hill, his servant, both had their weapons in hand. Hill carried a blunderbuss loaded normally with scraps of metal and pistol balls. Benson carried a cutlass in one hand and a short club in the other. Both nodded. Giles grinned and quietly drew his sword. With pistol in one hand and sword in the other he stepped round the corner and shouted at the dacoits. Then he fired his pistol and dashed at the remaining bandits. One man dropped, shot through by the pistol, though Giles had hardly aimed it, expecting only to startle the bandits. The roar of the blunderbuss was followed by the shouts of his two men. Lady Isabella was being dragged away by two of the retreating dacoits.

Giles ran at them slashing the arm of the nearest man causing him to drop his tulwar and grab his arm as it spurted blood. The other man dropped Isabella and attacked Giles, weapon raised to chop at his head. Giles blocked the strike and slipped his blade along that of the bandit. The two swords came together as the hilts clashed. Giles managed to push both swords up above the head of the dacoit. He pushed the man and, as the swords separated, his blade slashed a wound down the face of the man the point nicking the man's neck causing a great spurt of blood from his carotid artery. The man grabbed his neck in a vain effort to stop the bleeding.

The ambush broken, the survivors of the party were gathering themselves together, collecting their scattered property.

Giles assisted Lady Isabella to her feet establishing, that apart from bruises on her arms from the manhandling, all was well.

"Thanks to you, sir, I am unharmed. I fear that my trust in our escort was misplaced. "

Giles commented, gazing at the bodies of the unfortunate guards, "It appears that they did their best at least. I am happy to have been of service, miss." He bowed and turned to the others, making sure that they were all cared for.

Benson and Hill were standing back keeping an eye on the direction taken by the bandits.

Giles had been ahead of his caravan, now the remainder of the small group caught up and started lending a hand with the clearing up.

Isabella joined Giles where he stood, sword now cleaned and sheathed. "What is your name, sir?"

"I am Giles Masters, Captain of the frigate *HMS Watchet* currently refitting in Bombay. He bowed. "At your service."

Isabella curtseyed. "Lady Isabella Staunton, sir, grateful for your intervention, and saving my life."

So the two young people met. Isabella, who had been expected to marry Lord Patrick Simion, was free by virtue of the demise of his lordship from malaria, two days before the formal announcement was made. It seemed that the chastening experience of the brush with death had brought the lady to her senses rather sharply. For Giles there was no hesitation. The damsel in distress was undoubtedly the woman for him and over the next month both found the prospect of life apart impossible. They married during the voyage home, the wedding conducted by the captain of the East Indiaman *Shropshire* during a period of calm in the doldrums off the coast of Africa. Their three day honeymoon was made possible by the persistent lack of wind for the period.

With the return of the wind the couple were forced apart until the convoy's arrival in England.

For Martin, the introduction to Lady Isabella Masters the wife of Giles was a shock. He swiftly recovered when, with great aplomb, Isabella smiled happily at being introduced and announced to all present, "Captain Forrest-Burrows, please tell me you have not forgotten our meeting in Bombay, at the Governor's soiree, I believe."

The swiftly-recovering Martin replied gallantly, "Madam, how could I forget the most beautiful lady attending the gathering? My uncle is to be envied for his good fortune."

Lady Jane watched the proceedings with a speculative eye, but there was a twinkle there when she mentioned her new sister-in-law to Martin later. There was a moment during the evening when Isabella and Martin were alone. "I did not realize that it was you that had married Giles," he said carefully.

"Why should you, Martin. I was also a little shocked to meet you tonight. I presume, in our mutual interest, what happened in Bombay remains in Bombay?"

Martin bowed over her hand, relieved. He kissed it and said, "Oh. Yes. I really think that would be best."

Jennifer took Isabella under her wing in London. The two ladies found common interests and quickly became friends. Giles was happy to renew his acquaintance with

Martin and they saw quite a lot of each other over the next three   weeks.

Chapter twenty-three

Rumours and Ru

Martin was waiting for a call from Mr. Smith. When it finally came he was surprised to find that his task was apparently a simple one. His presence was requested to sail a yacht to Waterford. There was rumour of French attempts to arrange to land troops in Ireland for an alternative invasion of Britain. The failure of the Irish revolt, led by Wolf Tone in 1798, had been the inspiration for rumours of further attempts by the French to use Ireland as a way to invade England.

Smith had information that there were groups forming to raise troops for the Napoleonic army, with the possibility of their use against the English in Ireland.

With the ongoing turmoil in Europe there was still a recognized risk of a group of spies actively stirring up rebellion, with the possible intervention of the French using the French/Irish troops from the French forces. Since late 18th Century the French army had included an Irish Battalion which had been expanded to regiment size by 1808. The ranks had been filled by a variety of non-Irish men, including prisoners, who had been pressed into the British navy and captured by the French. Many hated their former countrymen for the treatment they had received. In general terms the Irish regiment had fought well and earned the approval of their leader, Napoleon. They had been raised in the first instance with the intention of backing the efforts of Wolf Tone, trusting the Irish troops would find support and encourage rebellion against the British Government. The failure of the Wolf Tone hadnever entirely convinced the Government that rebellion would not eventually happen.

Martin eased the tiller on the fifty foot ketch, calling to his servant Peters, below in the cabin. "Where is the food? Do I have to find another cook for this craft?"

Giles answered "Hold your horses, squire. Food doesn't cook itself. The damn stove has a mind of its own." Giles did not sound at all concerned. Peters just grinned and carried on with his preparations ignoring his Captain's complaint.

The voice from the fore-cabin gave them all a twinge of guilt.

The plea to stop discussing food whilst the speaker was dying of sickness could have melted the heart of a Greek statue.

Hill, Giles's servant eased himself out of the cabin door bearing a steaming bowl of stew in one hand and a lump of Soda bread in the other. Giles followed carrying his own bowl. "I am accustomed to throwing slave drivers in the brig," he muttered darkly.

Martin ignored the comment, and holding the tiller with his knee, dipped the bread into the stew and ate with relish.

Giles stretched his arms above his head and breathed deeply. "This is the life!" He said with a big smile. Sailing at this level is fun."

Round a mouthful of bread and stew Martin mumbled agreement.

With a smile Giles added, "Our companion is not too happy." He inclined his head toward the foreword cabin.

Martin smiled. "Saves on the provisions!" He said, "Mind you! Alouette was never a good sailor, and there is more movement in a small craft like this."

"Have you known her long?" Giles asked.

Martin thought a moment. "I first met her in '98, so ten or so years I suppose. We have been friends for that time."

"I confess she is a beautiful woman and I would have found it difficult to keep my distance. Of course, now I am married the matter would never arise." Giles sounded just a tiny bit wistful.

Martin smiled secretly, and got on with his lunch. The ketch, *Heron,* was approaching the Irish coast, the City of Waterford now visible from the deck of the boat. Martin anticipated arrival before dark.

There was considerable unrest reported within the city, owing to the impending imposition of a heavy tax on the glass manufacture for which the city was already famed. It amazed Martin how the Governments of his country always managed to antagonise the populace with taxes and laws which beggared common sense. *No wonder*, he thought, *these people are rebellious. We should have learned from the debacle with America!*

Waterford was a major harbor and industrial city, though from the harbor there was little sign of it. The quays were busy, but no more so than at any of many ports on the English coast. They tied up and Peters created a meal for all three of them. Contemplating Peters skills as a cook, Martin smiled to himself, Peters had been on Martin's first ship a countryman pressed into the navy. Peters had always been grateful for Martin's help, in writing to find out if his mother was safe and well. He had been serving with Martin ever since, Peters was rated bosun on his last ship, he like Giles had volunteered to accompany Martin on this mission.

Martin was pleased that Giles was here. Mr. Smith had been adamant that Martin should travel to Ireland with someone to watch his back. Alouette was well skilled in survival, but Smith insisted that their companion be someone who could not only look after himself but the others also.

In his travels in the far-east Giles had made a reputation for his quick thinking and skill with arms. The fact, that he was present when Mr. Smith called Martin to the Foreign Office, gave him the incentive to pull him into the plan for the excursion to Ireland.

Giles was delighted. His projected posting was as liaison with the army in the peninsular. Smith was able to promise him a ship on the completion of the task. For Martin, his ship would continue under the temporary command of Lieutenant, acting Commander, Reed. Martin would lose Reed when he returned to his ship. Reed would be given a command of his own. The Navy was expanding with the presence of Napoleon still conducting affairs in Europe.

Alouette appeared pale-faced but determined, and took her place at the table in the saloon of the ketch. Peters had prepared haddock fresh caught from fishermen on their way into the port. He had poached it delicately with herbs especially for the lady, who had eaten little since they had departed Milford Haven in Wales, two days ago. They were served by Alouette's servant/companion, Margaret.

Alouette thanked Peters for his thoughtfulness very graciously and thus added him to the ever lengthening list of her admirers.

Between them they agreed to stroll into the city, Martin and Alouette, with Giles acting as their servant/protection, in plain clothes of course to maintain as low a profile as possible. They were on holiday, and seeking crystal for their new home. They left the boat in the charge of Hill, Giles servant, and Margaret. Peters drifted along in the background. Just in case.

As they walked Alouette leaned on Martin, still a little weak after the voyage. She whispered so the Giles walking behind could not hear. "Martin, my dear, it has been a long time since we last enjoyed each other's company. It is a shame that Giles is your uncle. This could have been a joyous occasion for us both."

Martin whispered back, "Alouette, I am a respectable married man only just separated from my beloved wife. How could you suggest such a thing?"

Alouette giggled and said, "Am I no longer attractive to you then?" The artful catch in her voice made him immediately deny her suggestion, causing them both to laugh, he, as he realized she was gulling him, and she, because she had caught him out.

"Perhaps I should enquire of Giles if he would be interested?" Alouette whispered. Martin thought for a second or two then said, "Please do not. I fear he would be only too willing and that would make me jealous." He turned to her gravely.

She turned to him and smiled. "You know me too well, my dear. When you are near there are no others. In choosing my career I elected to follow a lonely life. You are an indulgence I cannot afford, yet I cannot deny." The warmth of her smile covered the sadness in her eyes. She hugged Martin's arm close as they made their way into the lights and sounds of the main street.

They sought and eventually found what they were looking for. The shop window glittered from the refracted light of the lamps that lighting the crystal displayed there.

The sign over the door suggested that John FitzGerald was a purveyor of glass and crystal to the nobility. Martin and Alouette entered the shop and started looking at the display.

There were two other customers in the shop, both on a similar mission apparently. "I am sure this would be the best piece," the woman said.

The man grunted and picked up an ugly vase, "Why not this?" He said.

"That is disgusting. The woman will think we don't like her."

"Well nor do we, so why not?" The man persisted.

"We may, or may not, like her." The woman looked at Martin and Alouette, decided they were not acquaintances, and continued, "By giving her something like that she will know that we don't like her. After all, she is the children's godmother."

With the matter resolved they shortly left the shop. The assistant approached Martin and Alouette to offer his services.

The man was tall, perhaps just short of Martin's height, with white hair over a rather youthful face. He smiled as he asked, "Sir, Madam? Can I be of assistance?" The accent was soft Irish, the voice warm and friendly.

Alouette said, "We were hoping to meet with Mr. FitzGerald?"

The white-haired man said, "He is only here during the lunch hour, perhaps you would like to see the private collection." The codes exchanged, the man went to the door and nodded to Giles who entered and stood waiting, while the man closed the door and locked it, turning the open sign to the side reading closed. He then snuffed the lights in the windows out, and drew the blinds. "My name is William Penney," he said quietly. "I was notified you were coming yesterday?"

Martin said, "What man proposes, the tide disposes."

The final confirmation of their identity established, William led the trio through the door at the rear of the showroom.

"Stop!" He said as he closed the door. There was a click as he opened the closed panel of a lamp and light exploded throughout the room, reflecting off silver and glass, crystal and mirrors.

All three visitors gasped. The room was about twenty foot long, the walls hung with mirrors of various shapes and sizes. A central table was arrayed with glass and crystal ware. At the near end was a table laid with bread and cutlery. Several chairs were around the table. As they stood taking in the scene, a round rosy face appeared through a door to the rear. "Should I bring the soup now?" The rich Irish accent sounded as warm as undoubtedly the proffered soup.

"Please, sit and eat. I will never hear the end of it if you don't."

The rosy face disappeared and, as they seated themselves, the woman appeared bearing a tureen that steamed as she placed it on the table mat next to the ladle already on the table. Disappearing once more, she returned with a plate piled with chunks of bread that were warm to the touch.

The Irish lady bade them eat, and seated herself next to William facing the three visitors. "And who will you be?" She said looking at them keenly.

Alouette answered for all three. "I am Alouette, and my companions are Martin and Giles. We sailed in today from Wales."

The Irish lady said, "I am FitzGerald. This is my brother, William. Eat and we will talk afterwards."

The soup was as good as it smelled, and the people ate the warm bread with gusto.

Afterwards William cleared the table and fetched hot toddy.

FitzGerald started talking. "You obviously gave the correct identification so we will dispense with the formalities. Call me Fitz. My husband was a career soldier in the British Army. A rifleman, he served in the Americas, mainly in the woods where he made friends with the Iroquois Indians. He returned here and was murdered by the rebels in '98. His murderers killed him because he had been a soldier, though here he was a simple tradesman. He had opened this shop with the monies he had saved over twenty years of service." She paused looking sad, "We had seven years between us, before he was ambushed and murdered by the Fenians." She paused. "I am Irish, and proud of it. I believe in a free Ireland, but there are ways of doing things. That means I am a sworn enemy of the extremists like my husband's murderers and, by the way, Napoleon's French. So I will co-operate with you and give you information about both. But I will not betray my country! Understood?"

Alouette said quietly, "Of course. I am French and my situation was similar to yours. My husband is now long dead and my country suffers under the gun. but I hope, one day, to return and live in peace and freedom."

Fitz looked up in surprise, then nodded, and looked at Martin eyebrow raised.

Martin smiled faintly and began. "We are here to check and confirm that the attempt to reinforce the Fenians with elements of the Irish Regiment from the French army has failed. We were assured that the French withdrew, but we are not completely sure. If any are still here, we could have an ongoing situation at our backs, while the war in Europe is facing us."

Fitz asked, "Are you here to take action, or just to report?"

"It depends on what we find, and of course, our abilities. If there is no problem, we visit and enjoy a holiday. If there is a problem, we will see at the time."

Fitz looked at the three people in front of her. Then she looked at William. "Tell them what you stumbled across."

William leaned back in his chair and started to speak, "I thought...."

Fitz said sharply. "Tell them!"

William started to speak hesitantly. "I was riding in the countryside north of the river. I have a place that I rent out to a market gardener. He keeps my horses there as part of the rental. I was over there exercizing the mare and realized that there was a lot of activity on the next door farmland. It was dusk, and I was walking the horse over the wet leaves from the trees of the copse. I could just see people in the field beyond the trees. I realized that they were training with muskets. There must have been twenty men at least.

There was a man in uniform with them who had a Tricolor around his waist. I was able to see another had a shako on his head.

"I got out of there in a hurry and, when I got back to the stable, spoke to my tenant. He was wary but I pushed him. He confirmed that he had been told not to go that way in the evenings. He realized that they were Fenians training, though he had not seen Frenchmen there. His family and children had been threatened if he said anything to the constable. He had made it clear that there was no way he would speak to the constable, since he realized that the constable was a member of the Fenians." He paused. "I was not sure of this, though we had suspected that it was true. Since then we have confirmed it."

Fitz took up the story. "We started to trawl the area for information and found out that the local rebels have been threatening people, extorting money and punishing people for being who they were. They were the same people who had murdered my husband."

She stood and walked over to the centre table. Reaching under the table top she withdrew an envelope. Returning to the table she passed it to Alouette.

Looking through the contents, Alouette passed the sheets to Martin, who looked at the names listed. "Are these known members of the Fenians?"

"All members or collaborators with the rebels, and most carry arms wherever they go. I have no doubts that among them are the men who murdered my Billy."

Martin replaced the lists in the envelope, and passed it to Giles who placed it in the inside pocket of his greatcoat. "Is there anything we can do to further the matter while we are here?"

"Two men have appeared recently. Both are, I believe, English. Both also appear to be expert swordsmen and pistol shots. I suspect they were deported to the colonies, but escaped when the ship stopped at Cobh to water before the long sea voyage. They have joined up with the Fenians. I guessed they had a grudge against the British for transporting them. I heard them called Rowland and Barrat."

Martin looked up sharply at the names. "If they are the two men whom I know, then they are indeed dangerous. I think it a good idea that we remain for sufficient time to recapture these men and send them off to the colonies as they deserve. Their crimes are blackmail and assaults on women. They use the threat of duelling with the women's husbands to force themselves on respectable women. Since their skill with weapons is well known in England, the women submit to save their menfolk from almost certain death."

Fitz looked at them intently. "And sir, how do you intend to deal with these dangerous men?"

"The last time I encountered Rowland I beat him with my hands, and kicked him into the street. This time will be the last time I soil my hands on him."

"In a duel?" William suggested.

"Certainly not. Whilst with a sword I am better than competent, with a pistol I'm not so sure, I'll take him in whichever way offers."

Fitz nodded slowly. "I do believe you will. We will have to find a way of placing you together."

Alouette interrupted at that stage. "In that case I shall see what I can do with the French trainers." She smiled and said in French, "It is the least I can do in the circumstances."

Fitz answered in the same language, then in English said, "There are places where people go. There a person could accidently meet a fellow countryman, or perhaps woman."

Chapter twenty-four

Playing the field

Fitz and Alouette strolled through the city centre, Giles and William walking behind them for protection. There was plenty of light through the area and, though the hour was early, night had fallen so the street and shop lighting was welcome. The coaching inn was a haven of warmth and light. The ladies were welcomed to the private dining room reserved for the respectable clientele, and specifically for the wealthier of the city dwellers who did not always wish to dine at home. The inn was popular with the widows and those whose husbands worked elsewhere and were therefore without the male company they might otherwise have enjoyed.

"Do you mean that this establishment is a place of assignation?" Alouette asked with a smile.

"Certainly not," Fitz replied with an answering grin. "Though I suspect it has been used thus on occasion. No. I can assure you that, because of the shortage of men here at present, it was tacitly decided that there should be provision made for the respectable ladies of the city to attend a restaurant of quality without the escort normally required elsewhere. The compromise reached made the 'White Swan' the first choice at this end of the city at least. There are other places that cater to the range of quality elsewhere in the city."

Alouette raised her eyebrow as they entered the inn, to be greeted by a well-dressed Maître d'hotel who accepted their cloaks and escorted them through the glass door to the ante room of the dining area. A maid appeared and offered small glasses of sherry or marsala. The pair seated themselves as the Maître returned and produced menus for them both. He indicated the small bell on the table in front of them. "Please ring the bell when you are ready to order, Mesdames." He bowed and left them with their sherry.

Alouette was intrigued. "I have never experienced such a thing in my life. How was it possible to obtain such freedom from established conduct?"

Fitz smiled grimly. "The women of this city gathered after the departure of the last infantry regiment from the area. I have never seen the like. The Colonel's lady was here to await a subsequent transport to India, The wives of those not permitted, or who could not afford to go, approached her to speak for them on the subject. Convention being what it was nearly two-thirds of the adult population remaining here were women. All were expected to wait quietly at home until husbands and lovers, fathers and brothers, returned. The small number who regularly visited between houses were a minority. The vast majority did not 'dine out' and, to go to a hostelry as we have done, labelled them prostitutes and subjected them to the unwanted attention of those men left behind.

"The Colonel's lady got the message and had the city council called to find an answer, though in the end the ladies themselves provided it. So the system was created. For any night except Friday and Saturday, the rule prevails.

For Friday and Saturday, the city belongs to the men. The rest of the week, women rule."

"Until the return of the regiment." Alouette said thoughtfully.

"Just so," said Fitz, ringing for the waiter to take their order.

Martin was alone on the boat, having sent Hill and Margaret off to obtain provisions from the fish quay. Two boats had just returned with their catch. He had been considering what he would wear, when he heard movement on the aft deck of the ketch. Taking knife and pistol he made his way to the forward entrance to the cabin. He left the lamp burning and once on deck his dropped to his knees, blessing the fact that he was wearing canvas sailing trousers. The tar between the planks of the deck would have ruined his dress clothes.

He was able to make out two men on the after deck of the boat, both dressed in black, and by the look of them not used to boats. Their actions were clumsy on the moving deck and neither had thought to wear soft shoes. In view of this he presumed that they were not local men, since they would have probably understood boats a little better, and made less noise.

In this he was correct. Both men were convicts who had slipped the leash at the same time as Barrat and Rowland. Freelancing, the pair were aware that the boat had recently arrived. They had watched the departure of two people earlier and seen only one person around. Happy that one man would not prevent them from stripping the boat of any valuables, if they had to kill him, so be it.

Allan and Carter were experienced at robbery in the east end of London. Their mistake was to underestimate the person they were up against.

Carter was in front and he was holding a club in his hand. Allan had a knife, the blade glinting evilly in the light of the lantern through the cabin window. Martin reversed the pistol in his hand and clubbed Allan over the head. He caught the unconscious man as he dropped, but the knife fell from his hand to hit the deck with a thud. Carter turned and swore at the shadowy figure behind him, "Be quiet, you idiot." He did not realize that the figure was not Allan.

Martin took advantage of the moment and stepped forward lifting the knife as he moved. With the point touching Carter's throat he said, "Let us collect your friend and step below."

He took the club and added it to the knife while Carter dragged Allan to the cabin door and through to the saloon. With his hands and ankles bound, Carter sat looking sullenly at Martin as he tied Allan.

"Now, let's have a chat." Martin said quietly.

Carter looked at him. "What about. We was just going to ask for a passage back to England. We missed out ship. Bloody skipper sailed early and left us on the quay."

"Coming back from overseas, where were you coming from?" Martin asked." The only ship through here during the past week or so was coming from Jamaica."

"That was it. We were coming back from Jamaica."

"Out there long were you?" Martin asked.

"Couple of years." Carter said.

"You were inside, were you?"

"No, we were out all the time."

"You seemed to have missed out on the sunshine there."

Carter's shoulders slumped, realizing he had been tricked. "What did you want to know?"

"You got away with Barrat and Rowland?"

"They could not manage on their own, so they got us to help, saying they would give us money when we got out. I reckon we were lucky to survive. The bastards tipped the boat when we came through the harbor entrance. Allan hadn't told them he could swim. He was my mate and he dragged me to a ladder. We got out of the water; they were gone.

"We laid-up in a storage shed overnight, managed to get our clothes dry beside a furnace. All we could find to eat was some potatoes. We had no money. That's why we were here."

Martin nodded thoughtfully. "Have you seen the other two since you came ashore?"

"Oh, yes. We saw them alright. They didn't see us. They were all dressed up in posh clothes, with swords and ladies all about. We decided to stay low."

Martin made a decision. He leaned forward and cut the bonds round his wrists. "Right then, I have some things for you to do. Cut your friend loose and tell him he can stop trying to kid me that he is still unconscious. I'll get some food for you both and then I'll tell you what I want you to do."

Carter looked at his unbound hands trying to decide what to do. Allan's voice came from his place on the floor. "Well, get a move on. Cut me loose. I'm bloody starving here."

Carter shook himself. "Always thinking of you stomach, greedy sod." But he bent down and wielded the knife to cut his friend loose.

When Martin came through with the bowl of stew and the lumps of bread, they were both sitting at the saloon table. Allan had a bump on his head but, apart from that, was none the worse from the pistol butt.

"While you eat this I will tell you what you will do for me. In return I will tell you what I will do for you. In the immediate future I will need you to observe and find out the whereabouts of your two erstwhile companions. I presume you will not feel the need to protect Rowland and Barrat. The reason for this exercise is to kill them both as they have attacked my family and others of my friends. Here they have murdered others already. Do you have any problem with this?"

Carter grinned. "I'm quite happy to see them gone. They left us for dead without a qualm. I'll help you put the knife in."

Allan was more restrained. "They never did pay us, for helping them escape and all.

"Then, when we were in the water, Rowland looked straight at me, ignored me and left me to die. They didn't know I could swim. I grabbed Carter and brung him ashore. I had decided that they would pay for that. We earned our part of the bargain, getting them out of the pokey. They owe us for that. I don't mind if you kills them. Wouldn't mind if I had a hand in it neither!"

Martin looked at the pair and was comforted by the fact that he had his pocket pistol and sword to hand.

"If all goes well there may be a way for you to get clear of pursuit to the Americas. I can probably arrange it if you like. Returning to England means you will always be looking over your shoulder for the hand of the law. In America you can forget that and make a new start if you wish. It is up to you."

In the 'White Swan' the two ladies were discussing tactics over their meal. In the corner of the dining room two men were having a meal and conversation in high good humour. Their voices rose and fell. Alouette realized that there were French words scattered throughout their conversation and made some effort to hear what they were saying.

As they got up to leave the dining room they were able to hear the conversation of the men. There was a misunderstanding over a word which one could not understand and the other could not explain. Alouette said, "Excuse me, gentlemen. What this gentleman is saying is, he has no opinion about Free Ireland. He believes it is an issue for the Irish to resolve."

She took Fitz's arm and they left the room, leaving the two men dumbstruck at the intrusion and also at the lady's ease of translation from French to English.

As the ladies reached the lounge of the hotel where they prepared to take tea before returning to the crystal shop, the men from the dining room appeared with the Maître.

He approached the ladies and said, "Pardon, ladies. The gentlemen wish to speak to you. I will be preparing your tea here while they make their request."

Fitz said, "They may approach."

The two men took the chairs opposite the ladies, and thanked them for their forbearance. The Frenchman started to speak in broken English.

Alouette held up her hand. "Please speak French if you wish. It will simplify the conversation." She spoke in French.

The man broke in to a flood of French that Fitz and his companion could not follow. Alouette listened and replied in equally rapid French. Then she turned to Fitz and said in English, "This gentleman is here to help train local militia in the use of the French weapons they carry. His English is not up to it and he asks if I could interpret on occasion when he is discussing the program with this other gentleman."

"Will there be a chaperone present?" She asked.

"They suggest you may wish to participate, at a fee for us both of course."

"It could be arranged. Though I would point out that, with my business, it would need to be at my premises, for me to take part."

Fitz turned to the maître who was serving the tea. "Thank you sir you have been most helpful. I think these gentlemen may be trusted. Please return to your duties with my thanks for your thoughtfulness."

"For you, madam, as always. It has been a pleasure." He bowed and withdrew, leaving the four people alone with their tea and conversation.

"Right," Fitz said, "You can now speak frankly, the militia in this country are not trained to use French weapons. So I conclude you are training rebels seeking independence from England. Am I right?"

The Irishman reddened. The Frenchman obviously only got one word in three and looked blank.

Fitz continued, "Michael Connolly, I have known your big sister for 20 years. I knew you had been in trouble further north. I had not realized you were back here stirring things up for us in your home town,"

"Mrs. FitzGerald. I apologise for trying to pull the wool over your eyes. I thought you would not recognize me, it's been several years."

"So are we to get the truth or not?" Fitz took no prisoners.

"You are right, Bridget. We are training believers to work with the French army." He leaned forward to speak confidentially.

Fitz held her hand up with blazing eyes. "You keep a respectable tongue in your head or this conversation finishes now. It's Mrs. FitzGerald to you!"

"S...sorry, Mrs. FitzGerald. I did not mean to be familiar. Tis just that at home Maureen speaks of you....."

"Your sister is my old school friend! What is this nonsense about the French army landing here? We have been through all that before and it ended in disaster. What makes you think this will work any better?"

"Well, we are training properly this time and making better arrangements for the troops to land secretly." Michael Connolly was getting most uncomfortable.

Alouette interrupted, "What did you really want of me?"

Connolly relieved, said, "We need to coordinate matters between the Captain here and our own leaders. So far it has been difficult. What Mrs. FitzGerald suggests would be very suitable if the offer is still on the table."

Alouette considered. "Perhaps you should introduce me to your leaders. I am now acquainted with the French side." She nodded at the Captain, "But I know nothing of your leaders."

Now relaxing, under the impression he was taking control of matters once more, Michael Connolly said, "That is easily arranged. We can take my carriage."

Alouette held her hand up at this. "You can stop right there. I will not be going anywhere in your carriage. You tell me where we can meet and I will tell you if it is acceptable or not."

"Come now, madam. My people are very important. They cannot be pushed about at the whim….."Connolly stopped, suddenly becoming aware of his mistake in his dealings with this lady, sitting helplessly and watching as Alouette allowed the Captain to assist her to her feet.

His misery was compounded by her words as she prepared to leave.

"Mr. Connolly, you go and speak to your superiors, whoever they are. Explain that if they truly need my assistance, they must send a grown man in a position to make arrangements to meet. Unless the place is public and acceptable to me, he need not waste his time. Am I clear, Mr. Connolly?"

Chastened, Connolly stood and confirmed that he would pass the message. He said his farewells, and departed accompanied by his French companion.

Chapter twenty-five

Where the wind blows

At the meeting in the glassware shop later that evening, Alouette was not so sure of her control of the situation. After all, they knew where she was but she had no idea where they were.

When the bell rang at the back door of the premises, Martin was immediately alert. He ushered Giles through the door into the dark passage to the stair to the upper floor. William answered the back door cautiously. A voice called saying the visitor was for the French-speaking lady.

He opened the door, pistol in hand. "Take care, sir. This is loaded."

"Well, you can put it away, for I'm no threat and I am here by invitation of the lady herself."

The man who entered was a big, broad-shouldered fellow with a mop of black hair, laughing blue eyes, and a ready smile that seemed to fill the room.

Alouette took one look and decided that this man was really dangerous. From the passage beyond, Martin and Giles sat and listened to the discourse between Alouette and the man who had introduced himself as Brian Casey.

"Why would I have the feeling that, if I asked for Brian Casey in this locality, they would have no idea who I was talking about?" Alouette sounded displeased. "If there can be no trust between us, I do not wish to know you, Mr. Casey!"

Her visitor stopped in his tracks, smile gone, his face like carved granite. Alouette saw the real man in those few seconds before the smile returned.

"Come now, madam. I have to protect myself and my family. Here, there are as many informers as there are patriots."

Alouette conceded the point. "I suppose the word patriot is open to interpretation as well?"

"Why now, lady? I am impressed by your perspicacity. There are few enough people around here who at least have the brains to appreciate the difference. I think you are right and I accept that patriotism depends on your point of view."

He indicated a chair. Alouette shrugged and nodded, and he seated himself.

"What did you want of me?" She asked. I am not a political person and, though I speak French, I am here to visit my friend, Mrs. FitzGerald. If translation is required I can do it, but I will not involve myself in any political activity."

"I have enough people involved in those matters. All you would be needed for would be translating orders for our French people to use training the local militia." Casey sat back, pleased with himself for edging round the core of this matter so skilfully. He was not pleased for long.

Alouette looked directly at him. "You are lying to me. Your very presence here is a danger to my friends. I think that if I do anything for you and your people I will be compromised and so will they. I believe you had that in mind from the start. You may leave as soon as you like, mister. Whoever you are. I told you before. If you have to lie to your friends, then whatever you are doing must be highly illegal and probably dangerous. It is obviously anti-government. So goodbye!"

Casey rose to his feet looking angry. "That is twice you have called me a liar, lady, and I will not stand for it." He swung round and knocked the pistol from William's hand. It hit the floor and went off with a bang. The ball flew through one of the glass displays, causing considerable damage, shattering several vessels.

The door burst open and two men rushed in from outside. Both had drawn swords in their hands. Through the gap in the part-opened door, Martin saw it was Rowland and another man, whom he guessed would be Barrat.

Casey grabbed Alouette by the arm. She did not struggle. She just looked coldly at Casey, then at the two men who had entered the room. "Were you worried I would attack you, Mr. Casey? You had these two thugs waiting to protect you, I presume." Two more men entered and stood behind Rowland and Barrat. The three rebels neither heard nor realized they were there.

Alouette said, "What's this? More problems, sir? I really cannot see why you should need my services with so many at your disposal."

Startled, Casey looked round at the newcomers.

"They are not my men." He stuttered."

"In fact," said Martin, coming through the inner door. "They are mine."

Rowland and Barrat started to turn round, but both stopped at the touch of the knife to their necks.

"Who might you be then?" Casey recovered fast, still holding Alouette's arm.

Martin's sword lifted and pricked the back of Casey's hand causing him to release his grip.

Rowland sensed a moment of inattention from Allan who was interested in what was happening elsewhere in the room. He knocked the knife aside and lunged forward at Alouette. Martin shouldered Casey aside. "Take him, Allan!" and flicked the blade of Rowland's sword aside, so that it missed Alouette completely. Giles grabbed her and pulled her out of danger. Martin engaged the sword of Rowland who had a pleased look on his face at the chance to kill this man who had beaten him so badly in London.

Allan had Casey under his knife in the corner. Carter had Barrat. Martin and Rowland fought back and forth at the other end of the room, boots crunching on broken glass as they stepped to and fro, blades flicking back and forth. Each looking for the opening that would allow them to inflict injury.

Unaccustomed to drawn-out sword fights, Rowland began to feel the pace. Long practice sessions did not prepare you for an extended fight to the death. For Martin the reverse was true. There were no breathers permitted when fighting for your life on the deck of a warship.

Sensing he was beginning to tire, Rowland became more and more desperate, his sword heavy in his hand. Martin slapped his sword across Rowland's blade and pierced his forearm.

Rowland cried out and dropped his weapon. He clutched his arm to stop the pulse of blood that came from the wound. Alouette grabbed a cloth from the table and hastily wrapped it round the wound, and used a table knife to twist the cloth tight and slow the bleeding. "Hold that!"

She said and went and fetched a roll of muslin that the glassware was packed in for shipping. Efficiently she wrapped the wound tightly using the original cloth as a pad, and holding it in place with the wrapping of muslin.

"There," she said, "You'll make it to the colonies yet."

There were few complications following the confrontation at the glass shop. Rowland and Barrat were given the choice of keeping their lives, and continuing their broken journey to the colonies, or an unmarked grave in the cold waters of the Atlantic. The cold eyes of their captor offered no mercy. Unsurprisingly, they chose to live and were detained in the local jail to await the next convict ship to call at Cobh. Allan and Carter, who now regarded Martin with awe, were despatched incognito from Bristol to London for examination and eventual employment, by Mr. Smith, who declared an interest in their qualifications for a place within the framework of his operations.

Martin, Giles, and Alouette, having left the ketch at Bristol, travelled more sedately to London and, having delivered their reports and Alouette to Mr. Smith, returned to their families.

HMS Diane was in Chatham having attention to her rigging after a skirmish with enemy ships during her Baltic excursion during Martin's absence. Acting Commander Reed, Martin's first lieutenant, was looking forward to his own command as soon as Martin resumed his place on the *Diane*.

It was three weeks later that the Lieutenant received his first command, the captured French corvette *Charlotte* was commissioned, renamed and classified as 24 gun sloop *HMS Diomede,* Lieutenant Hammond of the cutter *Daisy,* in command. Lieutenant Reed was given command of *HMS Daisy,* much to his delight.

HMS Diane was found to be suffering from stressed frames which resulted in their working loose where they were seated in her keel. The consequent leaking in the strained planking as a result meant major repair or breaking up. The entire crew were therefore transferred to the recently completed 38 gun frigate *HMS Fox,* a new bigger class of frigate carrying heavier guns, the 32x18pounder broadside guns being combined with the six 24pounder carronades. It was one of the complexities of the classification system used, that the two bow chasers and the pair of stern chasers were omitted from the designation of the class. All four guns were 12 pounders, and a significant enhancement to the ship's firepower. In addition the transferred crew were not regarded as sufficient in number for the bigger craft A draft of an additional 90 men including a replacement First Lieutenant, and two junior lieutenants arrived at the quayside in Chatham to report on board.

For Martin, the stern cabin was spacious after the rather more cramped quarters in his previous commands, with the curtained alcove for his sleeping berth, the desk, and the new cabinet with its secure storage for wine and glassware now safely attached to the bulkhead. So accustomed was he to the two stern chase guns that he hardly noticed them in his inspection.

Jennifer interrupted his survey, "Martin, my dear. Have you sufficient linen for the voyage?" Martin smiled fondly at his wife whose figure was beginning to show signs of the eventual arrival of a second child into their lives.

"My dear, I have sufficient linen to supply half the fleet, I do believe. In fact my servant has had problems finding space to store everything. Now I fear you must join Lady Isabella, for I am to interview my new officers. Your presence is guaranteed to distract them if you remain here."

Seated at his desk later that day he studied the man in front of him. Lieutenant Athol Donald was a burly Scot who had been captive of the French until his rescue by riflemen of the army in Portugal. His refusal to give his parole had meant he was imprisoned in the port of his capture. The relief of the port had been one of the early successes for the building army in Portugal.

He was older that the average having been in his rank for eight years. His previous commissions having been in line of battle ships, where, as Martin well knew, unless you were of the select few, the chances of promotion are scarce. The scions of the privileged families being first considered for advancement, while professional sailors like Donald were retained, prized for their expertise in ship handling and navigation.

"Well, Mr. Donald, you have seen the ship. What do you think of her?"

Mr. Donald pursed his lips and then said, "She'll do, sir. She has a good feel about her and the look of a flier."

Martin smiled. "Good. I will expect the watch lists to be organized and the ship ready to sail on the tide at noon tomorrow." He stood and held out his hand to the man before him." You are welcome aboard my ship, Mr. Donald."

"Thank you, sir. I'll not let you down!"

The orders were to join with Rear Admiral Sir Alexander Cochrane in the West Indies. The voyage across the Atlantic gave Martin the chance to shake down the new men who had joined the crew transferred from *HMS Diane*. He soon discovered that he had found a good man in Athol Donald. The two new younger lieutenants, James Haskall and William Bates were, but recently, midshipmen, both from ships of the line.

On the third day at sea, leaving the waters of the English Channel finally after battling contrary weather, he came on deck to find Mr. Donald walking the quarter deck with a small smile on his face.

Martin studied the other three ships comprising the small detachment en route to join the West Indies fleet. The cutter *Daisy*, now under her new commander Lieutenant Reed, was making headway, snapping at the heels of the Brig/Sloop *HMS Walrus* captained by Commander Brown. He had distinguished himself during the raids on the French invasion forces, when Martin was raiding Boulogne. The supply ship *Hastings,* was as usual finding it difficult to keep up. Her shape was designed for cargo not speed.

"Good day to you, Mr. Donald, a better morning I see. Tell me, you seem to have the deck. Where is Mr. Haskall?"

Donald looked aloft at the mizzen top. "There was a question of the security of the mizzen-topmast, sir. Mr. Haskall asked for it to be frapped to make sure it was not going to break under the stress of the past two days. I volunteered to take the deck while he made sure the job was properly done. I got the impression that he got little masthead practice on the *Indefatigable* and he decided that, if he were required to order others aloft, he should know what the problems were first hand, if you take my meaning?"

"And you volunteered to help him acquire this experience of course! I am pleased that you take your duties so seriously. I am sure Mr. Haskall will thank you for your efforts on his behalf. Please ask him to see me when he has completed his survey aloft. He must be finding life on a frigate considerably different to his time on a ship of the line."

Martin paced the quarterdeck for the next half hour. he then called Lieutenant Donald. "I will be in my cabin if I am needed. Perhaps you could produce the midshipmen's journals this afternoon. I will be interested to read what they have to say about our present orders. Oh, and dine with me tonight and perhaps one of the young gentlemen. I'll leave the choice to you."

With a small smile he went below and called for coffee.

The knock on the door reminded him that he had sent for Mr. Haskall.

"Enter!" He called.

His servant, Wells poked his head in. "It's Mr. Haskell, sir."

"Send him in, Wells,, and bring more coffee please."

James Haskall was nearly six foot tall and ducked as he entered the cabin. With his hat on he just managed to clear the deck planking above his head. He touched his hat and stood more or less at attention. His languid stance irritated Martin, but he had the impression that there was more to this man than met the eye.

"Stand straight, Mr. Haskall," Martin said quietly. "You are not at a coffee morning in Albany.

Haskall straightened up and hit his head on the cross beam.

Martin noticed and smiled to himself. Then he said "Perhaps you had better seat yourself. This will not take long, I hope."

Haskall removed his hat and seated himself on the chair opposite his captain.

Martin sat back and studied the young man before him. Six perhaps seven years his junior, Haskall had dark hair and fine features, an intelligent face Martin decided. He was slim but not skinny.

"Why were you aloft during your watch on deck?" Martin asked.

"I was worried about the state of the mizzen topmast, sir. I thought it might need frapping."

"I see, and where was the bosun at this time, perhaps the Sailing Master?"

"They were engaged elsewhere on deck."

"You asked the First Lieutenant to take the deck while you went aloft to check the mizzen topmast?"

"Yes, sir." Haskall was starting to worry.

"Are you aware of the duties of the officer of the watch on a naval ship, Mr. Haskall?"

"Yes, sir, but…."

"But, Mr. Haskall. If from your lofty position you observed some hazard almost under the ships bows, what would you have done?"

"Why I…."

"Mr. Haskall, just between us here, you are aware that with a skilled crew aboard there was no reason for you to leave your post on deck. In your position you are expected to exercise leadership and command men. It implies that your crew are competent to carry out your orders without needing your personal supervision. Trust your men, Mr. Haskall, and they will trust you!"

"I, I was never allowed to do anything without supervision.."

Martin sat back in his chair as Wells brought the coffee in. "Thank you, Wells. Another cup, please."

Wells brought an extra cup from the locker in the cabin, and withdrew.

"Coffee, Mr. Haskall? It's James, is it not?"

"Yes, sir. Please, sir."

"James, there are many things different between a ship of the line and a frigate. On this ship I expect my officer to act like officers. If a man fails in his duties on a small ship like this, it is noticed. It is also dealt with swiftly. If you wish to practice your skill at climbing the rigging, then off duty you are welcome to do so. I would point out though it can interfere with the duties of the crew. The First Lieutenant, Master, the bosun and I, are all here to deal with the fate of this ship, and all will be pleased to answer questions and give advice. You are expected to learn and lead the others junior to you. Take heed of today. Watch the way Mr. Donald deals with things. Cultivate the Master. His knowledge of sailing and navigation is second to none. Probably most important at the moment, the bosun knows every rope and hatch on this ship. He knows the men. Use his expertise and learn from him.

"The ship is a machine that works as well as its component parts, the crew, can perform. Each has his place and task. Find your place fit in, and you will do well." He rose to his feet. "Good day, Mr. Haskall."

Haskall saluted. "Thank you, sir. I will, sir." He ducked his head and left the cabin.

Martin sat down again and finished his coffee. Noticing the untouched cup left by Haskall he shrugged and drank that too. He thought Haskall would probably be alright.

William Bates was a different proposition, as junior he was berthed in the gunroom with the midshipmen. There was little to say of the man apart from the fact that the gunroom was kept in an orderly manner. It would be interesting to see Mr. Bates when he presented the books of the midshipmen today.

Bates was stocky and fair haired with a countryman's face. That was Martin's conclusion upon meeting Bates that afternoon. He had seen him on occasion after boarding, but had not really had any chance to study him or to gain an impression of the type of man he was. Seated in front of his captain, William Bates turned out to be a blunt, straightforward character who was at sea from choice, and had gained his place through the good offices of the squire in his village, a retired Admiral. From that time on, it seemed determined application had served him well. Together the two men went through the midshipmen's journals. In view of the short time they had been at sea most of the entries covered the time at anchor. There was an obvious difference in the presentation between those who could write well and the others who could not. The four were generally regarded by Bates as a typical gunroom. Some better than others, but as yet no one outstanding.

That evening Athol Donald and David Sessions appeared to dine with their captain. Sessions was the youngest of the four midshipmen. He had been accepted because his father was a former Lieutenant, wounded under Martin's adoptive father. The family was not poor, a fact that was reflected in the quality and tailoring of his clothing.

He was well mannered and made no mistakes with the cutlery. For most of the meal Martin and Athol Donald talked, periodically pulling Sessions into the conversation.

Toward the end of the meal Session asked a question of his two elders. "I have been told that this is the season the treasure galleon sails from Darien. I presume, since Spain is once more our enemy, we may interfere with her progress if we encounter her?"

Donald raised his eyebrow and left it to his captain to reply.

"We are most unlikely to encounter her, but, were we to do so, of course we would not allow her to pass unchecked. Her cargo would be a serious asset to the Joseph Bonaparte. In the present situation she would probably be heavily escorted."

Donald said, "I have heard that the Spanish colonies do not all recognize Bonaparte as king."

"Well, if we encounter her we will assess the problem at that time."

Chapter twenty six

Pirates

\

The small French convoy was battered by weather and from the look of it gunfire. The corvette was low in the water and afloat by virtue of the pumps alone, judging by the noise that could be heard at some distance. The larger ship was being repaired. Her damage appeared to be mainly from gunfire. The third ship was not French. At the sight of the three British warships it was making off rather foolishly, as Reed in his cutter flew in pursuit overhauling it hand over fist. The fleeing pirate from the distant African coast had depended on boarding the French ships, having pounded its victims with the two heavy cannon it carried. The battered French ships had been possible prey, but even the cutter handled as she was could be a match as long as she stood off and pecked away with her six pounder popguns, and her nine pounder bow and stern chasers. He would not have stood a chance in a straight fight. Because of her agility the *Daisy* could run rings around the clumsy-looking Pirate.

For Reed it became obvious when caught and passed the hidden side of the ship. She had suffered gunfire, and the hole in her side was being patched as she left the scene. *Daisy's* nine pounder bow gun hit the repaired section having bounced off the water. The ball smashed the patch and disappeared into the hull. Reed had been cursing the gunner for wasting his shot, until he saw the fluke result. "A golden guinea if you can repeat that shot," he called to the gunner. The men cheered and ran out the gun once more. This time they had to settle for smashing the starboard rail and cutting a swathe through the men swarming the deck. The blood ran in streaks down the side of the ships as she heeled in to the long waves. The water slopped into the hole that once more gaped in her side.

As *HMS Fox* ran out her guns the corvette struck her colors. On the bigger ship, reminiscent of a Spanish frigate, there was activity and apparently dissent, "Fire a shot over her bow Mr. Donald."

The crash of the gun resolved the dissention on the frigate. The Tricolor dropped as the halyard was cut.

HMS Walrus had boats in the water with a boarding party for the corvette, Martin ordered Donald to take Haskall with his party to the frigate, which they could now identify as the *Hermione.* She had originally been Spanish, though now obviously with a French crew and a French name.

On the deck of the *Hermione* Athol Donald realized that something was not right. The damage to the ship was mainly cosmetic. The Captain was in an ill-fitting coat and obviously upset at losing his ship, but there was a furtive aspect to his manner that did not go with his position in command. The second boat arrived with the marines and their sergeant. He spoke to Haskall. "I do not like this. There is something wrong. Damn it. This crew doesn't fit with this vessel. Lieutenant Haskall, I am going to see the captain." He turned and called the sergeant over. "Mr. Haskall, take over. Sergeant, have your men finish disarming the men on deck. Then herd them all forward and guard them. Mr. Haskall, have all the hatches closed and locked until either myself or the captain gets here. Do you both understand? Haskall, you are in command! Nobody comes on deck or goes below while I'm away!"

Lieutenant Donald scrambled down into the nearest boat. "Back to the ship, and put your backs into it."

Martin stepped onto the deck of the captured ship. He was immediately aware that there was something wrong. The crew members were all sitting around the windlass in the bows of the ship.

"Sergeant! Over here with two men. Bosun, with me. Open the main doors to the stern cabins!"

Peters walked to the barred door. Using the blade of the cutlass he carried, the bar dropped and the door swung open. There was noise from within. Two men stumbled out, both were bloody with wounds from sword cuts. The men were in French uniform, and when they saw the British uniforms, one turned and called to someone behind him. From within came a line of people including women and children. All the men were wounded in some way.

Martin spoke to the leader. "Who are you?" He asked in French.

The man wearily lifted his head. "I am Lieutenant Marquand, second in command of this ship. My captain had made an arrangement with these corsairs." He waved at the men at the bow of the ship. "Our captain ordered us to stop when the ship appeared. He was in command of the *Minette* corvette and he ordered them not interfere. The corsair opened fire and crippled the *Minette,* though she did manage to get some shots off and damage the corsair. I killed my captain when we were boarded. He greeted the Pirate and told them the ship the treasure and the women were there for the taking. I rallied the loyal members of the crew whom the boarders had not yet encountered. We managed to close the deck entries and they barred the doors to keep us below. I can only assume that they intended sailing the ship to their harbor." He stopped and leaned against the rail."

Martin called Peters and held out his hand. "Flask?"

Startled, Peters looked at his captain. "Sir!"

"Flask, Peters. I need the brandy."

Reluctantly, Peters rummaged in his waistband and found a small flask which he passed to his captain.

Martin passed it to the wounded Frenchman. He waited while the man drank some of the contents.

The man revived somewhat and continued his story. "I saw your ships coming and I thought perhaps they were more of these scum." He waved his hand at the seated men. "Then I saw your flag and realized we were saved."

There was a signal from *Daisy* asking for assistance.

Martin said to the sergeant. "Secure the prisoners. Mr. Haskall, take command. Peters, stay with Mr. Haskall and get the crew working."

Martin swung over the side and returned to the *Fox*.

They sailed over to the spot where *Daisy* was hove-to. The fleeing corsair was getting lower in the water as they watched. There were boats being dropped into the water all around her and an astonishing number of people filling them. As the frigate approached Martin used the speaking trumpet to call to Lieutenant Reed. "Stand away, Mr. Reed. These men are pirates and if you attempt to help them they will overrun your ship."

In response to the call, Reed's craft took the wind and drew away from the approaching boats.

On the pirate ship itself, with decks almost awash, a surge of people poured up on deck. Most of them seemed to be women.

"Take us alongside, Mr. Donald."

"Prisoners, sir?" The lieutenant enquired.

"Looks that way. Shall we find out?"

Already close, the *Fox* scraped alongside the sinking ship. The boarding net thrown over the side was soon covered in people climbing to safety, assisted by the *Fox's* crew.

The woman who took charge was dressed in what had once been an expensive gown. She approached Martin and to his surprise addressed him in English. "Thank you, Captain. We were destined for another fate, I assume. I was on a merchant trading vessel taking passage to England when we met the pirates. I am Mary Rankin, companion to Lady Sutton. My mistress insisted I wear one of her gowns so that I could stay with her when we were captured. Sadly, she has not survived. The captain desired her. For the past three days since we were captured, he used her himself. He then decided that she was not really to his taste and the crew were given their turn. We watched her thrown overboard, already dead, from all appearances. That was yesterday. This morning we came up with the French ship, and our ship was holed in the skirmish."

As she finished the sinking ship slipped under the waves, with a gurgle of air and a small explosion of dust and broken furniture as it sank out of sight. There were several boats full of men struggling among themselves.

As he watched one of the boats spun and started dashing towards the *Daisy* lying hove-to. She lay a quarter mile off and showed no signs of noticing the fast moving launch.

"Mr. Donald, ask the gunner to stop that boat." Martin's voice was calm.

Athol Donald looked at the fast moving boat and called out to the Master gunner. "Mr. Carson. Stop that boat, if you please."

The Master Gunner smiled and got the crew of the bow chaser to shift the gun a little and remove two of the quoins. He looked along the barrel nodded to himself and applied the match to the loaded gun. Taking his time, he stepped aside and nodded to Mr. Donald.

The gun crashed and jumped back against the retaining ropes. There was no sign of a splash, but the speeding boat stopped suddenly. Then the two ends folded upward, spilling the crowd of men into the water.

None of the other boats made any attempt to rescue the men struggling and sinking in the water, they all continued making their way toward the distant line of the African coast. After a while the disturbance in the water ceased. Martin sent the carpenter over to help with the repair of the corvette *Minette*. He also arranged for a party of the prisoners to be transferred to the corvette to man the pumps while the work was being done. Despite grumbling, the men went without trouble when they were reminded of the fate of their fellows, now no longer moving in the water.

The *Hermione* was seaworthy and, it seemed, loaded with bullion. In the circumstances Martin decided that it should be transferred to the *Fox*. With working parties under the supervision of Lieutenant Donald, the work of transfer was undertaken.

There was a truly astonishing amount, apparently the output of several mines for the past eighteen months.

"This will be a bone of contention for some time, I should imagine." Athol Donald commented.

"How so?" Martin asked with eyebrow raised.

"Which Admiral is in charge here? Will it be Cochrane in the West Indies, or are we still under Portsmouth?"

"Interesting, Mr. Donald. Now how many prisoners have we got and where do we put them?"

"I thought perhaps we could send the prizes to Gibraltar, and the prisoners with them. If we send *Daisy* with them she could bring our crew back with her."

"That makes sense, though I think we may need to find a place for the ladies. I am uncomfortable with our bilges stacked with bullion, however new our timbers may be."

"So it's Gibraltar for us all, sir?"

"Make the signal to the other ships. We can depart now."

The familiar shape of the Rock was on the horizon when the cutter came into view, beating south west as fast as her sails would take her.

The signals exchanged between her and *Daisy* quickly established that she was carrying urgent despatches for Captain Forrest-Bowers on *HMS Fox*.

In his cabin Martin opened the packet of orders and private mail.

Placing the private mail to one side he opened the sealed papers from the Admiralty.

The opening sentence informed him he was recalled to the Admiralty, for orders. The body of the letter stated that his recall was for assignment to special duty, and that his return was required with all despatch. Meaning as soon as possible!

Calling the Commander Brown to attend on board, Martin spoke to Mr. Donald. "We will not be calling at

Gibraltar, but proceeding direct to Portsmouth. My new orders specify, 'with all despatch', so I will pass command over to you, Commander Brow for the Gibraltar delivery of the prizes. While this wind holds there will be little to gain using a cutter, so *Daisy* will accompany us. If there are any problems I will transfer to her for the balance of the voyage and you will take *Fox* into Portsmouth. Call Haskall and our people from the prize. I will brief the Commander when he is aboard."

The knock on the door announced the arrival of Brown, and Martin gave him his orders. Though the need for a prize crew would make him short-handed, it was for a short distance only, so it would be a minor inconvenience.

Standing, watching Brown returning to his ship, Athol Donald approached Martin. "What about the ladies, sir?"

"I believe they were bound for England, were they not?"

"Yes, sir. They were."

"Then they may as well accompany us on this rush to Portsmouth, d'ye not think? After all, if we put them off at Gibraltar, there may be difficulty in returning them home."

"Just so, sir. I will inform the ladies of your decision."

"Is it any lady in particular, Mr. Donald?" Martin had a small smile as he spoke.

Donald flushed. "Well, sir. It does seem that Mistress Rankin shares many of my interests and we have discussed the possibility of meeting in the future."

"My impression is that she is a fine woman who would stand well as a sensible man's wife. You are not married, Mr. Donald?"

"Indeed I am not, sir, though mainly because the opportunity has not arisen."

"It seems fate has played into your hands on this occasion. Good luck, Mr. Donald."

"Why, thank you, Captain. And I hope your news was good as well."

Martin realized that having put his private mail to one side when he opened his orders, it was still on his desk unopened. Teasing himself, he took a turn around the deck before he descended to his cabin. Arranging the letters in date order, he opened the first.

Jennifer was happy to announce that she was never better and the new baby was kicking occasionally but expected now at term with no problems. Lady Jane was well and always asked after Martin. Giles was itching to return to sea, and Isabella was with child but still great fun to be with.

There followed other news about the estate at Eynsham and the progress of the new stables.

Martin opened the second letter and found a very different story. There had been trouble at the London house. A party had got out of hand and the subsequent fire had damaged both houses. It transpired that the incident had been arranged by Sir Paul Rowland, prior to his departure to the Colonies in irons.

Since no one had actually been hurt Martin was unworried. So he proceeded to the third letter. Jennifer started the letter but it was taken over by Lady Jane, the sad message being that the expected baby was no more. A fall had led to a miscarriage and Jennifer was quite ill.

Jane said that all was being done that could be done. She was in good hands. She finished by saying that she hoped the West Indies would not keep him away too long. As they all missed him.

With the news he had received, Martin lost no time. Handing command over to Lieutenant Donald he transferred to the cutter, *Daisy,* to make all speed to England. The urgency of Martin's need to get home was all that Lieutenant Reed needed, he drove the cutter to her limits. Martin was landed at Portsmouth after an anxious two-week race up the coast of Portugal and the English Channel. He lost no time hiring a post coach to London.

When he arrived after dark anxious and tired, Lady Jane met him at the door of their home, and it was then Martin realized, that there would be no good news awaiting him. She greeted him thankfully. Holding him back briefly before taking him to her daughter. "Martin, before you go in, the doctor was here earlier." There was a pause and her voice broke as tears ran down her cheeks. "There is no hope, my dear." She turned and took his hand. "She knows you are coming."

He found Jennifer in poor case, and though his appearance lifted her spirits, it was evident that there was nothing to be done. His beloved was dying, her face fine drawn and pale. He could not do more than be there, holding her.

Poor young Jane their daughter had no real idea what was going on, only that her mother had been ill and something awful was happening.

The following morning, aware that her father was sad, she did her best to cheer him, but could do little to lift his mood.

Around the sad household events were occurring, life progressed despite all. As the family mourned, the world elsewhere registered the news of another naval coup for a favorite Captain.

The cargo carried by *HMS Fox* caused considerable stir at the time. Despite the secrecy surrounding the transaction, word got about. Happily after the gold and silver was securely tucked away. Martin's share made him completely independent for life, and for Donald there was sufficient for him to contemplate marriage, providing the lady agreed.

In the case of the crew, most had more money than they had ever had in their lives. When the gazette published the story the people of England cheered. Already known for the exploits earlier in his career, Martin confirmed his place as a hero's in the public's eyes.

For this latest event his fame was assured. The announcement of the award of the Freedom of the City of London and a ceremonial sword was greeted with fervour by the people, avid for news of success after the years of war dragging behind the seeming invincible rollercoaster of the Napoleonic armies.

The knighthood seemed inevitable and was promptly bestowed. Through it all Martin stumbled, numb at the knowledge of his beloved wife, Jennifer's, desperate fight for life after the loss of her child.

As the news of Martin's situation became known, the wave of sympathy allowed him privacy and time to be with Jennifer during her last days.

Charles Bowers looked at his adopted son with sad eyes. Martin stood in uniform, the honors, newly awarded, glinting on the navy blue of his tunic. He was gazing out of the window.

He turned to Charles, his face calm, and said "I am eternally grateful for the fate that brought me here to be with my beloved when she left us. Our daughter I know will be cared for when I am away. Now please tell me why I was recalled from the West Indies?"

Charles looked at Martin gravely, then, "I was trying to do something about that, but I'm afraid I do not have the power as yet. The man you call 'plain Mr. Smith' was responsible for that. He has asked to see you as soon as you are able. I do not know why nor do I know of any reason for your employment rather than in command of a ship."

Martin smiled grimly, "For whatever reason I will be forever grateful to plain Mr. Smith for having me brought back to be with Jennifer during her last moments."

"I also am pleased that things worked out that way, though I object to the cavalier way he cancelled orders of the Admiralty, and makes use of naval personnel. He has asked that you be given time to arrange your life.

Later, alone in his room Martin stood at the window, he had seen his daughter Jane and said goodnight to her. Now, alone once more, he gazed out at an uncertain future......

The End

Counterstroke # 1....Exciting, Isn't It?

O'Neil's initial entry into the world of action adventure romance thriller is filled with mystery and suspense, thrills and chills as *Counterstroke* finds it seeds of Genesis, and springs full blown onto the scene with action, adventure and romance galore.

John Murray, ex-Police, ex-MI6, ex management consultant, 49 and widowed, is ready to make a new start. Having sold off everything, he sets out on a lazy journey by barge through the waterways of France to collect his yacht at a yard in Grasse. En route he will decide what to do with the rest of his life

He picks up a female hitch-hiker Gabrielle, a frustrated author running from Paris after a confrontation with a lascivious would-be publisher Mathieu. She had unknowingly picked up some of Mathieu's secret documents with her manuscript. Although not looking for action, adventure or romance, still a connection is made.

An encounter with Pierre, an unpleasant former acquaintance from Paris who is chasing Gabrielle, is followed by a series of events that make John call on all his old skills of survival to keep them both alive over the next few days. Mystery and suspense shroud the secret documents that disclose the real background of the so called publisher who is in fact a high level international crook.

To survive, the pair become convinced they must take the fight to the enemy but they have no illusions; their chances of survival are slim. But with the help of some of John's old contacts, things start to become... exciting.

Counterstroke # 2....Market Forces

Market Forces, Volume Two of the Counterstroke action adventure romance thriller series by David O'Neil introduces Katherine (Katt) Percival, tasked with the assassination of Mark Parnell in a hurried, last-minute attempt to stop his interference with the success of the Organization in Europe. As a skilled terminator for the CIA, Katt is accustomed to proper briefing. On this occasion she disobeys her orders, convinced it's a mistake. She joins forces with Mark to foil an attempt on his life.

Parnell works for John Murray, who created Secure Inc that caused the collapse of an International US criminal organisation's operation in Europe, forcing the disbanding of the US Company COMCO. Set up as a cover for money-laundering and other operations designed to control from within the political and financial administration, they had already been partially successful. Especially within the administrative sectors of the EU.

Katt goes on the run, she has been targeted and her Director sidelined by rogue interests in the CIA. She finds proof of conspiracy. She passes it on to Secure Inc who can use it to attack the Organization. She joins forces with Mark Parnell and Secure Inc. Mark and Katt and their colleagues risk their lives as they set out to foil the Organization once again.

Counterstroke # 3....When Needs Must...

The latest action adventure thriller in the Counterstroke series opens with a new character Major Teddy Robertson–Steel fighting for survival in Africa. Mark Parnell and Katt

Percival now working together for Secure Inc. are joined by Captain Libby 'Carter' Barr, now in plain clothes, well mostly, and her new partner James Wallace. They are tasked with locating and thwarting the efforts of three separate menaces from the European scene that threaten the separation of the United Kingdom from the political clutches of Brussels, by using terrorism to create wealth by a group of billionaires, and the continuing presence of the Mob, bankrolled from USA. An action adventure thriller filled with romance, mystery and suspense. With the appearance of a much needed new team, Dan and Reba, and the welcome return of Peter Maddox, Dublo Bond and Tiny Lewis, there is action and adventure throughout. Change will happen, it just takes the right people, at the right time, in the right place.

Donny Weston & Abby Marshall # 1 – Fatal Meeting

A captivating new series of young adult action, romance, adventure and mystery.

For two young teens, Donny and Abby, who have just found each other, sailing the 40 ft ketch across the English Channel to Cherbourg is supposed to be a light-hearted adventure.

The third member of the crew turns out to be a smuggler, and he attempts to kill them both before they reach France. The romance adventure. now filled with action, mystery and suspense, suddenly becomes deadly serious when the man's employers try to recover smuggled items from the boat. The action gets more and more hectic as the motive becomes personal

Donny and Abby are plunged into a series of events that force them to protect themselves. Donny's parents become involved so with the help of a friend of the family, Jonathon Glynn, they take the offensive against the gang who are trying to kill them.

The action adventure thriller ranges from the Mediterranean to Paris and the final scene is played out in the shadow of the Eiffel Tower in the city of romance and lights; Paris France..

Donny Weston & Abby Marshall # 2 – Lethal Complications

Eighteen year olds Donny and Abby take a year out from their studies to clear up problems that had escalated over the past three years. They succeed in closing the book on the past during the first months of the year, now they are looking forward to nine months relaxation, romance and fun, when old friend of the family, mystery man Jonathon Glynn, drops in to visit as they moor at Boulogne, bringing action and adventure into their lives once again.

Jonathon was followed and an attempt to kill them happens immediately after his visit. They leave their boat and pick up the RV they have left in France, hoping to avoid further conflict. They are attacked in the Camargue, but fast and accurate shooting keeps them alive. They find themselves mixed up in a treacherous scheme by a rogue Chinese gang to defame a Chinese moderate, in an attempt to stall the Democratic process in China.

The two young lovers, becoming addicted to action and adventure, link up with Isobel, a person of mystery who has acquired a reputation without earning it. Between them they manage to keep the Chinese target and his girlfriend out of the rogue Chinese group's hands.

Tired of reacting to attack, and now looking for action and adventure, they set up an ambush of their own, effectively checkmating the rogue Chinese plans. The leader of the rogues, having lost face and position in the Chinese hierarchy, plans a personal coup using former Spetsnaz mercenaries. With the help of a former SBS man Adam, who had worked with and against Spetsnaz forces, the friends survive and Lin Hang the Chinese leader suffers defeat.

Donny Weson & Abby Marshall # 3....A Thrill A Minute

They are back! Fresh from their drama-filled action adventure excursion to the United States, Abby Marshall and Donny Weston look forward to once again taking up their studies at the University. Each of them is looking forward to the calm life of a University student without the threat of being murdered. Ah, the serene life.... that is the thing. But that doesn't last long. It is only a few weeks before our adventuresome young lovers find that the calm, quiet routine of University life is boring beyond belief and both are filled with yearning for the fast-paced action adventure of their prior experiences. It isn't long before trouble finds the couple and they welcome it with open arms, but perhaps this time they have underestimated the opposition. Feeling excitement once again, the two youths arm themselves and leapt into the fray. The fight was on and no holds barred!

Once again O'Neil takes us into the action filled world of mystery and suspense, action and adventure, romance and peril.

Donny Weston & Abby Marshall # 4....It's Just One Thing After Another

Fresh from their victory over the European Mafia, our two young adults in love, Abby Marshall and Donny Weston, are rewarded with an all-expense-paid trip to the United States. But, as our young couple discover, there is no free lunch and the price they will have to pay for their "free" tour may be more than they can afford to pay, in this action adventure thriller. Even so, with the help of a few friends and some former enemies, the valiant young duo face danger once again with firm resolve and iron spirit, but will that be sufficient in face of the odds that are stacked against them?

And is their friend and benefactor actually a friend or is he on the other side? The two young adults look at this man of mystery and suspense with a bit of caution. Action, adventure and romance abound in this, the latest escapades of Britain's dynamic young couple.

Donny Weston & Abby Marshall # 5....What Goes Around...

Just when it seems that our two young heroes, Donny Weston and Abby Marshall are able to return to the University to complete their studies, fate decides to play another turn as once again the two young lovers come under attack, this time from a most unsuspected source. It appears that not even the majestic powers of the British Intelligence Service will be enough to rescue the beleaguered duo and they will have to survive through their own skills. In the continuing action adventure thriller, two young adults must solve the mystery that faces them to determine who is trying to kill them. The suspense is chilling, the action and adventure stimulating. Finding togetherness even among the onslaughts, Donny and Abby also find remarkable friends who offer their assistance; but will even that be enough to overcome the determined enemy?

Better The Day

From the W.E.B. Griffin of the United Kingdom, David O'Neil, a exciting saga of romance, action, adventure, mystery and suspense as Peter Murray and his brother officers in Coastal Forces face overwhelming odds fighting German E-boats, the German Navy and the Luftwaffe in action in the Channel, the Mediterranean, Norway and the Baltic – where there is conflict with the Soviet Allies. This action-packed story of daring and adventure finally follows Peter Murray to the Pacific where he faces Kamikaze action with the U.S. Fleet.

Distant Gunfire

"Border s Away!" Serving as an officer on a British frigate at the time of the French Emperor Napoleon is not the safest occupation, but could be a most profitable one. Robert Graham, rising from the ranks to become the Captain of a British battleship by virtue of his dauntless leadership, displayed under enemy fire, finds himself a wealthy man as the capture of enemy ships resulted in rich rewards. Action and adventure is the word of the day, as battle after battle rages across the turbulent waters and seas as the valiant British Royal Navy fights to stem the onslaught of the mighty French Army and Navy. Mystery and suspense abound as inserting and collecting spy agent after spy agent is executed. The threat of imminent death makes romance and romantic interludes all the sweeter, and the suspense of waiting for a love one to return even more traumatic. Captain Graham, with his loyal following of sailors and marines, takes prize ship after prize ship, thwart plot after diabolical plot, and finds romance when he least expects it. To his amazement and joy, he finds himself being knighted by the King of England. The good life is his, now all he has to do is to live long enough to enjoy it. A rollicking good tale of sea action and swashbuckling adventures.

Minding the Store

O'Neil scores again! Often favorably compared to America's W.E.B. Griffin and to U.K.'s Ian Fleming, and fresh from his best-selling action adventure, "Distant Gunfire," O'Neil finds excitement and action in the New

York garment district. The department store industry becomes the target of take-over by organized crime in their quest for money-laundering outlets. It would seem that no department store executive is a match for vicious criminals, however, David Freemantle, heir to the Freemantle fortune and Managing Director of America's most prestigious department store is no ordinary department store executive and the team of ex-military specialists he has assembled contains no ordinary store security personnel. Armed invasions are met with swift retaliation; kidnapping and rape attempts are met with fatal consequences as the Mafia and their foreign cohorts learn that not all ordinary citizens are helpless, and that evil force can be met with superior force in O'Neil's latest thriller of adventure and action, romance and suspense, mystery and mayhem that willl have the reader on the edge of his seat until the last breath-taking word.

The Mercy Run

O'Neil's thrilling action adventure saga of Africa: the story of Tom Merrick, Charlie Hammond and Brenda Cox; a man and two women who fight and risk their lives to keep supplies rolling into the U.N. refugee camps in Ethiopia. Their adversaries: the scorching heat, the dirt roads and the ever present hazards of bandit gangs and corrupt government officials. Despite tragedy and treachery, mystery and suspense while combating the efforts of Colonel Gonbera, who hopes to turn the province into his personal domain, Merrick and his friends manage to block the diabolical Colonel at every turn.

Frustrated by Merrick's success against him, there seems to be no depths to which the Colonel would not descend to achieve his aim. The prospect of a lucrative diamond strike comes into the game, and so do the Russians and Chinese. But, as Merrick knows, there will be no peace while the Colonel remains the greatest threat to success and peace.

When Needs Must

The latest action adventure thriller in the Counterstroke series opens with a new character Major Teddy Robertson–Steel fighting for survival in Africa. Mark Parnell and Katt Percival now working together for Secure Inc. are joined by Captain Libby 'Carter' Barr, now in plain clothes, well mostly, and her new partner James Wallace. They are tasked with locating and thwarting the efforts of three separate threats to the European scene that threatens the separation of the United Kingdom from the political clutches of Brussels, by using terrorism to create wealth by a group of billionaires, and the continuing presence of the Mob, bankrolled from USA. An action adventure thriller filled with romance, mystery and suspense. With the appearance of a new team, Dan and Reba, and the return of Peter Maddox, Dublo Bond and Tiny Lewis, there is action and adventure, mystery and suspense, romance and surprises throughout. Change will happen, it just takes the right people, at the right time, in the right place.

Sailing Orders

For those awaiting another naval story of the 18/19th century, then this is it. Following the life of an abandoned 13 year old who by chance is instrumental in saving a family from robbery and worse. Taken in by the naval Captain Bowers he is placed as a midshipman in his benefactor's ship. From that time onward with the increasing demands of the conflict with France, Martin Forrest grows up fast. The relationship with his benefactors family is formalised when he is adopted by them and has a home once more. Romance with Jennifer the Captains ward links him ever closer to the family.

Meanwhile he serves in the West Indies where good fortune results in his gaining considerable wealth personally. With promotion and command he is able to marry and reclaim his birth-right, stolen from him by his step-mother and her lover.

The mysterious (call me merely Mr Smith) involves Martin in more activity in the shadowy world of the secret agents. Mainly a question of lifting and placing of people, his involvement becomes more complex as time goes on. A cruise to India consolidates his position and rank with the successful capture of prizes when returning convoying East-Indiamen. His rise to Post rank is followed by a series of events, that sadly culminate in family tragedy.

Though still young Martin Forrest-Bowers faces and empty future, though merely Mr Smith has requested his services?

Available in print from
A-Argus Books
www.a-argusbooks.com

Available in ebook from
WEB Publishers Inc
amazon.com
barnesandnoble.com
smashwords.com

Made in the USA
San Bernardino, CA
19 January 2014